# ALL THE WRONG PLACES

Riptide Publishing
PO Box 1537
Burnsville, NC 28714
www.riptidepublishing.com



All the Wrong Places


Cover art: L.C. Chase, lcchase.com/design.htm
Editor: Delphine Dryden, delphinedryden.com/editing
Layout: L.C. Chase, lcchase.com/design.htm



ISBN: 978-1-62649-420-6

First edition
June, 2016

Also available in ebook:
ISBN: 978-1-62649-419-0

# ALL THE WRONG PLACES

# TABLE OF CONTENTS

# CHAPTER ONE

# BRENNAN

Once was chance. Twice was coincidence. Three times was a goddamn pattern.

I'd heard that expression before, and thought I understood it, but this morning it made a lot more sense than I cared to admit. Especially since I wasn't crazy about the pattern that I couldn't deny anymore.

Half-sprawled on my sofa, I stared at the dark TV screen. The ceiling. The window. The blank wall that probably needed some artwork or something. Maybe one of those pastel paintings my mom had all over her house. Or a photo. There was a shop down on Main Street that carried some cool prints of landscapes and animals and—

*And she's gone.*

No matter how many times I mentally changed the subject, the truth remained. Aimee was gone.

Question was, whose fault was it?

Technically, she'd initiated the breakup, but I would've dumped her had she given me a second to get a word in edgewise, because she'd fucked him *how* many times over the last few weeks?

Groaning, I leaned forward and scrubbed my hands over my face. I should've been crying or drinking or something. I was devastated, after all. A year and a half down the shitter. The woman I loved—gone. The heartbreak would probably show up soon, but right now I was a little preoccupied by the reason she'd given me for sleeping around.

*"A woman has needs, Bren,"* she'd said with a sort of apologetic shrug. *"He does things that you don't."*

Over and over, those words ricocheted around in my head. Needs? Things I didn't do for her? God, was I really that bad at sex?

Maybe I could've written it off and told myself she was just making excuses for cheating on me, but there was a small problem with that—she wasn't the first. She was the third. I'd confronted the first after some rumors had made their way back to me. The second had thrown it in my face while we were arguing about something. And Aimee, I'd caught red-handed.

All three had given me more or less the same excuse.

And now . . .

Now I just wanted to curl up and die. More than twelve hours had passed since I'd caught her, and I was pretty sure everyone in our social circle had already heard. My phone was blowing up. Or, well, it had been until I'd turned the little bastard off. And like Aimee, Billy Fallbrook—the guy who'd been balls-deep in her when I'd walked through the door last night—was part of the local skateboarding scene. Knowing her, she was doing damage control. Knowing him, he was bragging to everyone that he'd nailed her.

Which meant everyone and their mother probably knew by now what a lame idiot I was in bed.

I gritted my teeth, wondering if I really was about to throw up. I swallowed hard to keep my breakfast down, but that was getting tougher every time my brain helpfully replayed that image of Aimee riding a spread-eagled Billy Fallbrook on our bed.

Fuck. Maybe I should've watched for a minute or two. Learned from his techniques. Figured out where the hell I kept falling short with the women in my life.

*You're pathetic, Brennan. Fucking pathetic.*

Maybe, but I was getting desperate. Whatever I'd done for all three girlfriends, it obviously wasn't enough. I needed some kind of help. Or advice. Or . . . or some goddamn CliffsNotes.

What the fuck was I supposed to do? Hire a sex therapist?

*"So, I suck in bed. Help?"*

Was there a documentary out there?

*Yes, Brennan. It's called porn.*

Eh. That shit was about as boring as a documentary anyway. I'd probably fall asleep before I learned anything. Or just get depressed because my dick wasn't the same size as my forearm.

*Maybe . . .*

I folded my hands under my chin and stared at the wall. I wasn't paying for a damn therapist. I had no desire to watch porn. I was almost afraid to google "How do I have sex?" because I could only imagine the results.

I needed some help that wouldn't bill my insurance or clog up my computer with malware.

*Hmm . . .*

Well, there was a sex shop in town. Red Hot Bluewater or something like that.

As soon as the place's neon-lit storefront flashed through my mind, I was on my feet and heading for the door. I grabbed my wallet and keys off the coffee table and walked out of my apartment, down the stairs, and out to my truck.

*Red Hot Bluewater, here I come.*

I had to be at work in a couple of hours anyway, so I parked behind Skate of Juan de Fuca, the skate shop where I worked. I stepped onto my skateboard and wove my way down the sidewalk toward the sex shop two blocks away.

It felt weird, coming to this part of town so early in the day but not going into the shop or over to the skate park like I usually did before work. Today, I was on a mission. And besides, I didn't feel like kicking around with all of our mutual friends. Didn't feel like being around her, and there was a good chance she'd be there. Along with *him*.

I gritted my teeth and kept going, without even glancing in the direction of the park.

As I followed the sidewalk, though, I slowed down a bit, nervously eyeing the red-and-black sign up ahead. I couldn't tell what the sick feeling was now. Or rather, where the queasy betrayed feeling ended and the gut-twisting nervousness began. I'd never been into a sex shop before, and I sure as hell had never gone into a place to ask for advice about how to keep my girlfriend—or, well, hypothetical future girlfriend—satisfied.

Especially since I wasn't even sure where to start. Where had things gone wrong? She always came. Didn't she? Or had she been . . . faking it?

Well, if she'd faked it, she deserved an Oscar, because that woman always came harder than either of my previous girlfriends.

My previous girlfriends who'd also deemed me a dud in bed.

My cheeks must've been glowing red. I couldn't remember ever being this humiliated in my life. I hadn't even brought my phone with me because I was mortified at the thought of turning it on and seeing a million texts from people who now knew I couldn't turn *her* on.

She'd never complained about my technique. Not once. Neither had Alejandra, though Kasey had occasionally made passive-aggressive comments about me buying her a dildo or something for Christmas so there wouldn't be so much pressure on me. But I'd thought Aimee was satisfied. She always wanted to have sex.

Or, well, she *had* always wanted to have sex. For the first year, she was constantly initiating it, and I rarely turned her down. But the last six months . . .

The nausea nearly lurched up the back of my throat, and I gulped hard to once again keep my breakfast where it belonged. How had I not seen the signs?

Too late now. Only thing I could do was figure out where I'd gone wrong, and see if I could maybe *not* disappoint the next girl who came along.

Parking was a bitch in Bluewater Bay, and the spaces in front of most shops were full. There were open parking spaces in front of the sex shop, though. So, that must've meant nobody was here? This time of day, it wouldn't be that busy, right? When *did* people go to sex shops, anyway? Seemed like the kind of thing you'd do at night, under cover of darkness. Unless all the daytime customers were cowards who parked over at Walgreens or the bank. That might've explained the random cars sometimes parked behind Skate of Juan de Fuca—people hiding their cars while they browsed porn? Something.

In front of the sex shop, I kicked up my board and tucked it under my arm. For a minute, I stared the place down and tried to psych myself up. The windows were covered in black paper. As progressive as this town was, I supposed Bluewater Bay wasn't quite ready for street-facing displays full of dildos and condoms. Hell, Juan de Fuca caught flak for having mannequins on skateboards without helmets and pads, so the moral vigilantes must've had a field day with this place.

A sign on the door said *No One Under 18 Permitted* in big, red letters.

*Here goes nothing.*

Heart thumping, I opened the door and went inside.

Two steps in, I halted and stared at my surroundings. What . . . the hell . . . was all this shit?

The lingerie and condoms, I understood. But some of the . . . tools? Toys? Whatever they were, I thought they belonged in an operating room. Or an interrogation room.

*Okay, so apparently I* am *clueless, because holy fuck.*

The place even smelled alien. Like a mix of herbs, fruits, leather, rubber, and . . . I wasn't even sure I wanted to identify all of it.

My dick didn't hold a candle to most of the dildos. Well, that might've been a clue about my girlfriends' problems. I hadn't thought I was lacking in size, but if the "power dong" and "hole buster" were anything to go by, maybe there was an anatomical issue I had overlooked. Okay, so Kasey had once said my cock was clearly the karmic result of some horrible thing I'd done in a past life, but I'd *thought* she was joking. I supposed—

"Can I help you find something?"

The smooth male voice damn near made me jump out of my skin, and I spun around like an idiot in a haunted house instead of that same idiot in a sex shop. Leaning over the counter, seemingly unaware of the penis-shaped lollipops next to his arm, was a guy with a black ponytail and dark eyes fixed right on me. I thought he was Middle Eastern—didn't see a lot of people with olive skin like that around here.

And he was still staring at me, waiting for an answer to his question.

I cleared my throat. "Um . . . I . . ."

"Also, do you have any ID on you?" He grimaced apologetically. "We've had some issues with minors, so . . ."

"Yeah. Yeah. Sure." I fished my wallet out of my back pocket, pulled out my driver's license, and handed it to him.

He took it, looked it over, and slid it back across the counter. "You're good. Sorry about that. We—"

"No, I get it. Don't worry." I stuck my license back in my wallet and into my pocket. "I still get carded for R-rated movies, so it's cool."

He laughed. "You too?"

"All the time." I rubbed my chin, which I hadn't had to shave since yesterday. "Damn baby face."

"I know, right?" He folded his arms and leaned on them. "So, what can I help you find?"

And suddenly I wasn't laughing anymore. Shit. Nerves. Hello. What could I say without sounding like an idiot? Why did I even care what this guy thought of me? He'd probably seen and heard things in here that would've blown my mind while he didn't bat an eye. This was, after all, a guy who worked in a place that sold penis-shaped lollipops—*Now in Banana Flavor*, apparently.

I shook myself and pulled my gaze away from the candy. "To be totally blunt? I'm having some issues with my girlfriend. And I guess I thought . . ." I glanced around the shop, my shoulders sinking as my stomach turned to lead. "I don't know what I thought."

"I assume you mean problems in bed."

Heat rushed into my cheeks. Staring at the lollipops because they were easier to focus on than him, I nodded. "Yeah."

"So . . ." He absently tapped a pen on the counter. A pen with a big plastic dick on it. Of course. "If you don't mind my asking, what kinds of problems?" He paused. "So I can help you narrow down a solution, I mean. Not . . . not trying to pry."

"Well . . ." I thumbed the peeling tread on my skateboard. "What do you have for people who thought they knew what they were doing in bed, then realized they didn't?"

"Ouch. Hmm. Well, fair warning, I'm not a sex therapist or an expert." He chuckled. "I just sell the tools."

"Hey, I don't need a therapist. If you can point me toward the right tools"—*and maybe show—no,* tell*!—me how to use them*—"we're good."

"That's what I'm here for." He came around the cash register and motioned for me to follow him. I fell into step behind him, and we moved toward the far end of the shop. At a large bookcase, he stopped, and gestured at the shelves that were crammed with books. "Any of these could help, so I'd suggest browsing through it and seeing if anything sounds like what you need."

"That's just it." I stared at the books, my heart sinking. "I . . . I don't know. I have no idea what the problem is."

"That's perfectly okay." He waved a hand at the bottom shelf. "It's not all techniques and things like that. We've got books that may as well be textbooks on human sexuality." Turning to me, he lifted his eyebrows a little. "Could be worth it to read through and see if something resonates."

I scanned the titles, and nodded. Then I looked around the rest of the shop. "It's funny. Up until last night, I thought I knew what I was doing. Now, I feel like a clueless virgin."

He watched me for a moment. "If it's not too personal . . . what happened?"

*Too personal? We're standing in the middle of a store full of fake penises, talking about my sex life.*

"I caught my girlfriend." I swallowed. "Ex-girlfriend now. With another guy. And she said it was because I didn't fulfill her 'needs.'" I made the sharpest, bitterest air quotes ever. "Whatever the fuck that means."

His posture stiffened. "That sounds to me like an excuse to cheat."

"That's what I thought when the girl before her made the same excuse. And the one before her."

He grimaced. "Wow. Well. Excuse or not, cheaters are . . ." He pressed his lips together, then shook his head. "Anyway."

"All I know is, *something* was wrong, and I'm hoping there's something here that can help me fix it."

He shifted his weight. "All right. Giving her the benefit of the doubt—which, for the record, I don't give to cheaters—maybe you two were mismatched somehow."

I wasn't sure how I felt about him being angry at her on my behalf. Vindicated wasn't the word. Maybe kind of relieved that he hadn't laughed me out of the store for being such an absolute dud that she'd had to resort to whatever Billy had going for him.

I sighed. "So I'm mismatched with her and the two before her?" I shook my head. "Whatever's going on, I'm the common denominator."

He started to speak, the tightness in his features making me wonder if it was something snide, but he hesitated. Then he shook himself, and his expression relaxed a little. "Well, it might mean you haven't figured out what you want enough to find a partner who matches."

"Oh." Not surprising—the answer was that I was clueless about something. I'd just figured it was about women, not myself, but what the hell did I know?

He tilted his head. "There's nothing wrong with that, by the way. Some people take years to find exactly what it is they need with a partner."

"That's encouraging."

He pursed his lips as he scanned the shelves around us. "For starters, I think we need to find your kink."

I bit back an incredulous request for him to repeat that, catching myself an instant before I would've sounded as stupid as I felt.

He turned to me. "What kind of stuff do you fantasize about?"

"Fantasize . . ." I avoided his gaze, staring at a rack of magazines, but not really looking at them as I kept working at that peeling tread on my board. "I don't . . ."

"It's nothing to be embarrassed about," he said softly. "Just might, you know, help me steer you down the right aisle."

I glanced up and scanned the signs on the ends of the various aisles. Lingerie. Dildos, Dicks, and Vibrators. So Much Lube. Kinky. Kinkier. Kinkiest.

The answer was down one of those aisles?

"I, um . . ." I gestured at them. "None of that stuff."

"Okay, fair." He shrugged. "Do you watch porn?"

"I have, but it's boring as hell. Maybe I'm watching the wrong kind?"

"What kind have you watched?"

I had to think about it for a minute. I was pretty sure the last time I'd looked at porn, I had to use my mom's credit card to get past the "prove you're eighteen, asshole" screen. If memory served, I'd been more excited about *accessing* porn than watching it.

"I don't know," I said. "Two people fucking?"

He gave a quiet laugh. "Well, that rules out orgies, and presumably BDSM?"

"Never watched anything with S&M in it. Or orgies."

"So, what you did watch . . ." His eyebrows rose a little. "Did you enjoy it?"

"Always thought it was kind of boring, to be honest. It's all fake."

"Yeah, a lot of it is. You ever tried amateur?"

"No . . ."

He watched me for a moment. "Let me ask you this: are you into men?"

"What? No!" I shook my head. "I mean, one of my exes convinced everyone I'm gay, but . . . no. I'm not."

"Okay. Are you into women?"

"Huh?" I laughed. "Of course I am. That's why I'm here. To figure out how to not be a loser in bed with a woman."

"Right, but . . ." He absently ran the backs of his fingers along the edge of his jaw. "Okay, well, to put it more bluntly, what do you think about when you jerk off?"

Fresh heat rushed into my cheeks. "Um . . ."

He smiled warmly. "It's nothing to be embarrassed about. Trust me—I've heard it all."

"It's not that. I mean, okay, it kind of is, but . . ." I pretended to be interested in a couple of weird metal objects whose purpose I wasn't sure I wanted to figure out. "I don't really think of anything when I jerk off."

"You don't think of anything at all?"

I hesitated, then met his eyes. "Is that weird?"

"Well, no." He folded his arms loosely and shifted his weight. "But I think it might be telling."

"How do you mean?"

"Let me ask you this first: *why* do you jerk off?"

I studied him, trying to figure out what the hell he was getting at. "Because I have a boner? And I want to go to sleep?" God, could this conversation get any weirder?

"But not because you're thinking of someone?"

I shook my head.

"Have you ever thought you might be asexual?"

"Uh . . ." I blinked. Yep. The conversation could get weirder. "Come again?"

"Asexual. Maybe you're . . . not into sex."

I shifted my weight. "That's a thing? People can be asexual?"

"Yep. It's not just plants anymore." He smiled, and something about his expression gave me permission to laugh, which was good—it meant I was breathing again.

"But if I was asexual, I wouldn't jerk off, would I?"

"Maybe, maybe not." He shrugged. "Some people do. I do."

I jumped like he'd smacked me. "So . . . you're asexual?"

He nodded. "That's why I started wondering. Some of the stuff you said, it sounded pretty familiar."

"How come I've never heard of people being asexual?"

"A lot of people haven't. It's only been the last few years that it's really been acknowledged." He scowled. "Isn't terribly *accepted*, but it's a start."

"So it's just . . ." I rocked from my heels to the balls of my feet, wondering where all this nervous energy was coming from. "People who don't like sex?"

"Well, not necessarily." He half shrugged. "Some asexuals want nothing to do with sex. Some will do it if their partner is into it, and they'll still enjoy it. And some people aren't interested in sex unless they have a really strong emotional bond with someone."

"So, even though I like sex, I'm still . . ."

"From what you're telling me, that's my guess." He held my gaze. "When you and your girlfriend did have sex, did you ever initiate it?"

I thought back, and now that he mentioned it, I couldn't remember being the one to initiate it. Narrowing my eyes, I said, "So what you're suggesting is, it *was* my fault she cheated."

"No!" He shook his head. "No, not at all. But it—"

"I mean, what the fuck am I supposed to tell the next girl? We can date, but I don't do the sex because I'm asexual?"

"Look." He patted the air, and his tone was quieter and gentler than before. "There are plenty of options for asexuals. There are—"

"Shit." I shook my head and took a step back, inching toward the door. "No, I think coming here was a bad idea. I'm not good at sex, but I *want* to be."

"Because you want sex?" he asked softly. "Or because you want to be able to please your partner?"

"What's the difference?"

We locked eyes. He didn't say anything, and I wondered if he didn't have an answer, or if he wanted me to put the pieces together. Nervously, I tugged at that piece of tread again, and when it snapped, I jumped. Swallowing hard, I moved the board under my other arm.

"I, um . . ." I took another step toward the door. "I have to go."

I turned and hurried out. He didn't follow me or try to stop me.

I dropped my board to the sidewalk, stepped on it, and got the hell out of there.

"Hey, Brennan." My boss, Colin, snapped me out of my thoughts. When I turned, he gestured into the back room. "Got a shipment of wheels. You know what to do."

I got up off the stool behind the cash register. "On it."

While he manned the register, I went into the back. This part of my job was pretty easy—open the shipment, match everything to the packing list, put the new merchandise in with the back stock or out on the shelves if there was room. Most of this would end up on the shelves. We'd been running low on this particular brand of wheels for almost a month, especially the fifty-one- and fifty-three-millimeter sizes.

I cut the tape on the box and started pulling out sets of wheels, checking them off as I went. The whole time, though, my brain was elsewhere. Good thing this was mindless work, because I was busy thinking about everything the guy at the sex shop had said earlier.

Asexual? Since when were *people* asexual? How the hell did that work anyway? And how the hell was *I* asexual? I could get a boner. I could use it. I came every time. Almost every time. More often than not. I liked the things my girlfriends had done for me when they weren't out doing them for other guys.

Shaking my head, I collapsed the empty shipping box and tossed it on top of a two-foot stack of flattened boxes. Then I opened the next one and started inventorying wheels again.

And of course, my brain went right back to Red Hot Bluewater. The more I thought about our conversation, the more I kind of felt like a dick for walking out the way I had. Maybe the guy had been a bit blunt, but he *was* trying to help. And it wasn't as if he'd laughed me out of the shop or said something was wrong with me.

*"For starters, I think we need to find your kink."*

How we'd made it from there to asexual—that was the part that blew my mind. The fact that we'd been standing there in a room full of porn and sex toys, having a straight-faced conversation about it, was . . . weird. And he'd said he was asexual too. But he jerked off? And he worked in a sex shop?

Mind blown.

Except . . . what if he was onto something? He'd seemed like he genuinely wanted to help me figure out my problem, so I didn't get the impression he was fucking with me.

I glanced around to make sure Colin hadn't wandered back here. Then I pulled out my phone and googled "asexual."

My jaw dropped as I stared at the screen. There were thousands of results, and none of them seemed to be about houseplants. Skimming over it, I was inundated with terms I was pretty sure I hadn't seen in high school biology.

Graysexual? Demisexual? Cupiosexual? Apothisexual? The fuck?

"How's that shipment coming?" Colin's voice startled the shit out of me, and I shoved my phone into my pocket just before he poked his head into the stockroom. "I've got someone looking for Radial Red in fifty-two."

"Uh." I'd seen three sets of those not thirty seconds ago. Where were— There. I grabbed the sets of Radial Reds, double-checked that they were fifty-two millimeter, and tossed them to him. "They'll be in the system in two seconds." I held up the packing list. "All I need to do is punch this in."

"Great. Thanks."

Well, the graysexuals and asexuals and whateversexuals were going to have to wait, apparently. When I got home tonight, I'd google this shit and actually read it.

For now, asexual or otherwise, I had work to do.

# CHAPTER TWO

# ZAFIR

Two days after he came into Red Hot Bluewater, I still couldn't get Brennan out of my mind. Or was it Brandon? Brennan. Brendan, maybe? Pretty sure it was Brennan. I'd only given his driver's license a quick look, though. Brandon? Brennan?

Whatever his name was, he hadn't come back in. Not that I'd expected him to, but I hoped that meant he was finding all the answers he needed. It had taken me months to get my head around the concept of being asexual, and what that meant, and where I went from there. I didn't envy him, because I'd been there, done that, no thanks, keep the T-shirt.

I kept wishing he would come back into the shop. I wanted him to find the answers and accept who he was, and if I could help, I wanted to.

That wasn't the only reason I perked up whenever the bell on the front door jingled, though. It was probably just the novelty of running into another asexual in this town. Bluewater Bay had plenty of queer people, especially since they'd started filming *Wolf's Landing* here, but the ones on my end of the spectrum didn't seem to be all that common. Or, well, they didn't come strolling into the sex shop very often, anyway. Big shock.

It was also possible I'd been wrong about Brennan, and I wanted a second chance to talk to him so I could either clarify things or apologize for screwing with his mind. He'd pinged asexual to me, but I was no sexuality psychic. And the more I thought about it, the more I had to admit there *might've* been some wishful thinking involved. Another asexual in Bluewater Bay? Yes, please!

And what would I do if he did come back? Direct him toward a few more answers, then clock out and wave good-bye because

I wouldn't have time for anything else before I sprinted out the door to go pick up my kid or work my second job.

Muttering a few curses, I looked at the clock above the door. According to the legs of the leather-clad Tom of Finland character, it was ten fifteen. Only two minutes since I'd last checked.

Today was going to be a long one. Full shift at Red Hot, then on to Old Country Pizza, where I delivered pizzas for that inflexible asshole who always smelled like cigars. Tomorrow, same deal. My next day off from both jobs was . . . I couldn't even remember. Too depressing to think about.

Maybe it was time to ask both my bosses for a little simultaneous vacation time, even if it meant working double shifts to make up for the unpaid days off from Old Country. I needed a breather. Maybe some social interaction with someone who wasn't buying a pizza or a dildo. As it was, I'd barely had time to go to the asexual social group out in Port Angeles, and hadn't been to the bigger one in Seattle since last year.

Between my jobs and my son, there just weren't enough hours in the day. My social life was nonexistent. The closest I came to one these days was at the mosque we attended. Tariq liked the other kids, and the adults were nice when they weren't needling me about the lack of a maternal figure in my son's life. Or my lack of attendance, since "I barely have time to grocery shop or breathe" didn't seem to fly.

Finding time to socialize with other people like me? Yeah, right.

Which was probably why I kept an eye on the shop's front door, hoping Brandon—Brennan—would come back just so I could talk to *someone* who got it. Or was in the process of getting it.

At the very least, it would be a distraction from a monotonous morning of precisely nothing happening. Chin on my hand, I leaned on the counter and scanned the store, looking for something to do. Tuesdays were slow as hell here. They'd be slow at my other job too, which meant not a lot of tips, and the boss might cut drivers loose. Great. A tighter budget. Totally what I needed these days.

But at least working at Red Hot was relatively low stress. As far as retail jobs went, it didn't suck as hard as it could have, and Violet was a saint when it came to being flexible for a single parent.

The only real downside? Slow days. Like this one. When there was nothing to do but stand around.

And wait.

For something.

To happen.

I drummed my fingers on the counter. So . . . fucking . . . *boring.*

The UPS driver came. The FedEx driver came. The mailman came.

No customers, though.

I shifted my gaze toward the shelves of sex toys I'd restocked this morning. How many dildos would it take to build a tower all the way to the ceiling? The Tower of Dildylon? The Leaning Tower of Phalluses? The Eyeful Tower?

*Please, someone, come through that door . . .*

No one did. Of course.

I took out my phone and started browsing. Violet didn't mind as long as my daily task list was done and there were no customers in the store. And it passed the time.

I'd just started reading some clickbait article about celebrities and their pets when the bell on the door jingled.

*Oh yes. Finally! Someone's—*

I nearly dropped my phone.

"Oh hey!" I set the phone down so hard, it slammed against the counter and I startled myself. "Uh, hey. How are you?"

"I'm good." Brennan smiled shyly as he tucked his skateboard under his arm. "Didn't catch you when you were busy, did I?"

"No, not at all." I cleared my throat, folding my hands on top of my phone. "So, um, you're back." *Smooth. Real smooth.*

"Yeah. I . . ." He rubbed the back of his neck. "I've been thinking about everything you said last time I was here. And, uh, I was on my way to work, so . . ." He gestured up the street. "I don't work very far from here. So, you know, thought I'd swing in."

"Oh." I paused. "I, uh, I'm sorry if I threw too much at you the other day. It's—"

"No, it's cool." He waved his hand. "I did a lot of thinking afterward. And looking around on the internet."

"Did you?"

He nodded, scanning our surroundings uneasily. Then he met my gaze. "One minute, I think you're right. The next, I . . ."

"Don't know what to think?"

"Yeah. That. How'd you know?"

"Been there." I grimaced. "I can probably relate more than you think."

"I figured. That's, uh, why I came back, actually." He pulled in a deep breath as he gave the shelves and merchandise another sweeping glance. "I have . . . so many questions."

"Well." I flattened my palms on the counter and stood a little straighter. "That's what they pay me the big bucks for, so ask away."

He gulped, rolling his shoulders. "Man, I'm not even sure where to start."

"You said you did some looking on the web, right?"

Brennan nodded. "A few hours' worth, yeah."

"Anything in particular you want to know about?"

"Is 'all of it' too broad?"

"It's kind of hard to know where to start, but I get it, believe me." I whistled. "It's overwhelming."

"Seriously."

The bell on the door jingled, and I glanced over as a couple of guys strolled in, hand in hand. About three seconds later, a redheaded woman walked in looking like she was on a mission.

*Really?* Now *you all start coming in?*

Brennan glanced at them, then turned to me. "I guess I should, um, let you get to work."

Disappointment tugged at my chest. "Yeah. Sorry. It's just me for the next few hours, so . . ."

"I need to get to work myself anyway." He swallowed. "I was mostly coming in to see if I could buy you a drink or something later. To apologize for being kind of a dick the other day, and to ask you about all of this."

"Oh. I . . ." That wasn't what I'd expected. We had customers ask us out and offer to take us for drinks all the time, and the creepy undertones were enough to make my skin crawl. But nothing about Brennan's request pinged as anything except innocent and genuine.

He rocked from his heels to the balls of his feet. "If that's not cool, it's fine. I don't want to monopolize your time or anything." He glanced again at the other customers. In a quieter voice, he said, "I just feel completely fucking clueless."

"Well . . ." I moistened my lips. "I'm not off from my second job until probably nine."

"That's okay. I'm usually up late."

I wanted to jump at the offer—how long had it been since I'd been out with anyone?—but I hesitated. My son was at my sister's tonight, since she covered for my babysitter once or twice a week, and he was staying overnight. So it really didn't matter if I got home at ten thirty or midnight. Did it? What was the harm?

I smiled. "Sure. You know where the Captain's Lounge is?"

Brennan's lips quirked, and he seemed to lose focus for a second, but then he nodded. "Yeah, yeah. I know where it is."

"I can meet you there a little after nine if you're sure that's not too late."

His eyes lit up. "Great. Sounds great. I'll see you there."

"Definitely."

He started to go, but hesitated. "Oh. I just realized I didn't catch your name."

"Zafir."

"Zafir? Interesting name."

I laughed. "Says everyone who ever tries to spell it. It's Lebanese. And you're . . ." Was it Brennan or Brandon? "Brandon, right?"

"Brennan. How did— Right. My driver's license."

I nodded.

"Well. Um. Zafir, you said?"

"Yep."

"See you this evening."

And with that, he was gone.

The Tom of Finland clock said it wasn't quite eleven yet, so I still had way too many hours left before I met up with Brennan. Chances were, the time would move even slower from here on out.

But that was okay. Now I had something to look forward to.

# CHAPTER THREE

## BRENNAN

*I wonder if this is what a blind date feels like.*

Sitting in a booth on the bar side of the Captain's Lounge restaurant, drumming my nails on both sides of my glass and staring at the door, I was beyond restless. The handful of other people sprinkled throughout the mostly deserted bar must've thought I was crazy. Or hopped up on Monster or something. I just couldn't sit still.

Zafir was ten minutes late.

Then fifteen minutes late.

As the half-hour mark crept up, I flagged down the waitress and paid my bill. I could take a hint.

I didn't know what I felt right then. He was a stranger. He owed me nothing. But I was disappointed. He knew things I was struggling to understand, and asking him face-to-face was somehow less intimidating than posting behind the cover of a screen name. I wanted a human being to talk me through this shit, so I could maybe believe I wasn't fucked up. It was a lot easier to believe there was nothing wrong with me if someone was looking me in the eye and saying, "Don't worry, dude—I'm just like you."

Kinda hard to do that if he didn't show up, though.

The waitress thanked me for coming in, and as she left with her tip, I picked up my skateboard and started to stand.

And right then, Zafir flew in through the door. I froze. He saw me and hurried toward the booth.

"I am so sorry." He took off his hat, which matched his embroidered black Old Country Pizza shirt. "We got crazy busy tonight, and we had to do a huge run to one of the soundstages, so . . ." He groaned. "Anyway, I realized a bit too late I didn't have your number, so I couldn't text you and—"

"It's okay." I smiled and eased myself back onto the bench, gesturing for him to take the other. "I don't have anywhere to be tonight."

"Okay." He exhaled and dropped onto the bench. A few strands of black hair had fallen out of his ponytail, and he brushed them out of his face. "Anyway. Sorry I'm late."

"Don't worry about it. I appreciate that you came at all." I gestured at the bar. "Can I buy you a beer?"

"Well, not a beer, but I could go for a Coke."

"Not a drinker?"

Zafir shook his head and tapped a small pendant hanging below his collar. "Muslim."

"Oh." I straightened and gave the pendant—a crescent and star—a double take. "I didn't realize . . . I guess—"

"Relax." He smiled. "You met me where I sell sex toys and porn. Most people don't immediately guess that I'm Muslim."

"You did say you were . . ." I winced. "Damn. You told me where you're from, and I—"

"Lebanon. I was born in Lebanon."

"Right. You said that. Sorry, I—"

"Brennan." When I met his gaze, he patted the air with both hands. "Chill. I've thrown a lot of info at you. I don't expect you to be an expert at Zafir trivia."

"Fair enough. Uh . . . drinks. Right." I flagged down the waitress again. She gave me a puzzled look, but didn't comment. She just took our orders—Cokes for both of us—and left again.

"So . . ." I hesitated, not wanting to sound like an idiot. "How long have you been in the States?" Eh, it was a good enough icebreaker as any.

"I've been here since I was three."

"Explains why you don't have an accent."

Laughing, he nodded. "Yes, it does."

The waitress came back with our sodas. As Zafir took a deep swallow from his, he looked around at the maritime-themed restaurant—the weathered driftwood; the faded black-and-white photos on the walls of boats, fish, and seagulls; and even an old helm suspended above the bar.

He set the glass down and wrapped both hands around it. "Man, I haven't been here in ages."

"I've never been here."

"Really?" He shifted his attention to me. "You're missing out. My ex and I used to come here all the time."

"Yeah?"

Zafir nodded, a faintly nostalgic smile on his lips as he gazed around the room again. "He was a fish-and-chips junkie, and this is one of the best places to get them in this town."

*He?*

"I didn't know that. Might have to try them sometime."

"I'd order them now, but . . ." He made a face. "I can't eat anything after a shift at Old Country."

"You can't?"

"Ugh. No. Everything tastes like grease and garlic. I mean, except . . ." He raised his glass. "Coke or water usually tastes fine. Half the time, the first thing I do when I get off shift is shotgun a bottle of water or two."

"That I believe. I worked in a burger joint for about six months, and I don't think I've ever drunk that much water in my life."

"Right?" He took another drink. "So which burger place was it?"

"Oh, a little locally owned shop out in Port Townsend. They folded a few years ago."

"Seems like a lot of the best ones do." He gestured at our maritime-themed surroundings. "Aside from this one. It'll probably be here till the end of time."

"Probably, yeah." I ran a finger around the rim of my glass. "So you came here with your . . . ex-boyfriend?"

"All the time."

"So you've . . ." I shifted in my seat, not sure how much to pry. After all, he was here to answer my questions about asexuality, not his sexuality. Which happened to *be* asexuality. Right? "You've dated men?"

He nodded. "And women."

"Does that make you asexual or bisexual?" I genuinely expected him to roll his eyes or sigh at my dumb, annoying questions, but he didn't.

"I'm asexual," he said. "But biromantic."

"Biromantic?"

"Mm-hmm. Means I can develop emotional and romantic connections with men or women." He shrugged. "I'm just not *sexually* attracted to anyone."

I blinked. Had that been covered on the sites I'd looked at last night? Oh hell, like I could remember most of that—my brain had turned to mush after three pages. "I've . . . never even . . ."

"Most people haven't."

"Oh." I started to speak again, ready to fire off another question, but hesitated. "You really don't mind this, do you? Meeting a total stranger so I can pick your brain?"

"If I did, I wouldn't be here." He smiled again, and there was something about him that relaxed me. Like every time I met his eyes, the warmth in his expression calmed me down. I was sure I was asking the stupidest questions ever, but so far he'd patiently met every one with an answer.

"Seems like you know a lot about this," I said. "I mean, not just from experience. Like, you know . . . all of it."

"I did a lot of reading about it. That's actually why I'm totally happy to answer any questions you have—I'd have cut off my arm to have someone there who was like me. Reading about it, you learn a lot, but then you feel isolated and . . ." He squirmed in his seat. "I just would have had a much easier time if there'd been someone I could talk to. So . . ." He gestured at me. "That's why I'm here."

"I . . . Thanks. I really appreciate it."

"Don't mention it."

We locked eyes for a second, but I broke contact and glanced up at the bar. Clearing my throat, I fidgeted. "This is all . . . I mean, you barely know me, but—"

"Brennan."

My teeth snapped shut, and I turned to him.

There it was again—that subtle, gentle smile. "Relax. I don't bite."

"That's . . . good." I chuckled. "I guess I just get so overwhelmed. I've been thinking about all this almost nonstop. About being asexual."

"Well, let me ask you something." He sat up straighter, folding his arms loosely behind his mostly empty glass. "Do you think you *are* asexual?"

"That's what I keep trying to figure out." I surreptitiously glanced around, not sure why I cared if anyone else could hear us. "I guess what it comes down to is, I don't mind having sex. I just don't . . . I don't really care if I do."

Dark eyes locked on me, he nodded. "That's pretty much textbook asexual. Believe it or not, being asexual really doesn't mean we're all disgusted by the idea of sex."

"Right. I . . . I gathered that much. But I . . ." Rubbing a hand over my face, I muttered a few curses. "It's so confusing. And weird."

Zafir nodded. "Believe me. I get it. " His cheeks darkened. "That . . . may be why I came on a little strong the other day. It's not very often someone comes strolling in, wondering why their sex drive doesn't match everyone else's, and I realize we have something in common."

"No, no. You were fine. I don't know. I guess it was just a lot to take in. I thought I was fucking up with the women I've dated, and it turned out my sexual orientation wasn't what I'd always thought it was."

"Happens to more people than you would imagine." He brought his drink up to his lips again. "That's why we have groups, too. There's one over in Port Angeles and a few out in Seattle."

"Groups? Like support groups?"

"Kind of." He shrugged and took a drink. As he set the glass down, he went on. "The groups I belong to are just people who like to get together and *not* go out drinking and looking to get laid."

*Groups like that exist?*

"Wow. I guess I didn't realize there'd be that many people like . . . um . . ."

"Like us?"

I nodded.

"More than you think, especially now that it's getting out there that we exist in the first place. There's a ton of info on the internet these days." He paused. "I can, uh, give you my email if you want me to hook you up with some good sites? Or if any questions come to you after tonight?"

"Sure. Yeah."

We pulled out our phones, exchanged contact information, and put them away again.

"So . . ." I rolled my shoulders, not sure why I was getting all tense like this. "This whole asexuality thing is a spectrum?"

"A broad one, yep."

"Yeah, I gathered." I blew out a breath and shook my head. "Seemed all nice and cut-and-dry, and then there's all this stuff about graysexual, and demisexual, and . . ."

"Apothisexual, abrosexual . . ." He nodded. "Yeah. It was all kind of overwhelming when I first started looking into it."

"But how do you figure out which one you are? I mean, there was so much—"

"Brennan. Brennan." He sat up a bit and flattened his palms on the table. "Don't sweat it. You don't have to figure out which one you are."

"But . . . I mean, it's . . ."

"Chill. They're just categories and labels. They're for people to look at and say, 'Hey, that's me—I'm not the only one!' But if you don't see you in any of them, it's okay. They might not fit, or you might not have figured yourself out yet. I promise—it's totally okay." He tilted his head. "So, what else do you want to know?"

"Well . . ." I played with my straw, racking my brain for more questions. I knew there were plenty in there, but I was still processing everything he'd already told me, and couldn't quite come up with anything else to ask him. Not directly, anyway. "Okay, kind of off-topic, but I have to ask. Why do you work in a sex shop?"

Zafir laughed. "So my paychecks make it out the door."

"Huh?"

"I'm not qualified for much besides retail and food service. That place gives me a hell of an employee discount, but I don't have much of a reason to use it."

"That's . . . pretty smart. I probably should've thought of that."

"Yeah? Where do you work?"

"Not that far from you, actually." I gestured up the street. "Skate of Juan de Fuca. The skate shop."

"Oh." He glanced at my board, which was leaning on the table beside me on the bench. "I guess that makes sense."

"Yeah." I chuckled. "And no, my paychecks do not make it out the door in one piece. But the store cosponsors me, so . . ."

"You're a skateboarder? Like a professional?"

I nodded. "Semipro. Trying to go pro, but it's a long road. Getting sponsorships and all that is a pain in the ass."

"Wow. My son would lose his *mind* if he met you."

"Yeah?" *You have a kid?*

"Oh, absolutely. He keeps begging me to take him to the skate park so he can learn, but . . ." Zafir grimaced. "I don't know. I'm not sure if I'm ready for that."

"How old is he?" *Seriously? You have a kid?*

"Nine."

If I'd been drinking just then, I'd have sprayed it across the table. I could barely fit it in my head that he had a kid, but a nine-year-old? Jesus.

Not my business, though. "Eh, that's not that young. I've been skating since I was five."

He raised an eyebrow. "And how many times have you gotten hurt?"

"Uh, well . . ."

"Yeah. Exactly."

"It kind of comes with the territory, but we do wear safety equipment and stuff." *Err, sometimes.*

That eyebrow climbed even higher. "So where's your helmet?"

"Uh . . ."

"Mm-hmm."

"Okay, we make sure the kids wear safety gear." I chuckled. "And hey, I've only broken three bones as a skater."

His eyes were suddenly huge. "Only? Oh, that's very encouraging."

"Being a dumbass, I might add, and not wearing safety gear. There's a reason all the kids at our park *have* to wear gear—we've all done enough stupid shit, we know what happens."

"I see," he muttered into his drink.

Typical parent. I'd had these conversations with my parents too, not to mention the parent of every kid who came into the skate shop.

*None of whom look like Zafir.*

Which gave me pause. He had to be about my age, so either he had a super young kid or he'd started pretty young himself. Except hadn't he just said the kid was nine? And wasn't he . . .

Wait a minute.

I cocked my head and folded my hands on the table. "Okay, back up a second. You're asexual too, right?"

Zafir nodded.

"But you have a kid?"

"Yep. Paid a little too much attention in biology, I guess."

"Paid—" I eyed him. "Come again?"

He shrugged. "When they were telling us about reproduction and all of that. I was fascinated with the whole asexual reproduction thing. So I concentrated really hard on dividing, and bam! There he was. My kid."

I snorted. "You are so full of shit."

"No, it's true!" He gestured at himself. "Why do you think I'm so short? I was six three before Tariq came along." Shaking his head, he clicked his tongue. "Last time I paid that much attention in school, let me tell you."

I burst out laughing. "Idiot."

He chuckled. "Okay, okay. The truth is, I didn't know what I was back then." His expression turned serious, but the gentle warmth in his eyes remained. "I was dating a girl, and we were dumb, hormonal kids, so . . ." He lifted one shoulder. "We did what dumb, hormonal kids do, and nine months later . . ." He waved his hand. "I'm seventeen with a baby."

I whistled. "Wow. You've made it work, though. That's impressive."

"Didn't really have much choice, did I?"

I didn't know him nearly well enough to ask why he and the mother didn't give the baby up for adoption, so I just nodded. "I guess you didn't."

"But yeah, I've made it work. He's a good kid." Zafir laughed self-consciously. "Not sure where he got the brains, because he sure didn't get them from me."

"What do you mean?"

"I mean I've never exactly been the academic type, let's put it that way. My son?" His smile was a combination of shy kid and proud father—broad, glowing, with a hint of red in his cheeks. "I'd go bankrupt if we didn't have a good library in town."

"Ah, so he's the kid who stays up all night reading under his blanket with a flashlight?"

"Yes. *Exactly*." Zafir rolled his eyes, but chuckled. "I'm constantly on his case to put the book down and go to sleep. Which, I mean . . . I want him to read. Maybe one of us can actually get a decent education, you know? But he's gotta sleep too."

I laughed. "I was like that. If he's anything like me, he'll figure out how much sleep he can do without."

"I hope so. He hasn't yet, let me tell you." Zafir shifted. "And who knows? Maybe I'll let him give skating a try."

"Hit me up if you want to. And I can help him get some of the better skate gear." I wrinkled my nose. "You don't want him falling on cheap shit."

"I'd just as soon he didn't fall on anything, but okay. I'll take a look." He grimaced. "See if I can afford it."

I waved a hand. "It's not that bad. I can hook you up for not a lot of cash. Don't worry."

"Cool." Zafir smiled. "Thanks."

"Don't mention it."

The conversation fell into a lull, and we both paused for long swallows from our sodas. I sat back, a little more relaxed than I'd been when he'd first come in. He was easy to talk to, so that was a plus. If I could get these questions out of my head, maybe we'd get somewhere.

"So, going back to the asexual thing . . ." I drummed my fingers on the table. "If it's not too personal, where do *you* fall on the spectrum?"

"I kind of go back and forth between graysexual and demisexual."

"You go back and forth?"

"Mm-hmm. I lean more graysexual—not into sex one way or the other—but sometimes I do get sexually involved with people. I just have to be *really* into someone emotionally in order to want sex with them. So . . . a little demisexual, I guess."

"Oh. So you . . . you do get involved with people? Physically?"

He nodded. "If I'm in a relationship with someone who's sexual, then yeah. My ex-fiancée and I had sex all the time."

"You—" God, I wasn't sure how to deal with someone so blunt and candid about his sex life, but then, he worked in a place where shyness probably didn't fly. I cleared my throat. "You did? Really?"

"Mm-hmm." He gave a quiet, almost bashful laugh. "We were polar opposites when it came to sex drives. I could take or leave it, but she had a pretty serious libido. So any time she wanted it, I gave it."

"And that didn't bother you?"

"Not at all. I wanted her to be happy. Part of making her happy meant having a lot of sex." He paused. "I mean, it was understood that if I wanted to *not* have sex, we wouldn't, and she was fine with that."

I chewed my lip, not sure how much of an open book he really wanted to be. I had questions, but we barely knew each other. The fact that we were being this open at all was still kind of weird.

"For the record," he said, studying me as if he could see right through me, "no, we didn't break up because of our sex drives."

I blinked. "Oh. Yeah, I kind of wondered."

"A lot of people do." He shook his head and went for his drink again. "Having mismatched sex drives doesn't make things easy, but no, it isn't why we split." Right before he took a sip, he added a bitter, "There are plenty of other ways for someone to make a man feel inadequate."

I eyed him, but didn't push that issue. We definitely hadn't known each other long enough to go down that road, especially since it seemed like the wound was still tender.

I cleared my throat. "Have you ever had a relationship end because of . . ."

Sighing, Zafir nodded. "I'm not gonna lie. Some people think they're okay with it until the rubber meets the road. But that kind of applies to anything. And even if two asexuals start dating, they might not be sexually—or, well, asexually—compatible either."

"How so?"

"Well, if one falls in love with the other, and it turns out they're demisexual, so they start wanting to have sex with the other, and the other is apothisexual and is repulsed by sex . . ." He lifted one shoulder. "It might not work, you know?"

"Can it work if someone's asexual and the other person isn't? Like, can it *actually* work?"

"Sure. It's just up to the couple to figure out what works and what doesn't." He held my gaze for a moment, and smiled subtly, as if he could see my brain scrambling from trying to process all this. He sat up, resting his elbows on the table and clasping his fingers together. "It's honestly not as crazy and complicated as it sounds. Think of it this way: people approach sex like they do carnival rides."

"Carnival— What?"

He laughed. "Stay with me. So, you've got people who go to the carnival and want to go on every ride a dozen times. They're the ones who get off the roller coaster, and they enjoyed it so much, they can't wait to get on the next one. Or, before the adrenaline's even worn off, they're back in line to ride it again."

I nodded, not entirely sure where he was going with this.

"Think of those people as sexual people." Zafir lowered his hands to the table and folded them, looking me right in the eye. "Asexuals, we're the friends who come along to the carnival, but aren't really into the rides. And we're all different about it. Some get green and feel like they're going to barf just looking at a ride. There's no way in hell anyone's dragging them on. Not happening."

He paused, and I nodded. *Go on.*

"Not all asexuals are like that, though," he continued. "Going back to the carnival ride analogy, some aren't really interested, but, eh, your girlfriend's going on it, so you go with her, and you do actually have a good time, but after one or two, you'd just as soon go play some games or something. Or maybe you have no desire to go to the carnival at all, but since your girlfriend wants to go, you do too, and you really do get into it. But when you're single again, you drive by the carnival every day on your way to work and don't even notice it's there." He chuckled. "It's not a perfect metaphor, but it makes sense, right?"

"It's starting to." I drummed my fingers beside my drink. "Or . . . you think the rides are fun, but you don't get as crazy excited as the person you're with, and then everyone tells you you're doing it wrong?"

"Exactly. The point is, there's no one way to do a carnival. And there's no one way to be asexual. Or sexual, for that matter." He leaned closer, lowering his voice. "So, what happened with your girlfriends . . .? My theory is that you weren't doing it wrong. It's just not what you were wired to *want* to do."

I stared at the table between us for a while, letting it all sink in. I'd never heard of asexuals until recently, and I'd never thought about any of what he was saying, but it all made so much sense, I couldn't believe it had taken me until this moment to understand it all. Of course I was asexual. How the hell did I ever think I wasn't?

Because I didn't know what an asexual was before I met Zafir. But still. It seemed so *obvious*.

When I looked at him again, he tilted his head slightly, brow pinched with unmistakable concern and sympathy. "So, is this making a little more sense?"

"Some of the pieces are kind of coming together. Slowly." I shifted, folding and refolding my hands, and laughed bitterly. "Funny—the girls in high school always said they liked me because I didn't push for sex. If anything, *they* were pushing *me*. I guess now we know why."

"You're not the first guy I've heard that from." His lips quirked. "My friends all thought I was gay for a long, long time." He laughed quietly. "Some of them still do, actually."

"Really?"

"Well, to be fair, I have dated men. And the people I hung out with in high school can't even figure out what 'bisexual' means, so I'm not about to explain 'biromantic asexual' to them." He shrugged. "They can think what they want."

"Fair enough."

Zafir smiled. Then he glanced at his watch and scowled. "Crap. I didn't realize how late it was." He met my gaze. "I should probably go get some sleep so I can take my kid to school at the crack of dawn."

"Yeah, no problem." I gestured for the waitress to bring the new check. To Zafir, I said, "Thanks again for coming. I really appreciate this. I was just hoping to clarify a few things, but you've been . . ." I exhaled. "A much bigger help than that."

He smiled. "Don't mention it. I'm happy to help you skip over that shitty phase I went through where I thought something was wrong with me. Email me or come by the shop anytime."

"I'll do that. Thanks." I paused. "And, um, like I said, if you want me to help your son get started skateboarding—safely—you know where to find me."

Zafir nodded. "I'll keep that in mind."

# CHAPTER FOUR

# ZAFIR

A few days after my late-night drink with Brennan, it was business as usual at Red Hot Bluewater. And since it was Friday afternoon, I was knee-deep in a new shipment of bondage accessories. The typical grind—sorting and counting them so they could be displayed in the shop. *So* exciting.

Violet leaned into the stockroom. "Honey, you've got someone asking for you."

"I do?" Oh, please don't let it be that creepy lady asking about stain removal again. "Who?"

She glanced over her shoulder, then back at me, and shrugged. "Some kid with a skateboard."

In a heartbeat, I was on my way to the door, but stumbled when my foot caught on a pile of bondage harnesses.

Violet smirked. "Someone you know, I take it?"

"Um . . ."

She laughed, patting my arm, and gently shoved me toward the sales floor. "Get out there."

"Yes, ma'am." I hurried past her, and sure enough, Brennan was standing there in the shop, eyeing a rack of sounding equipment.

As I came out of the back, he turned and smiled. "Hey."

"Hey," I said.

"Sorry to pester you, but—" He held up a catalog with a skateboarder on the cover. "I thought you might want to have a look at this. See what kind of safety gear I can get for your son if he still wants to skate."

"Oh. Awesome." I took the catalog from him and thumbed through it. "Not that I have any clue what most of this is for."

Brennan smiled. "Trust me—a lot of it will make sense when you really look at it. Don't worry about the custom boards or anything like that, but look at the safety gear and basic boards."

I nodded. "Cool. Thanks."

"Don't mention it." He chewed his lip, rocking from his heels to the balls of his feet. "I, um, don't have to be back at the shop tonight. Do you have a dinner break or anything soon?"

My heart sped up. It was early yet, a good hour before I usually took my break, but . . .

I glanced past him at Violet. She grinned as she nodded and waved toward the door.

*You're the best, V.*

Smiling, I faced him again. "Yeah. Just let me clock out really fast." I stepped into the back and put the catalog on the desk where I wouldn't forget it. Then I clocked out and rejoined Brennan in the front.

"See you in a bit, Violet," I called over my shoulder.

"Have fun, sweetheart."

I glanced back at her, and she smirked before returning her attention to the shelf she was stocking. Fortunately, Brennan didn't seem to notice her teasing tone, or at least didn't feel the need to question why my boss was ribbing me about going somewhere with a guy.

As we stepped outside, I said, "I don't have a ton of time, but there's a deli around the corner that's really good."

"Leo's Deli?"

"Yep."

"Sweet. I love that place."

We walked a few doors down and into the deli, which was deserted. There, Brennan ordered a turkey and Swiss sandwich, and I went for a salad.

As we sat down at a table by the window, he glanced at my meal. "You a vegetarian?"

I shook my head. "No, no. But I do try to keep halal."

"Keep . . . what?"

"Halal." I tore the salad dressing packet and started smothering the salad in balsamic vinaigrette. "Basically means we can only eat meat from animals that were slaughtered a certain way."

"Oh. Is that kind of like kosher?"

I laughed softly. "Not really, but . . ." I shrugged. "Close enough, I guess."

"Sorry." His face colored. "I don't know any of the rules about Muslims. I don't know *anything* about Muslims. So, if I sound like an idiot—"

"Relax." I smiled. "You're not patting me down or giving me the side-eye, so you're fine."

"Do you really get that a lot?"

"Not a lot, but it happens. Airports suck, and whenever something goes to hell in the Middle East, everyone either wants my opinion or my apology."

"Wow. That must be fun."

"It can be. Once in a while."

His eyebrows shot up. "Seriously?"

"Seriously." I laughed. "There was this one time I was out with my sister, and some guy started ranting and raving about how he didn't serve in Iraq so people like me could steal all the jobs in his country." I rolled my eyes. "We told him like six times we were from Lebanon and not Iraq. Finally my sister pointed at me and said if the guy really wanted a job, I could probably hook him up with a dildo-selling gig."

Brennan choked on his drink. "Really?"

"Yeah." I laughed. "He left us alone after that."

"Smart." He coughed a few times, took another drink, and cleared his throat once more. "I usually get stopped at the airport, but that's what I get for carrying a bunch of gear and tools through security."

"Gear and tools?"

He nodded. "I fly to competitions sometimes, and I've been paranoid ever since a buddy of mine had a bunch of stuff stolen from his checked bag. Including a custom board."

"Can you even *get* that stuff through security?"

"We have a pretty comprehensive list of what we can and can't take through." He shook his head. "Makes packing before a trip kind of a pain, but it keeps me from spending the whole flight wondering if anyone helped themselves to stuff I need at the competition."

"I totally get that." I skewered a piece of lettuce and a tomato. "I wonder if I could get anything like that past TSA."

Brennan snorted. "Good luck. I compete against this one dude out of New Mexico. He's originally from India, I think, and it's become a running joke. Whenever we see him, we have to ask him about getting searched." He met my gaze, and cringed a little. "I mean, I know it's racist as fuck that they do that, but—"

"Trust me, I get it. There are some guys at my mosque who travel for business all the time. It's aggravating, and they've all missed flights because of it." I shrugged. "But sometimes you have to laugh, or else you'll drive yourself insane."

"That applies to most things, don't you think?"

"It does. Very much so." I paused. "So when is your next competition?"

"Coming up pretty soon, actually. I'll be gone next Friday until Monday."

I smiled. "Fingers crossed for you."

"Thanks."

"I'd say 'break a leg' but I have a feeling—"

Brennan burst out laughing. "Yeah. No. That's not what you want to have happen at a skating competition. We all get hurt enough, thank you very much."

I nearly choked. "What?"

He put up his hands and shook his head. "Don't freak out. Your kid isn't going to be skating at this level anytime soon."

"Still . . ."

"The thing is, when you're trying to get into the X Games like I am, falling means . . . falling. *Hard.*" He picked up his drink. "At Tariq's level, you occasionally land on your ass, dust yourself off, and keep going. So, don't let what I do make you worry too much about him."

"You're assuming he won't want to get to your level."

The corners of his mouth rose in a lopsided grin. "Well, if he takes a few minor spills and still wants to do it, then he must be serious."

"Yeah. That's what I'm afraid of."

Brennan's smile was gentle, his tone reassuring. "I mean it—I'll make sure he learns to do it safely. Scout's honor."

As queasy as I was over the whole idea, I couldn't help taking that offered reassurance. "I appreciate it. Just don't break him. Okay?"

# CHAPTER FIVE

# BRENNAN

On my way to the skate park the next day, I glanced at my watch. I didn't have to be at work for another couple of hours. If I swung into Red Hot Bluewater, I could say hi to Zafir, and still make it to the park to do some skating before I had to clock in.

Hopefully he wouldn't think it was too weird. After all, yesterday he'd thought it was *so* weird and awkward, he'd felt compelled to spend his lunch break with me. And besides, he might have some questions about the catalog I'd given him. Couldn't hurt to swing in and make sure I hadn't confused him beyond repair.

Only one way to find out. With my board tucked under my arm, I pulled open the black-papered glass door and stepped into the sex shop.

The place was empty except for the older lady behind the counter. No customers and no Zafir. But he'd been in the back room yesterday, so maybe he was just out of sight.

As I walked up to her, she looked at me over her glasses. "Can I help you?"

"Yeah, um . . . is Zafir around?"

She shook her head. "Sorry, honey. He's off today. Is there something I can help you with?"

"No, that's fine." Why was I so disappointed? "I'll just shoot him a text. Thanks."

She smiled and went back to what she'd been doing.

I headed back out, and after the door had shut behind me, I sighed. Well, apparently I'd have more time to skate today after all. So I headed up the street.

First things first, I'd swing by the shop to pick up my helmet. I was admittedly a slacker about wearing it when I was just out skating, but if I was going to work on some jumps on the half-pipe, I needed a brain bucket. Not that I'd learned that the hard way or anything.

When I got to the shop, I put my board under my arm, pulled open the door, and—

Stopped dead.

Blinking in disbelief, I said, "Zafir?"

At the counter, he turned around, eyes wide. Then he smiled. "Oh hey."

"I . . . didn't expect . . ."

"I just brought my son in." He gestured over his shoulder. "One of your coworkers was showing me a few things to get him started." He smirked. "Guess now that I've brought him in here, I have to follow through, right?"

"Well, I'm not gonna say no . . ."

"Of course you're not." He rolled his eyes. "I'm still not sure about all this, though. I know you said he's going to start out slow and easy, but I could do without him doing . . ." Zafir gestured at some of the posters above the cash register, which showed several of the guys from the shop performing extreme tricks at competitions. "Kind of asking for a broken arm, isn't it?"

"Nah." I pointed at one of the posters. "And it took me fifteen years to be able to do a flip like that."

"You can do—" He squinted a bit. "Wait, *is* that you?"

I grinned. "That's me."

"Wow." He whistled. "That is impressive."

"Thanks. And like I said—you don't have to worry about him doing that kind of thing for a while."

His eyes widened, and he looked up at the poster again. "Not for a while. Define 'a while.'"

"*Years*. Trust me, there's a *lot* of skating between learning how to stand on a board and . . ." I gestured at the poster again.

"Hmm." He gazed at it for a moment. Then he turned toward the other end of the store and called out, "Hey, Tariq!"

A kid turned around from looking at a display of skating magazines, and trotted over to us. "Yeah?"

"This is my friend Brennan. Brennan, my son, Tariq."

Yeah, that was definitely his kid. Tariq's skin was a tad lighter, but he had the same dark eyes and jet-black hair. He was in that same gangly stage as my ten-year-old nephew—all knees and elbows, and even though he wasn't very tall yet, he had feet that hinted he'd be towering over his dad in a few years. If Zafir was anything like my sister, he was tearing his hair out over buying new shoes every other day.

"So, Brennan's a skater." Zafir hesitated, looking just a little bit tentative and a little bit queasy. Then he swallowed as he gestured at me. "He said he could give you some lessons if you really want to give this—"

"Yeah!" Tariq jumped on the balls of his feet. "Really? Can I?"

Zafir took in a deep breath through his nose. Slowly, he nodded. "You can give it a try, yes."

"Awesome!"

I grinned at the kid's enthusiasm. "Fair warning, though—scheduling a lesson might take a little while. We both have retail schedules. I've got a competition in Portland next week, and one in Reno the week after, so I'll be in and out of town a little bit."

Tariq's eyes bugged out. "You compete? At skateboarding?"

I smiled. "Yeah. Trying to go pro."

"Whoa!" He looked up at his dad. "That's so cool!"

Zafir laughed. "Yeah, it is pretty cool."

"Have you ever been to the X Games?"

I nodded. "I've been to them, but didn't *quite* qualify to compete."

"Whoa." Tariq's eyes got even bigger. "Can I come watch one of your competitions?"

"Tariq," Zafir said.

"It's okay." I turned to Zafir. "You guys are more than welcome to come. There aren't any on the Peninsula, but we sometimes have them over in Seattle or Tacoma."

"Please, Dad?"

Zafir looked at me, eyebrows up as if to ask *You sure about this?*

I nodded.

"Okay." He shrugged. "Maybe if there's one nearby."

"Cool!"

"I'll let you guys know," I said. "I know it's a bit of a drive."

"I'm sure we can swing it." Zafir gazed at his son for a moment, then asked me, "So, it really wouldn't be too much to ask for you to give him some lessons? Just, uh, something to get him started?"

"No problem!" I smiled. "I'd be happy to."

His lips pulled tight. "I can't afford to pay much. I'm really—"

"Dude." I put up my hands and shook my head. "Don't sweat it. I like working with kids and new skaters. And besides, after everything you've done for me lately? We'll call it even."

Zafir's forehead creased. "Really?"

"Sure." I smiled. "Once our schedules line up, just bring him by the park." I gestured up the road toward the skate park. "I can hook him up with some used gear and stuff too, the first few times. So you're not coughing up money for something he won't keep doing."

"Thanks. I . . . I really appreciate it." He turned to Tariq. "We should probably get going. You ready?"

The kid nodded. "Okay."

"Feel free to email me if you've got any questions." I paused, realizing how similar that sounded to our parting words the first time we met. "About, you know . . ." I gestured at the boards hanging on the wall behind me. "Anything."

Zafir smiled. "I will. We'll definitely be in touch. Again."

"Looking forward to it."

And I was. I really, really was.

# CHAPTER SIX

# ZAFIR

Getting Tariq, Brennan, and me in the same place at the same time so my son could have skate lessons turned out to be insanely complicated. Tariq was patient, though. Whenever I reminded him that I hadn't forgotten, he just nodded and smiled and said, "I know, Dad. It's okay."

Eventually. We would all make our schedules work *eventually*.

In the meantime, I saw quite a bit of Brennan. Every chance we had, we each made excuses to "happen" by the other's shop. After a week or so, it had become a routine part of the day. Brennan came by during his lunch or dinner breaks, and we'd either eat in the back room or go to one of the restaurants nearby. I swung by the skate shop on the way to work, and sometimes on my way from one job to the other. If he was working the closing shift while I was delivering pizzas, he and his coworkers would order, and they'd specifically request me as the driver.

If I was off, I'd come by the skate shop. At first, it was to ask more questions about giving Tariq lessons, but that didn't last. Half the time, we didn't even mention skating.

When he came into Red Hot, he sometimes had new questions about asexuality, but those were fewer and further between. Instead, we just talked about whatever.

I hadn't realized how much our visits had become part of my day until he was gone. The competition in Portland took him out of town for a few days, and the one in Reno wasn't far behind. I was surprised by how much I missed him. We texted almost constantly, but it just wasn't the same.

Through all of our texting, though, we realized we finally had that coveted weekend day off—when neither of us had to work and Tariq wasn't at school. The poor kid could finally have that skating lesson we'd been promising him.

But that wasn't for a few days yet. And as I stocked shelves in Red Hot's leather aisle, I could barely concentrate because tonight, during the sliver of time between my two jobs, I'd finally get to see Brennan.

I finished putting a couple of ball gags on a rack, then went to the end of the aisle to hang up some strap-on harnesses. As I headed back to get another box of new merchandise, Violet looked up from her clipboard and tilted her head.

"You're in a good mood today."

Laughing, I shrugged. "That's not a bad thing, is it?"

"No, but I know you, and it's mildly suspicious."

"Mildly— What?"

She chuckled. "Well, with as much as you keep checking the time and squirming, I'm guessing you've got something to look forward to after work." She glanced at the clock. "Why don't you wrap up what you're doing, and take off a few minutes early?"

I blinked. "Really?"

Violet nodded. "Get out of here, sweetheart. Have a good time." She shifted her attention back to the clipboard, and that was the end of it. She didn't ask questions and I didn't offer answers.

I finished stocking the last few items on my list, and fifteen minutes before I was supposed to leave, I said good-bye to Violet. She always insisted on paying me even when she let me take off early, so I didn't bother clocking out—she'd take care of that when the time came.

And yeah, she was right. I was excited. After not seeing Brennan for the better part of a week, why wouldn't I be?

*But . . . why* am *I?*

Oh who cared? I enjoyed hanging out with him. Didn't really matter why.

I strolled into Skate of Juan de Fuca and hoped I didn't look like too much of a grinning idiot as I approached the counter.

The burly biker-type guy behind the register glanced up from a magazine. Then he craned his neck toward the back room. "Hey, Bren! Your friend's here."

"Be right out," came the answer.

The guy smiled, and I returned it.

Something clicked in the back room. Then something scuffed, like a shoe skidding on laminate. Another click. Another scuff.

A second later, Brennan came hobbling out on a pair of crutches, and my jaw dropped.

"What happened?" I asked.

The other guy snorted, rolling his eyes, and wandered into the back where Brennan had come from.

Brennan laughed sheepishly, some color blooming in his cheeks as he leaned on his crutches. "Well, the good news is I came in third."

"Oh did you?" I eyed the black boot encasing his left foot. "What did the other guys do? Break *both* their legs?"

Brennan chuckled and shook his head. "No. And it actually didn't happen while I was competing."

"So . . ."

He cleared his throat, his cheeks getting even brighter. "Well, let's just say some of us were fucking off in the hotel parking lot, and I kind of wiped out."

Someone in the back room laughed. "'Kind of'?"

"Hey!" Brennan twisted around. "No comments from the peanut gallery."

One of the other guys—wearing a backwards cap and baggy shorts, of course—stepped out of the back, holding up his phone. He looked right at me, grinning. "You want to see the video?"

"Uh . . ." I glanced at Brennan. "N-no. That's okay. Not when my son's about to start skating."

Brennan shot his coworker a pointed look. "Don't you have work to do?"

The guy sighed dramatically. "Man, you take the fun out of everything."

"Except filming parking lot bloopers, right?"

His friend laughed. "Yep." He slapped Brennan's shoulder hard enough to make his already compromised balance wobble. "Never a shortage of those with you around." To me, he said, "It was a classic Brennan Cross moment. Absolutely kill it when it counted, then bust his ass doing an elementary trick off a four-inch curb."

Brennan muttered something obscene. After the guy had disappeared into the back again, Brennan turned toward me. "Anyway.

I was screwing off and being an idiot, and got a nasty sprain. And this." He held up his arm, revealing some vicious road rash on his elbow. "Not my most graceful moment."

I sucked in a breath through my teeth. "And it was a basic trick, you said?"

He held my gaze, and must've heard the concern I didn't say, because he hobbled a little closer and lowered his voice. "Not that basic. Nothing Tariq will be doing anytime soon." He paused. "If you're this worried, are you sure you want him to start skating?"

"To be perfectly blunt?" I folded my arms loosely and shifted my weight, avoiding his eyes. "No. I really don't. But . . . I know I can't protect him from everything." I took a breath and made myself look at him. "This is what he wants to do. And I'll get over it." Eyeing his crutches, I swallowed. "Eventually."

"I could always teach you first. So you can see just how basic and harmless it is for a beginner."

I pursed my lips. "That's . . . a possibility."

He smiled. "Tell me when and where." Then his features scrunched into an adorably apologetic grimace. "Err. Maybe give me a week or two. Sorry."

"It's okay." I laughed. "But fair warning—next time you see Tariq, don't be surprised if he wants to hear every detail of the competition and—" I gestured at his leg "—that."

Brennan shrugged. "Part of skating is telling war stories. I'm game."

"Well, you two will have plenty to talk about when you give him his—" I paused. "Crap. I suppose his lesson on Sunday is probably out."

"Aww, damn. Yeah." Brennan clicked his tongue. "I'm sorry."

"It's fine. Though . . ." I chewed my lip.

"Hmm?"

"Well, feel free to say no," I said. "But since we both have the whole day now, you and I *could* go over to Seattle and check out that asexual group. They meet Sunday night."

"Oh." He stood a little straighter, crutches creaking quietly. "That could be interesting."

"If you want to go, I'd be happy to drive. Since your foot is out of commission and all."

"Cool. I'll cover gas."

"Awesome." I grinned. "I'll email them and let them know we'll be there."

On Sunday morning, at eight thirty on the dot, I parked in front of Brennan's apartment. As he came outside, he carried his crutches, though he still limped heavily on the booted foot.

"How's the ankle?" I got out and came around to open his door.

"Sore. That's why I'm bringing these." He held up the crutches. "Hopefully I won't need—" He did a double take, and presumably saw Tariq in the backseat. "He's coming too? To the asexual thing, I mean?"

I shook my head. "No, he's spending the day at my sister's in Port Angeles. We'll drop him off on the way out of town."

"Oh. That makes sense." He paused, his expression turning sheepish. "Not that I didn't want him around or—"

"It's okay," I said as I took his crutches. "I probably should've mentioned it."

We exchanged glances, and both smiled. Then he got into the front seat, and once he was situated, I handed his crutches back.

By the time I was getting in on my own side, Tariq was already asking him about his injuries.

"You want to see the video?" Brennan asked as I buckled my seat belt.

I glanced at him, and he gulped.

"I mean if that's okay with your dad," he quickly added.

Chuckling, I waved a hand. "It's fine." I put the car in reverse. "I just don't want to see it."

"You're driving," Tariq said. "You can't watch videos."

"See?" I sighed dramatically. "I can't watch. Gotta drive."

Brennan glanced at me again, and I shrugged. While I drove us out of the parking lot and onto the highway, Brennan thumbed through his phone.

"Ah, here it is." He twisted around in his seat. "Okay, so I was supposed to be doing a kickflip and then jumping that curb. But . . ."

Though the volume was fairly low, I could hear the click and scrape of wheels on pavement. Someone's breath caught. Then there was a grunt. Lots of cursing—definitely Brennan. And someone—probably the guy who'd offered to show me the video in the first place—laughed and said, "Dude, that shit's going on the internet!"

"Fuck you," Brennan ground out, the pain in his voice palpable.

"Whoa!" Tariq laughed. "How bad did it hurt?"

"A lot." Brennan pulled his phone back but stayed turned around, facing Tariq. "You ever fallen off a bike or something, and it doesn't hurt right away, but you know it's going to?"

"Uh-huh," Tariq said.

I squirmed uncomfortably—I knew that feeling too.

"I didn't even get that." Brennan shuddered. "Soon as I hit the pavement, it *hurt*."

"How come you weren't wearing a helmet?" Tariq asked.

"Uh . . ." Brennan cleared his throat. When I glanced at him, his cheeks were so red I couldn't help laughing.

"Yeah, Brennan." I tried to sound disapproving, but failed miserably. "Why *weren't* you wearing a helmet?"

"Um." He shifted a bit. To my son, he said, "Because I'm a dumbass. And you want to see just how dumb I was?" He handed his phone back to Tariq again. "Watch really close when I fall."

The wheels clicked on the pavement again. *Scrape. Click. Click. Scrape.* The grunt made my skin crawl, and as did the pained cursing.

"See that?" Brennan asked. "You see how close my head came to the bumper of that car?"

My throat tightened. I gripped the wheel and focused intently on the road, thankful I couldn't see what was on the screen.

"If I'd fallen the other way, I'd have smacked my forehead right on it." He set the phone on the console. "I got lucky."

"So you're going to wear a helmet next time?" Tariq asked.

Brennan hesitated. I glanced at him again, and suppressed a smirk. I faced the road, and he turned toward the backseat.

"Yeah," he said. "I'll be wearing a helmet next time."

I pressed my lips together. The next time he strolled into Red Hot without a helmet, he was going to hear about this.

All the way to Port Angeles, which was about thirty miles out of Bluewater Bay, Brennan and Tariq chattered about skating. Brennan showed him some less horrific videos, mostly from his competition, as well as some older ones.

It couldn't go on forever, though, and before too long, I pulled into my sister's driveway.

"Here we are."

Leyla was outside with my niece and nephew, her hijab fluttering in the breeze as she watched the kids play. She waved at us, and I waved back before I put the car in park.

I'd barely shifted gears before Tariq was out of the car and sprinting toward his cousins.

"Bye, Tariq!"

"Bye, Dad!" he called over his shoulder.

"Really heartbroken, isn't he?" Brennan asked.

I laughed. "No kidding."

Leyla came up to the window. "I'm taking them to the beach today, so he should be totally worn out by the time you get back."

"Perfect." I gestured at Brennan. "By the way, this is my friend Brennan. Brennan, my sister Leyla."

She ducked a little lower so she could see him, and they exchanged waves.

"Hi," Brennan said.

"Hi." She smiled. "You really going to put up with—"

"Hey." I waved a hand at her. "He knows what he's getting into. Shut up."

Leyla smothered a laugh, and Brennan snickered.

"All right." She paused to tame a piece of her hijab that kept getting away in the wind. "I'll see you two tonight."

"See you tonight. Thanks for taking care of him for me."

"Anytime."

As she went after the kids, I shifted into reverse.

"I take it he doesn't mind staying here," Brennan said.

"Hardly." I backed out of the driveway. "He adores my sister, and her kids may as well be his siblings. It's when I tell him it's time to leave that he's not thrilled."

"Ah, yeah. I can see that." He paused. "So does your whole family live around here?"

"Just my sister. My parents live near Seattle."

"You close to them?"

I winced.

"Sorry," he said quickly. "I . . . If it's too personal, we don't—"

"It's okay." I glanced at him and managed a slight smile. Facing the road again, I said, "My dad and I have . . . never really gotten along. And it just got worse after I told them Tariq's mother was pregnant."

"He didn't approve?"

I laughed humorlessly. "Not of his unmarried sixteen-year-old son knocking up a non-Muslim girl, no. And 'non-Muslim girl' is putting it nicely compared to the way my dad worded it."

Brennan blew out a breath. "Ouch."

"Yeah." I sighed. "I was actually supposed to go with him that year to do my hajj."

"Your what?"

"Hajj." I glanced at him again. "The pilgrimage to Mecca."

"Oh right. Right. Sorry."

"It's okay." I flashed him another quick smile.

"That's . . . the one all Muslims have to do, right?"

"Well, at least once in our lifetime, if we can afford it." I scowled. "So, my dad was taking my brothers and me. We had our plane tickets and everything, but he canceled mine. He said when my son was old enough to come with me, then maybe I'd be mature enough for my hajj."

"Wow. That's harsh."

"Right?" I rested a hand on the wheel and the other elbow below the window. "But, I mean, maybe this means I can go with my son, and it'll be my first time and his. I would've liked to go with my dad, but . . ." I shrugged.

"And even after all this time, he still doesn't approve?" Brennan asked. "I mean, it's been, what? Ten years?"

"Pretty close." I paused for a moment to pass a pickup truck that was going twenty under the damn speed limit. As I eased back into my lane, I went on. "It took him a long time to get over the fact that I'd gotten a girl pregnant. After Tariq was born, he did get a little better, especially once I was raising the baby on my own. But then he was always on my case about not being a devout enough Muslim, and I was like, 'Dad. Back off. I'm trying to juggle high school and a newborn. Pretty sure Allah will understand.' And that . . . didn't go over well. We got into some huge fights about it, and I finally moved to Bluewater Bay to stay with my sister."

"And that's where you've been ever since?"

I nodded. "It was supposed to be temporary, but I liked it out here. Back before the TV show came to town, the cost of living wasn't so bad compared to where I grew up, and there were some jobs available that I could get once I finished my GED." As soon as I mentioned it, my stomach tightened. I could look people in the eye and tell them I'd been a teenage father, but dropping out of high school was still a sore spot on my pride. Clearing my throat, I shifted in my seat. "So, uh, even after my sister moved to Port Angeles, I decided to stay."

"Can't blame you. I love that town." He paused. "Have you been working at the sex shop since you moved there?"

"I've changed jobs a few times. Been there for the last four years, though." I laughed dryly. "It wasn't my first choice, but Violet really liked me, and she promised me full-time hours every week so I'd have benefits. On my own, I could probably wing it in whatever neighborhood and without insurance and hope for the best, but not with a kid."

"Yeah, I can understand that. But you have the second job too?"

Sighing, I nodded again. "I'd rather not, to be honest. The chain that owns Red Hot has spectacular benefits, but I still need the side job to earn enough that I can live in a better area so Tariq can go to a good school."

"Oh yeah. Good point." He was quiet for a moment. "Okay, so I gotta ask. You're Muslim. And you're asexual. But you work in a sex shop. How does that work? I mean, besides the paychecks making it out the door. Doesn't it, I don't know, bother you?"

"Well, no." Some heat rushed into in my cheeks. "Let's just say I'm not the perfect Muslim. My family would shit themselves if they knew I was working at Red Hot, I've dated men, I'm not great at the whole praying five times a day thing . . ." I shrugged. "And the things they do know about—well, between being a lazy Muslim and a single dad, we're always butting heads about something."

"Are you at least on speaking terms with them?"

"Off and on. But it's kind of touchy. My mom doesn't like how I'm raising Tariq. My dad's always on my back about something." I rolled my eyes. "Last time we talked, he was annoyed that I keep my hair long but I won't grow a beard." I scratched my chin and wrinkled my nose. "I hate facial hair."

Brennan laughed. "Yeah, me too. Can't grow it anyway."

"Yeah?"

"Uh-huh. I'm twenty-five and can still get away with not shaving for three days."

"Lucky," I muttered. "I can grow it. I just hate it. So it makes things kind of tense with my dad."

"Yeah, I guess it would. That sounds rough."

"Just a bit." But discussing my family situation was going to get depressing fast, so I asked, "What about you? You from Bluewater Bay?"

"I grew up in Port Townsend. Moved . . . man, almost four years ago now." He whistled. "Time flies."

"It does. What brought you to Bluewater Bay?"

"The skate shop, believe it or not."

"Really?"

"Yeah. I was trying to go pro, and the people I was skating with in Port Townsend couldn't get their shit together. But I really liked the group in Bluewater Bay, and the owner said he'd hire me and sponsor me."

"And that's what you've always want to do?" I asked. "Skate?"

"Since I was a kid." He laughed softly. "It's addictive. I know that's not what you want to hear before I teach Tariq, but there it is."

"Eh, I'm getting a little better about the idea. As long as he learns how to do it safely."

"He will." Brennan saluted playfully. "I promise."

# CHAPTER SEVEN

# BRENNAN

A few hours and a ferry ride after we left Bluewater Bay, we were in Seattle. The boat had been great—gave me a chance to get out of the car and stretch, especially since my leg was getting kind of sore. And it was a clear, sunny day, so we had a gorgeous view of Seattle and Mount Rainier as we slowly sailed toward the waterfront.

Now that we were back in the car and leaving the ferry terminal, I was extra thankful Zafir had driven. There must've been a game or something today—the terminal was down by the football and baseball stadiums—because there were cars *everywhere*. We had to wait through four red lights to get past the first intersection.

"Ah, I love this city." Zafir paused as he turned onto a slightly less crowded side street. "Could do without the traffic, but I love the city."

"Yeah, it's nice here. Except all of that." Seattle *was* a cool city and all, but the traffic and some of the weird streets and intersections could go straight to hell. I turned to him. "You come out to Seattle very often?"

"Not really. You?"

I shook my head. "Almost never. I used to come down for concerts and shit when I was younger, but it's such a hassle to get all the way out here, go to a show, and come back. I sometimes compete here, though."

"Do you?"

"Mm-hmm. Actually, now that I think about it, I've got a competition in this town pretty soon. If you and Tariq want to come, I'm sure I could get my hands on some tickets."

"He'd love that." Zafir glanced down at my foot. "Are you going to be able to skate by then?"

"It's not for a couple of months yet. If I'm not skating by then, I'm pretty screwed." I paused. "But if I do have to bail on competing, I'd still be happy to take you guys. Tariq seems like he'd enjoy it."

"He would. I can't tear him away from the TV when the X Games are on."

I laughed. "Sounds like me."

"*Great.*" He sighed dramatically. "And I'm going to let the two of you hang out."

"I never said I wouldn't be a bad influence on your kid."

"Mm-hmm." He glared at me, but then laughed. "Okay, so we've got tons of time to kill. Want to just grab some coffee and relax for a while?"

"That sounds great to me."

He pursed his lips and tapped the wheel. "Let's go over to Fremont. There's always a shop or two with good coffee and empty tables."

He was right—though two of the Fremont neighborhood's coffee shops were jam-packed with people, we pulled up in front of one that was nearly deserted.

"That's not a bad sign, is it?" I asked. "An empty coffee shop in Seattle?"

"Only one way to find out."

"Great. I'll go grab a table while you park." Getting in and out of the car with the boot and crutches was a pain in the ass, but I managed. While Zafir drove off to find parking, I went inside.

If the smell was any indication, the emptiness of the shop was not a bad sign. The coffee smelled amazing, and one whiff of their pastries made my mouth water.

The barista looked at me, and did a double take at my crutches. "Oh! Do you want to have a seat and we'll bring something out to you?"

"No, no. It's okay." I smiled and stopped in front of the counter. "Light crowd today?"

"This is normal. Tonight, it'll be wall-to-wall people." She gestured at one end of the shop, and I turned to see a small stage.

"Oh, so everyone comes out for . . . music?"

"Yep. And poetry slams on Tuesdays."

"Gotcha." I looked up at the menu on the wall. There were a ridiculous number of options, but I finally narrowed it down to a cappuccino and some flaky-looking little pastry with chocolate in the middle.

"Go ahead and have a seat," she said after I'd paid. "We'll bring it to your table."

"Great. Thanks." I hobbled over to a table by the window, and was just sitting down when Zafir walked in.

"I swear," he grumbled. "There is no parking in this town."

I leaned my crutches against the wall behind me. "You've just been spoiled by Bluewater Bay."

"The parking sucks there too."

"But not as bad as it does here."

"Hmm, yeah. True." He glanced at the menu above the counter. "Have you ordered yet?"

I nodded.

"Let me get something for me. I'll be right back."

He returned a minute later with both cups of coffee, a piece of pie, and my pastry, the plates and saucers balanced carefully on his arm and hand.

"Need help with that?" I started to get up.

"Nope, I've got it." Somehow, he managed to put all three things on the table without spilling a drop or losing a fork.

"Impressive," I said. "You must've waited tables before."

"Yep." He chuckled. "And I can get pizzas from my car to someone's door, while slipping and sliding on ice, without screwing up the toppings. I may not have many talents, but transporting food is apparently one of them."

I laughed, slicing off a piece of the pastry with my fork. "Well, I'm the type who can sit down on the couch with a bowl of cereal and wind up wearing it."

"That used to be me. But delivering pizzas and waiting tables . . ." He shrugged.

"Maybe I'm in the wrong line of work."

We munched on our pastries and sipped our coffees for a little while. When my cup was empty, Zafir went back up to get refills for both of us.

I glanced at my watch. We still had a few hours yet before the asexual group met, but my stomach was already doing somersaults. What was I supposed to talk about with these people? Would they think I was a fraud? Accept me? Interrogate me to make sure I really belonged?

Shit. Maybe this wasn't such a good idea.

"You okay?" Zafir put our fresh coffees on the table and sat down. "You look twitchy all of a sudden."

"Yeah, I'm . . ." I pulled my coffee toward me, but didn't drink it yet. Just letting it cool. Or something. "Thinking about the meeting we're going to."

"What about it?"

"I'm kind of nervous about it, to be honest."

Zafir lifted his gaze, his eyes as gentle as they'd been the first time we'd met. "Why?"

"I'm . . . I guess I'm not quite sure what I'm doing? Or if I really am asexual?"

"Don't worry about it." That always reassuring smile came to life. "It isn't like they'll quiz you or kick you out. And non-ace people come to these things sometimes anyway."

"They do?"

He nodded. "Sometimes people will bring a friend. Maybe someone who's trying to understand, or maybe they just need some support the first time they show up."

"Sort of like what you're doing for me?"

"Kind of." He reached across the table and squeezed my forearm. "Relax. You'll be fine. And if you don't click, it isn't like you have to go back."

"Well true." I rolled my shoulders, not sure why they were so stiff. Probably from my crutches, though they'd been okay the last few days. "So, um, while we're here, I'm kind of curious about something."

"Shoot."

I shifted in my seat. "You said before that your ex-fiancée had a high sex drive. But that wasn't an issue at all in your relationship?"

Zafir shook his head. "I loved her. I enjoyed making her happy." He shrugged. "Sex wasn't my first pick for ways she could make *me* happy, but I wasn't opposed to it as long as she didn't push me when I really wasn't into it. Which she never did."

"So . . ." I hesitated. "If it's not too personal—what happened?"

His lips tightened. "We broke up when she found a guy who didn't have a kid and did have"—he made air quotes—"'the potential to do more than stand behind a cash register.'" Zafir rolled his eyes, and his tone was bitter as he added, "The really shitty irony is that I'd been saving to go back to school, and I dipped into that to buy her ring."

"Wow. Ouch."

"Yeah." He stared into his coffee cup. "So that was rough. On me and Tariq. It's a damn good thing my sister lived nearby."

"How so?"

"Mostly because she took Tariq to play with his cousins, go to the beach, whatever, while Megan and I dealt with moving her out of the apartment." He exhaled. "And even after things quieted down, she was kind of my lifeline. Kept me sane. Which . . . well, that's what she's done for a long time. I don't know how I would've survived Tariq's toddler years without her. When he was really little, she sometimes took him off my hands when I was too stressed out and needed a break."

It was hard to imagine Zafir reaching that point with his son, but infants and toddlers were pretty draining. "Must've been great having that kind of support system."

"Oh yeah. This whole parenting thing is no joke. Especially when you're on your own."

I shifted a little, studying him, trying to read him even before I asked my question. "What about Tariq's mom?"

Zafir tightened his jaw. I was about to tell him to forget I'd asked, but he quietly said, "It's just me and him. Has been since he was two months old."

"Really?"

Zafir nodded. "She was gung ho about keeping him—we'd been in agreement about that from the start—but she found out newborns are a lot more work than she expected, and . . . here we are."

I chewed the inside of my cheek. "So, no contact? Nothing?"

"She signed away her rights." His tone was flat, but calm. "Every once in a while, she'll email me and ask how he's doing, but she hasn't seen him since he was two."

"Seriously?" My jaw dropped. "She just dropped off the face of the earth and doesn't see her own kid?"

"Well." He pursed his lips. "It's not quite that simple. Every now and then, she contacts me and wants to see him, but until she either takes me to court or promises to *stay* involved with his life, she can forget it." He scowled. "Tariq's had enough people treat him like his life has a revolving door on it. It bothers him that she's out of our lives, but he has no memory of her, or of her leaving. He doesn't need to experience her abandoning him again when he's old enough to know what's happening."

"That seems fair," I said, barely whispering. "I just . . . I can never get my head around someone abandoning their kid in the first place."

"I know. And . . ." He sighed. "It wasn't entirely her fault. She's not a bad person. We were both overwhelmed, plus we were living with my parents, which only made things worse." Gaze distant, Zafir swallowed. "Then when the baby was about six weeks old, she got hit with some really bad postpartum depression. That, on top of trying to keep up with school, take care of the baby, and have my parents browbeating us the whole time . . . she just couldn't handle it. So she moved back in with her parents, and they encouraged her to sign her rights away."

"And she did?"

He nodded.

I shook my head. "Jesus. That whole thing—it must've been hell for both of you."

"Yeah. After she left, it was better in some ways, worse in others." He paused. "Don't get me wrong. I love my son, and I wouldn't trade him for the world. But we both would've been a lot better off if he'd come along, say, now instead of then."

"I get that. I totally get that."

"It was the way it was meant to be, though," he said quickly. "So . . . it is what it is. Allah's plan."

I nodded. "And when Tariq was born and you were raising him on your own—you were going to school at the same time?"

"Well, I . . ." He lowered his gaze, and I thought his face darkened a little. "The punchline is that I have a GED. Couldn't *quite* pull off that last year and a half of high school when I was trying to raise him. My kid had to come first, you know?"

"Of course." I whistled. "My hat's off to you. Seriously. That you were able to take care of him when you were, what, seventeen? That's impressive."

"I turned seventeen two weeks before he was born," Zafir said quietly. "And it wasn't like I had a choice. It was either take care of him, or he was going up for adoption." He tapped his fingers beside his cup. "Sometimes I think I was selfish, keeping him when someone else could've given him a better start, but I think I've done okay. He's happy. He's healthy." Zafir lifted his drink as if in a toast. "Can't really ask for much more than that, can I?"

"No, not at all." I grinned cautiously. "And to be fair, I've got a high school diploma and half an associate's degree, and I'm working in retail too. So." I shrugged. "It isn't like the diploma is an express ticket to a corner office."

"Fair point." He smiled and seemed to relax a little. "Of course, you've also got the skating going for you."

"Pfft." I waved a hand. "This isn't baseball. Going pro doesn't mean much unless you start getting video game endorsements or something. And I'm already old enough, that probably won't happen."

"Old enough?" He blinked. "You're twenty-five, right?"

I nodded. "Yep. And there are seventeen-year-olds with major endorsements under their belts. Guess I should've stuck with snowboarding—at least they go to the Olympics now."

"You were a snowboarder before?"

"I was an 'anything where I can stand on something and go fast' guy."

Zafir burst out laughing, which made my heart speed up for some reason. "I'm not surprised. You kind of seem like that type."

"Hey! What's that supposed to mean?"

"Well, I've literally never seen you without your skateboard except when you've been on crutches."

"Okay. Fair." In fact, it felt really weird not having it with me. These crutches were bullshit.

Zafir sipped his coffee. "So why'd you give up snowboarding?"

"Because I hate being cold."

"Really?" He laughed again. "That's it?"

"How many more reasons do you need?"

"Fair." His expression turned more serious. Resting his elbows on the table, he said, "So, as long as we're getting personal . . . I'm kind of curious about your relationships."

I shifted uncomfortably. "What about them?"

"Well, when you came into Red Hot the first time, you'd said they'd cheated on you."

"Yeah, because I sucked in bed."

Zafir didn't laugh. "But . . . what were the relationships like otherwise? I mean, were you happy?"

That was a good question, wasn't it? Was I happy with any of them?

"Well." I ran my knuckles back and forth along my jaw, then folded my hands on the table. "I thought I was. But after we broke up, I do kind of remember feeling like I was free. You know, like I didn't know I was being suffocated until I suddenly wasn't."

Zafir grimaced. "Wow. So, not happy?"

"I guess not." I leaned back and looked up at the ceiling. "I am apparently the worst person ever when it comes to picking out women."

"What were they like?" he asked quietly.

I swallowed. Then I shifted my gaze to the window and stared out at the street. "Kasey was just . . . I don't even know why we dated. You ever had one of those relationships?"

"Uh-huh. The kind where you split up and wonder what you were on for the entire relationship?"

"Yes. Exactly." I met his eyes. "The funny thing was, the sex was about the only thing I enjoyed. Obviously I was the only one." I sighed. "After her was Alejandra. We were friends for a long time, and as soon as we started dating, the whole thing went downhill. It was like once we realized we had no chemistry at all, suddenly we couldn't stand to be around each other. It was weird."

Zafir nodded. "That happens. And it sucks."

"It does. And after her was Aimee. You know how that turned out."

"Yeah."

"On the bright side," I said with a shrug, "now I have a better idea of who I am. So, I guess I can't complain too much."

He smiled faintly. "There's always a silver lining, isn't there?"

Nodding, I held his gaze. "Yeah. There is."

We shifted to more pleasant subjects, and at some point Zafir went up for yet another coffee refill. And those pastries were pretty damn good, so we split another one. We bitched about jobs, chatted about the various TV shows we were both *way* behind on watching, and he smiled proudly when he talked about Tariq.

Zafir glanced at his phone, and jumped. "Oh crap!" His eyes bugged out. "It's almost five!"

"What? Already?" I grabbed my phone, and sure enough, it was quarter till. "When does that thing start?"

"Five thirty. And traffic's going to be a nightmare, so we'd better leave now."

"Got it." I started to get up, but my foot—which had been aching mildly all day—suddenly hurt worse. A lot worse. I dropped back onto the chair, grabbing the back of the boot as if that would do any good. "Shit . . ."

"You okay?"

"Yeah. I think I've been sitting too long without putting my foot up."

"Maybe you should put it up now." He looked around. "I'm sure we can find another chair to use."

"But we've gotta go."

Zafir gestured dismissively. "You need to take care of your foot first. If we're late, we're late."

"Okay, but . . . Do you think the shop will mind?" I glanced at the stage. "They've got a band coming in later. She said it would get crowded."

He pursed his lips. "You know, we could go to the group another time. Maybe tonight, we could just stay here and relax. They've got sandwiches and stuff, so we can have dinner, and it'll give you a place to put your foot up."

"Are you sure? You brought me all the way out here, and—"

"And the last thing you probably need to do is hobble down a steep hill on that foot."

The thought of it made my stomach turn.

He nodded toward the stage. "Maybe the band will be a good one."

"Want to stay and find out?"

"Sure." He hesitated. "I'm a little tight on cash. I'm not—"

"My treat."

Zafir's head snapped toward me. "What?"

"I'll buy. You've been letting me hammer you with questions, and you brought me all the way out here for a—"

"For a group that we're going to miss."

"Still." I smiled. "I got it. Don't worry."

"I . . . Thanks. I really appreciate it."

"Don't mention it."

He helped me put my foot up on the chair, and the barista even brought me a bag of ice. Then Zafir ordered us a couple of sandwiches, and we hung out while people filed in to find seats for the band's performance.

Without the meeting hovering over my head, I relaxed a bit. Good food. Good music, as it turned out. Really good company.

Maybe we didn't need to come all the way to Seattle for this. We could've found all of this in Bluewater Bay. We could've saved ourselves the trip.

But I was glad we hadn't.

# CHAPTER EIGHT

## ZAFIR

I'd heard a lot of really shitty bands play at coffee shops, but this one was pretty good. We ended up staying until after eleven, and Brennan bought one of their CDs before we hurried out to catch the ferry.

Fortunately, we made it in time.

In my car in the ferry line, Brennan swore as he scratched under his boot. "I am so ready to be out of this thing."

"How much longer do you have to wear it?"

"Eh, another week or so, tops."

"Any physical therapy after that?"

"No. My doc has this wild idea I'm going to stop skating for a few months, though." He chuckled and adjusted one of the Velcro straps. "Fat chance."

"You're going to skate on an injured ankle?"

"Well, when you say it like that, I sound like an idiot."

"If the boot fits . . ."

"Shut up."

We exchanged glances, and both laughed.

He gazed out the windshield. "Oh hey, they're loading."

As if on cue, all around us, engines turned over and taillights started coming on. I started my car, and when my line moved, followed it onto the boat. I put the car in park, then killed the engine again.

Brennan twisted around, looking at something outside the car. "I'm going to go up and find the bathroom. Be right back."

"Do you need help? Getting up the steps, I mean?"

He shook his head and unbuckled his seat belt. "Nah. I'll be fine. They've got handrailings, right?"

"Of course."

"Well, as long as the boat doesn't rock too much, I should be okay." He tapped his crutches. "I don't think I'll bother with these, though."

"Are you sure?"

"Yeah. On stairs, it's a lot easier without them."

"Okay. Just, um, send me a text, I guess? If you need help?"

"Will do."

He got out and limped toward the stairs. The seas were fairly calm tonight, fortunately, and he made it without too much trouble.

I watched until he disappeared and the big steel door had shut behind him. Then I took out my phone and texted Leyla. *On the ferry now—will be late.*

She sent back a picture of Tariq, sprawled out on the couch and sound asleep.

I smiled. Trust her and her kids to run him into the ground and wear him out. He'd sleep well tonight, that was for sure.

I hadn't meant for us to stay over here so late. Usually, I left the group around nine and was home by midnight. Tonight, it would be at least two.

Tariq wouldn't mind either way. As long as he got to hang out with his aunt and cousins, he was happy.

And I sure didn't mind. An entire day with just Brennan? No complaints. Hell, where were all the other people like Brennan in Bluewater Bay? Or even on the Olympic Peninsula?

And why was I latching on to him so hard?

Well, okay, that made sense. Of course I was latching on to him—he was the first asexual I'd met in my zip code in recent memory.

As the ferry pushed off and started across Puget Sound, I leaned against the headrest and watched the dark water and the little sparkles of light in the distance.

I still couldn't believe I was even considering letting him teach Tariq to skate, especially after he'd gotten hurt. I barely knew him. And letting him teach Tariq meant letting Tariq skate. Letting him do exactly what had put Brennan in that boot.

My heart flipped just thinking about it. So this was what my mother felt like when we were kids.

Footsteps—one normal, one heavy—caught my attention. I turned just as he opened the passenger door and got back in. "Holy crap, it got cold out there!" He shut the door and shivered. "Jesus."

I laughed. "The sun's down and we're out on the water. What do you expect?"

"Yeah, yeah."

I glanced around to make sure none of the ferry workers were nearby, and then turned on the engine. As I cranked up the heat, I said, "Let me know when you're warm enough so I can shut it off again."

"Will do."

"You did okay on the steps? With your boot?"

He nodded. "The boat rocked a little while I was on my way down, but . . ." He shrugged. "It wasn't that bad. Looking forward to losing the damn thing."

"And I'm still supposed to let you show Tariq how to skate."

He chuckled, rubbing his hands together in front of the heater vent. "It'll be *fine*. Promise."

"Yeah, yeah. I'll admit—I'm overprotective."

"Eh, beats the alternative." He sat back and sighed. "Okay, I'm good. Not cold anymore."

I killed the engine. The heater stopped, but the car stayed pleasantly warm.

"Anyway," I said. "Yeah, I know I'm overprotective. Way too paranoid and all that. I swear, every time he wants to do something that might give him so much as a bruise, I can hear my mother coming out of my mouth." I laughed, rolling my eyes. "Not gonna lie—I'm a parent who'd like to send his kid out into the world wrapped in titanium armor over bubble wrap padding."

"But you've said you'll let him skate, so you must not be that overprotective."

I gazed out at the dark water, tapping my nails on the steering wheel. "I am, but I don't actually say it, if that makes sense. Like, it scared me to death to teach him to ride a bike, especially when it came time to take off the training wheels, but I still let him."

"I think that's most parents, isn't it?"

"Maybe." I shifted in my seat, resting my elbow on the steering wheel. "The thing is, I grew up in an *oppressively* strict household.

Like, if there was the slightest possibility of something being dangerous, my mother wouldn't let us."

"Really?"

"Yep. After she turned her back one time and my brother fell down a couple of porch steps when he was like two, she panicked. From then on, she was adamant about protecting all of us from any kind of danger. I swear, any time we saw a commercial or an article about some new childproofing thing, we all face-palmed because we knew it would be adopted in our house the second it was available."

"Oh God." Brennan groaned. "You had *that* mom."

"Uh-huh. And of course, we all still managed to get banged up, so she'd just get even more strict, but she had no clue that she was making it worse." Sighing, I shook my head. "Every scare tactic news article meant new rules, and every new rule meant all of us rebelling even harder."

"As kids do."

"Right? So, we had to wear every piece of safety gear available if we got on a bike. Tree climbing? Not a chance. When we were teenagers, she heard that kids staying out late were more likely to get into trouble, so we had insanely strict curfews." I laughed humorlessly. "We weren't allowed to even have friends of the opposite sex because she'd read about twelve-year-olds giving each other STDs."

"Jesus. Seriously?"

"Uh-huh. So, in the end, my brother got on a friend's motorcycle without a helmet and split his head open. My sister broke her arm falling out of a tree. My youngest brother stayed out so late he fell asleep at the wheel." I exhaled, turning toward Brennan. "And I knocked up my girlfriend."

He watched me in the low light. "So basically, you have your mom's overprotective instinct, but you don't want to restrict him so much that he rebels and hurts himself?"

"Exactly." I pressed my head back against the headrest, staring out at the water. "Every time that instinct comes up, I fight it back down and remind myself Tariq *needs* to skin his knees and elbows. It's part of being a kid. If I let him take some lessons from an experienced skateboarder, then he'll probably fall a few times. Get some scrapes and bruises. From there, he'll either decide skateboarding isn't for him—"

"Or he'll continue, but with a healthy respect for how hard the pavement can bite."

I shuddered at the thought of Tariq hitting the pavement, but nodded. "Yeah. Exactly."

"That seems perfectly sane to me. I mean, I'm not a parent, but I see a lot of kids at the skate park. Some parents let their kids wipe out occasionally. You know, the 'rub some dirt in it and get back out there' parents." He shrugged. "And then there are the ones who refuse to let their kid even think about going on any of the ramps or learning tricks. When those kids show up with their friends and no parents, we pretty much put 911 on speed dial because we know something bad is going to happen."

I sat up. "What do you mean?"

"I mean, those are the kids who think, 'Hey, Mom's not watching, so I'm going to get on the half-pipe and do some of that cool stuff she won't let me do.' We try to stop them, but sometimes you don't realize it's happening until he breaks his arm."

I shuddered.

Brennan held my gaze. "I'm not a parent, and I'm no expert. But it sounds like you've got that balance, you know? Between being protective and being too protective. You let him take risks, but don't let him do things that'll get him seriously hurt. You know, enough that he knows that if you say not to do something, there's probably a reason for it." He smiled shyly. "Seems like Tariq's a lucky kid."

"Thanks."

He was quiet for a moment, then asked, "So, he's going to be grown-up and out of the house before you're forty. What are you going to do?"

I blew out a breath. "Haven't really thought that far ahead, to be honest. The past few years have just been about making ends meet and taking care of Tariq."

"You think you'll go back to school? Start a career?"

"I don't know." I shrugged. "I have thought that maybe once Tariq is old enough to be on his own after school, I'll go back to school myself. *Inshallah*."

"Huh?" He eyed me. "That last part? Inshall . . . what?"

My cheeks burned, though I wasn't totally sure why. "It's an Islamic thing. It means 'if it's God's will.'" I turned to him. "So like if we say we're going to do something in the future, we add that as kind of a nod to Allah. We're acknowledging that we know our plans aren't, you know, entirely up to us."

"So, like knocking on wood?"

"Well, a little less superstitious and more submitting to God's will, but close enough."

"Oh. Cool." He smiled. "Learn something new every day."

I returned the smile. "So. Yeah. That's as far ahead as I've thought. I don't even know what I'd study at this point."

"I've taken some online courses at one of the universities in Seattle. If you want the information, I can email it to you."

"Sure. That'd be great."

I was more relieved than he could imagine that he'd just taken the casual mention of Islam in stride. I tried not to bring it up too often with him or anyone else because that had a tendency to derail conversations and turn them into heated debates. But it was part of who I was, and it was naturally going to come out once in a while.

Every time my religion had entered a discussion, though, Brennan had approached it with nothing but curiosity. He never rolled his eyes or said anything snide. Even though he didn't fully understand my beliefs, he'd simply accepted them as part of me.

*An asexual man who's good with my son and doesn't bat an eye at me being Muslim? Is this even possible?*

*Please let this be real. Inshallah.*

## CHAPTER NINE

# BRENNAN

It was almost two when Zafir pulled into Leyla's driveway. I stayed in the car—my ankle was throbbing like mad now, so he insisted I just relax while he went in to get Tariq.

As I waited for them, my mind wandered through the last several hours. I was a little disappointed we hadn't made it to the asexual group, especially since it was anybody's guess when we'd have the opportunity again. Still, the day hadn't exactly been wasted. Quite the opposite. I was tired, and my ankle was sore, and I was ready to just face-plant in my pillow, but I still felt kind of . . . high? It was a little like when the adrenaline was tapering off after I'd competed—I was wrung out and completely done, but still kind of giddy. Like I desperately needed to sleep but wasn't ready for the day to be over.

At least it was better than feeling sorry for myself and pining for Aimee. Had I been pining for her? Now that I thought about it—not really. I'd been pining for that year and a half where I'd been cruising along in a relationship, taking for granted that things would never change and that I knew who I was. Ignorance was bliss, apparently.

But now she was gone, and my ego was healing because I'd found out some things that had never occurred to me, and I was grinning like a dumbass in the passenger seat of Zafir's car because we'd just spent the most awesome day together. My life felt like it had flipped on its head overnight. Everything seemed different now than it was a month ago. Or even a week ago. And I liked it. A lot.

The door opened, and Leyla stepped outside to hold the storm door. Then Zafir followed, his son in his arms. They were backlit, so I couldn't make out anyone's features, but Leyla's hijab gave her away, and Zafir . . . well, I pretty much knew his shape by heart now.

Slowly, balancing his son in his arms, Zafir came down the front steps. Tariq wasn't a big kid, but Zafir wasn't a big guy either. I would've offered to carry him, but with my ankle in that stupid boot, I was a little off-balance. Getting myself down the stairs would've been enough of a challenge without being scared to death I was going to drop Tariq. Today had been a good day—didn't need to end it on a sour note by breaking Zafir's kid.

After Zafir had cleared the steps, his sister jogged past him and opened the car door.

I twisted around as Zafir gently set Tariq in the booster seat.

"Another year," Leyla said, "and you won't be able to carry him like that."

Zafir groaned as he buckled the seat belt over his sleeping son. "Another year? More like another month."

"He's growing fast."

"Explains why my back is all jacked up."

I chuckled. "Could just be you getting older."

"Hey." He playfully wagged a finger at me. "That'll be enough out of *you*." He stood, rubbing his lower back gingerly, and exchanged a few words with Leyla in what I assumed was their native language. He hugged her, and as she headed toward the house, he got back in the driver's seat.

He started the engine. "Sorry that took so long."

"Nah. Wasn't that long." *But I'm glad you're back.* I turned around again. "He really is out cold, isn't he?"

Zafir smiled fondly at him. "Always happens when he spends the day with his cousins. Even when I don't pick him up at—" He glanced at the clock. "Two forty-five."

"Rough life."

"Right?"

We both laughed.

Zafir drove us back into Bluewater Bay. At my apartment, he stopped on the curb and put the car in park. "Well, even though we didn't make it to the group, I had a good time today."

"Me too. I think I needed to get out of town and *not* be skating for once."

"Yeah. I needed a break too." He smiled. "Next time, we'll make it to the group, though. Promise."

"Sounds great." I glanced back at Tariq. "You gonna be able to get him into your apartment?"

Zafir shrugged. "I'll wake him up if I have to. He won't be happy, but he'll just fall into bed and pass out anyway."

"Him and me both."

He laughed. "Right?"

"Well, I should . . ." I reached for the door, but hesitated. I didn't want this to be over yet, but it was starting to get really late. And Tariq was still snoring away in the booster seat, so Zafir was probably itching to get the wiped-out kid home and put him to bed.

"Anyway." I smiled. "Thanks again. For taking me out to Seattle."

"You're welcome. Even if we did waste the trip in a random coffee shop."

"I don't know. I wouldn't call it a wasted trip."

He held my gaze for a moment, then smiled too. "Neither would I, now that you mention it."

We locked eyes. My heart sped up for some reason. I wasn't sure what I was supposed to say or do right then, but throwing a "bye" over my shoulder and bolting out of the car didn't seem like the answer.

"Well." He nodded toward the backseat. "I should get him home."

"Yeah. Of course. I'll see you soon?"

He smiled. "Definitely."

"Great. Good night."

"Good night, Brennan."

We exchanged one last smile, and then I got out of the car. It wasn't the most graceful exit I'd ever made, but at least my boot and my crutches didn't make enough noise to wake up Tariq.

Finally, I was on my feet, leaning on my crutches because my ankle had had enough, and I shut the car door. Zafir waved. I waved back.

And then he drove off while I hobbled up to my apartment, smiling like an idiot the whole way.

After I'd let myself in, as I went through the motions to get myself ready for bed, I was lucky I remembered to lock the door and didn't put hair gel on my toothbrush or something. My mind was just . . . not here.

Why, I had no idea, but I kept replaying that moment when Zafir had gently eased Tariq into the car. For some reason, it made my heart flutter a little. He kind of had that effect whenever I saw him with Tariq. Maybe I was just a sucker for devoted parents. Watching Aimee with her nephews had always been cute. Kasey and her roommate's daughter had been too.

But there was something about Zafir with Tariq that made my breath catch. Was it because he was a man? Maybe because they had a warmer relationship than I'd ever had with my own father? Or because I was pretty sure that in his position—taking on parenthood alone before I could even vote—I would have torpedoed everything and made an absolute mess? Of course I'd only seen glimpses of them, but from everything I had seen, Zafir was exactly the kind of father I aspired to be when that time came for me.

And he'd pulled it off since he was seventeen. Shit, when I was seventeen, I was getting baked off my ass in between falling *on* my ass at the skate park. While I was bumming cash off my folks and weed off my friends, Zafir was parenting. On his own. And now he had a smart, respectful, healthy, thriving son who he'd gently carry out to the car even though his back obviously wasn't happy about it.

Why it stood out to me so much, I didn't know, but there was just something so endearing about watching Zafir shift into father mode.

Or any mode, for that matter.

*Am I going crazy? Probably.*

I grinned to myself.

*Fine. I'm enjoying it, so bring it on.*

Nothing in the world bored me more than hanging out at the skate park without a skateboard.

But, a week after my trip to Seattle with Zafir, there I was again—standing on the edge of a ramp with some of my friends, my foot still in that dumb boot. We were up on the big half-pipe, which was much less crowded than the other ramps and the two smaller pipes. This one was reserved for those of us registered for upcoming competitions. It was one of the perks of being sponsored by the shop.

Not that I was doing much with it today. My board was at home where it had been since I'd come back from my last competition. I wouldn't have even come here, but my buddy Sven wanted someone to look at his form. So I stood off to the side, well out of the way while he and another skater took turns.

I was definitely ready to get out of this boot and back on my board. I needed to practice before the next competition, but it also made me stir-crazy when I couldn't skate. Plus I knew Tariq was chomping at the bit for those lessons I'd been promising. Once I was out of the boot, I'd at least be able to show him a few things.

A few more days. Then I'd be back on my feet.

Someone skated up beside me and skidded to a stop. When I turned, so did my stomach.

"Hey." Aimee flipped her board and leaned it against her leg. "Can we talk for a minute?"

I glanced at Sven. He gestured for me to go ahead—*fucking traitor*—so I nodded, and we walked over to one of the picnic tables.

She stood, but I took a seat to get some weight off my foot.

"What's up?" I asked.

"I need to come get my stuff."

Oh sweet Jesus. Finally.

"Okay. When?"

"Whenever." She shrugged. "I'm moving in with Shannon and Emma. They gave me the keys already, so I just need to move my crap over there." She glared at the boot on my foot, then back at me. "But I guess you aren't going to help carry anything."

*You fucked another dude in our bed, and you thought I was going to carry your shit?*

I moistened my lips. "Sorry."

"I'm sure," she muttered.

I ground my teeth. No way in hell was she going to make me feel guilty for not helping her out. This was her choice. Not mine.

She fidgeted, tapping her nails on the edge of her skateboard. "So who's that guy who keeps coming by the shop?" Her lips twisted as she cocked her head. "I never saw him before."

I swallowed. "Just a friend."

"Yeah, but who the hell is he?"

"I don't think my social life is really any of your business anymore."

Her eyebrows climbed her forehead. "Oh."

I exhaled. Okay, maybe I'd sounded more like a dick than I'd intended. "Sorry. I'm . . ." I shook my head. "Look, he's just a friend. And I'm teaching his kid to skate."

"Oh."

"What did you think he was?" I smirked. "My boyfriend?" My throat tightened, and my mouth suddenly went dry.

*Why would I throw that out there? Put that thought in her head? What does it matter if she* does *think Zafir's my boyfriend? He isn't, so what does it matter? God, why did I say that?*

She just rolled her eyes, though. "No. I was just curious because I'd never seen him before, and suddenly you're joined at his hip." Glaring at me, she snidely asked, "Why? *Is* he your boyfriend?"

"No!" I sighed dramatically. "Jesus, Aimee."

"Hey, you're the one who said it."

"He's a friend, okay? So, when did you want to come by and get your stuff?"

She folded her arms loosely and shifted her weight. "When are you working this week? It might be, um, easier if you're there, so we can separate stuff."

Well, that saved me from suggesting that I didn't completely trust her anymore to be alone in what was now *my* apartment. "My schedule's all over the place. I'm closing tomorrow and Wednesday, but I have to see my doc on Wednesday." I tapped the boot. "About this stupid thing."

She pursed her lips. "Could I come by tomorrow morning, then?"

"How long do you think it'll take?" I asked. "I have to be at the shop by two."

She scowled. "I'll come by around nine, and if there's anything left when you have to leave, then we'll figure it out."

I nodded. "Okay."

"Cool." She smiled thinly, but her eyes didn't follow suit. "See you tomorrow."

*Yeah. Can't wait.*

About ten minutes to nine the next morning, it occurred to me that I hadn't asked Aimee to please not bring Billy to help her move. Fortunately, when she showed up—at almost nine thirty because fuck being on time—she was by herself.

Neither of us said much. I let her in, and then did my best to stay out of her way. She'd brought a few boxes up from her car, and went room to room collecting her things. She'd already moved her clothes and skating gear out, so there really wasn't much left. Between us, we didn't have a ton of stuff, and besides dishes and towels and things like that, we hadn't bought a lot as a couple. Since she was moving in with roommates and I was staying here by myself, she left most of the household stuff for me.

At a little past eleven, she carried the last box out, then came back in to go through the apartment one last time.

"I guess that's everything." She stopped in the kitchen where I was rinsing out my coffee cup. "So, um. I'll see you around."

*More than I'd like, but that's what I get for dating a skater.*

"Yeah. See you around."

One more beat of uncomfortable silence, and she was on her way out.

She'd almost made it to the door when I remembered we'd forgotten one thing, and I hurried—as fast as my boot would allow—to the kitchen doorway.

"Aimee."

Hand on the doorknob, she turned around.

I held out my hand, palm up.

"What?"

"Your key."

Rolling her eyes, she dug into her pocket. Her keys jingled in her hand, and she quickly took the house key off the ring before shoving it into my palm.

"Thank you," I said.

She muttered something, then turned to go. I didn't stop her this time. A second later, she slammed the door hard enough to rattle the apartment.

"Whatever," I grumbled into the empty room. This was her decision. If she wanted to be pissed, that was her problem.

Not three seconds later, though, there was a light knock. Had she forgotten something?

Swearing to myself, I went to the door and opened it.

On the other side was a very different woman than the one who'd just stormed out. Her shoulders sagged beneath her hoodie, and she kept her eyes down.

"Bren, can we talk?"

"Didn't you just—"

"Yes. And I'm sorry." She finally met my gaze. "That's actually what I wanted to say. I'm . . . What I did to you was shitty. You have every right to hate me for—"

"I don't hate you," I said quietly.

"Why not?"

I shrugged, wondering when something like that had started requiring so much effort. "It hurt, but . . ." How to explain it? I wasn't even sure why I didn't hate her.

She took a breath and pushed her shoulders back. "Look, I shouldn't have done what I did. I wasn't happy, and I should've just said something and called it quits instead of letting you find out like you did."

Shifting my weight, I resisted the urge to fold my arms, and instead hooked my thumbs in the pockets of my jeans. "I guess the part I don't get is why."

"Why, what? I mean, which part?"

"Why didn't you just talk to me if you were unhappy?" I hesitated. "Was it really that bad, being with me?"

Color bloomed in her cheeks as she dropped her gaze to the welcome mat between us. "I was just frustrated, you know? I felt like you didn't want me. And he . . ." She absently toed the edge of the mat. "He made me feel the way I needed to."

"Oh." We were quiet for a while. An uncomfortably long time. At a loss for anything else to say, I murmured, "I'm sorry too, then. For making you that miserable."

Aimee released a heavy sigh. "I think I screwed up more than you did. So . . . I'm sorry."

There was a time when I'd have lashed out and told her where she could store her apology—preferably elbow-deep in Billy's ass—but I had to admit, our breakup had been a blessing in disguise. It hadn't been fun by any means, but things were looking up.

"Apology accepted," I said. "And I mean it: I don't hate you."

She met my gaze again, and studied me. Then a smile slowly formed. "Thank you." She rocked from her heels to the balls of her feet and glanced over her shoulder toward the parking lot. "I'll, um, get out of your hair, I guess. I still need to unload everything."

"Okay. Take care."

"You too."

We stood in silence, as if she were as uncertain as I was about what we were supposed to do at this point.

Then she stepped across the welcome mat and hugged me gently. "I'm glad we talked."

Hugging her back, I said, "Me too."

She let me go, and after we exchanged smiles again and a couple of quiet "good-byes," she headed out to her car and I went back inside.

I sank onto the sofa and released a long breath. Carefully, I propped my foot up on a pillow on the coffee table, then leaned back and spread my arms along the back of the couch.

So this was my place now. Not our place. Mine. She was really gone. Her name was off the lease. Her stuff was out of the house. Her key was here and she wasn't.

A few months ago, we'd had one of those big fights that made me think we were about to call it quits. She'd stormed out, slamming the door just like she had today, and stayed at a friend's house.

*A friend's house. Right. Bet that "friend" did more than listen to her bitch about me.*

All night long, I'd been scared shitless we were done. But then she'd come back, and we'd talked enough to calm some of the tension. Then there'd been makeup sex for some reason—I'd never really seen the point, but it was better than fighting—and we'd never talked about it again. Next fight? Same thing. A week later? Again.

Why the hell had I been so afraid that any one of those fights would be the end? I should've just told her we were done so I could've started getting over her.

Ah well. Couldn't change the past. She was gone now, though, and not a moment too soon.

The rent was going to be pretty steep unless I took in a roommate. I wasn't sure I wanted to live with anybody else right now, though. In the short time since she'd left, I'd kind of gotten used to having the place to myself.

Maybe if I got desperate. Sven was always complaining about his roommates, and Kim was dying to move out of his parents' place.

Not yet, though. I'd enjoy having my own space for a little while.

Well, as much as I was ever here, anyway. Lately, my free time had been split between work, Zafir, the skate park, and . . . Zafir. I pretty much came here to sleep and shower, and then I was gone again.

Still, it was nice to come back and have this quiet place to myself. I could actually be alone with my thoughts for a little while. Which would've been a lot nicer if those thoughts didn't keep drifting to the woman who'd just given me her key.

It was probably because I'd been so busy and preoccupied lately, hadn't really had much opportunity to think about how I felt about Aimee. The weirdest part was that now that I had that opportunity, I felt . . . nothing.

It wasn't numbness or denial. Not like when she'd first left and I'd been so shell-shocked I couldn't make sense of my emotions. It wasn't even a sense of peace now that we'd talked.

I just didn't care. It was over, and it was in the past, and I was perfectly happy with my post-Aimee life. Sure, I missed the early days when we were together every waking moment or texting if we had to be apart. But looking back now, I realized those days had ended long before I'd caught her on another guy's dick.

The fact was, even though I'd loved her, we'd been miserable for a long time. Being together had become routine. Something that was *known*. The idea of breaking up had terrified me because it was unknown.

That unknown turned out to be spending a lot of time with a guy I hadn't even met until the day after Aimee and I split. Suddenly I had this friend who was cool as shit and had this awesome kid and had helped me figure out something I hadn't known about myself, and . . . Aimee who?

I closed my eyes and smiled. Would I be this okay if I hadn't wandered into Red Hot Bluewater to fix my ego the day after Aimee left?

Maybe. Maybe not.

But I had wandered in, and now? I was definitely feeling okay.

In fact, I felt pretty fucking good.

CHAPTER TEN

# ZAFIR

Any time I had to work the day after I took Tariq to the mosque in Port Angeles—a few times a month, which was less often than I would've liked—I was always hit by how surreal it was to have the job I did. Last night, I was keeping an eye on Tariq, making sure he properly performed the *wudu*—washing his hands, feet, and face before prayer. Today I was kneeling by the magazine rack at Red Hot, switching out last month's pornos with this month's.

I chuckled to myself, and just hoped for the millionth time that my dad didn't find out what I did for a living.

Just before noon, when I predicted Brennan would be strolling in any minute to grab lunch, the shop's phone rang. I nearly sprinted for the back, but then I remembered my boss was in the shop today, and she answered.

"Red Hot Bluewater, Violet speaking." Pause. "Just a second. Zafir!"

I swore under my breath, then called out, "Be right there." I set the stack of *Bra Busters Monthly* in my hand next to the mostly empty box, and toed it behind the rack so no customers—what customers?—would mess with it. Then I went to the counter and picked up the phone. "This is Zafir."

"Hey, it's Kelly." My babysitter's voice made me cringe—*don't bail, don't bail, don't bail*... "I'm sorry, hon. I've got to cancel on you today."

Oh shit.

"You—" I pinched the bridge of my nose, racking my brain for alternatives. "Okay. Okay. Uh, thanks for letting me know."

"Sorry about that! It should just be for today, though. Tomorrow, we'll be good."

*But what do I do about tonight?*

"Okay. No problem. I'll give my sister a call."

After we'd hung up, I called Leyla.

"Hey," I said. "Are you free tonight by any chance? I am desperate for a babysitter."

She sighed. "Sorry. I've got two fevers here, and I'm pretty sure you don't want Tariq getting whatever this is."

"*Shit . . .*"

"Why? Is everything okay?"

"Yeah, I . . ." I bit back a string of curses. "I have to work at Old Country tonight, and Kelly just canceled."

"Oh no! I wish I could help, but . . ."

"It's okay." I scrubbed a hand over my face. "I'll . . . I'll figure something out."

"Good luck."

We hung up, and my heart rate shot through the roof. There was no way I'd find somebody on this short notice. Nobody I could trust *and* afford.

"Everything okay?" Violet asked.

"Just need to find a babysitter for tonight."

She grimaced. "Go ahead and take a few minutes."

"Thanks." I moved into the back and started scrolling through my phone. I tried texting a few people, but the answers were the same.

*Sorry man, gotta work.*

*I'm in Oregon this week—sorry!*

*Can't—my kids are sick.*

The shop's front door jingled. Shit. I needed to get back to work. Violet was counting on—

"Is Zafir around?"

Brennan. Damn. We were supposed to get lunch, but there was no way I could drop everything and go while this was up in the air.

Sighing, I went back out front.

When he saw me, he smiled. "Hey."

"Hey." I frowned. "I'm gonna have to bail. I'm sorry. I need to find a babysitter stat, and I'm not having any luck."

He raised his eyebrows. "What happened?"

"My babysitter bailed at the last possible second. Leyla's not available." I raked a hand through my hair. "Shit. If I can't find someone, I'm going to have to call in to my second job." I could already hear my boss ripping me a new one over it, and cringed at the thought of losing that paycheck. Quite possibly permanently.

Brennan cleared his throat. "Maybe . . . maybe I could watch him for a few hours."

I turned to him. "What?"

"I'm off work tonight." He shrugged. "Don't have any plans."

Gnawing the inside of my cheek, I hesitated. "You really wouldn't mind?"

"Of course not. I mean, I don't know if I'd trust me with, like, a toddler because I don't know how toddlers work, but . . ."

I laughed. "Hey, if I managed to keep a toddler alive, anyone can." Turning serious, I said, "I hate to impose, though."

"Impose?" He waved a hand. "Come on. He's nine, and he digs skateboarding. We'll be fine."

"Okay, but . . ." I pulled out my wallet and offered him a few twenties. My last few. "Here's some cash if you guys want to get something to eat and—"

"Zafir." He closed my fingers around the money and pushed my hand back. "It's okay. My apartment's right down the road. We can even order from Old Country so you can come by and check on him."

I held his gaze. "Are you . . . are you sure?"

"Absolutely." He smiled. "You know, I could give him one of those skate lessons we've been talking about."

I gulped. My skin wanted to turn inside out at the thought of Tariq stepping onto a skateboard without me there to keep an eye on him, but I'd promised myself a million times not to be that oppressively protective.

"Okay," I croaked. "Yeah. Um. Just . . ." *Be careful? Really? If you have to tell him that, you'd better not be leaving Tariq with him at all.* No, I trusted him. He was a good guy, and he was good with Tariq, and Tariq would have a blast with him tonight.

I slowly released my breath as I rolled my shoulders. "You're a lifesaver. Seriously."

"Don't mention it. Do you need me to pick him up somewhere, or—"

"Shit. The booster seat. Your truck's a two-seater, do you know if it's okay for—" I shook my head. "You know what, I have no idea. It might be easier if we just switch cars."

Brennan's eyes widened. "You'd trust me with your car?"

"I'm trusting you with my kid, Brennan. If I didn't trust you with my car, I sure as hell wouldn't let him go with you either."

"Point taken."

"I'll pick him up from school. Should I just meet you by the skate shop, and we'll switch cars?"

"That works." He raised his eyebrows. "And you're sure you don't mind if I take him to the skate park? Just to give him a few pointers?"

I mulled it over again for a minute. Brennan knew what he was doing on a skateboard, and he wasn't a reckless idiot. I didn't have any illusions of him sending Tariq down a huge ramp with no helmet on, though the mental image did make my stomach turn.

"It's fine." I gulped. "Just, um, be careful, all right? He's still at that age where he thinks if something looks easy, it *is* easy."

"Don't worry." He chuckled. "My boss says skateboards are the great equalizer—everyone thinks they're the next Tony Hawk until they actually get on the board and see how hard it is. He'll crawl before he runs. We all do."

I slowly released my breath. "Okay. You're a lifesaver. Thank you."

"Don't mention it." He inclined his head a bit. "So does this mean you don't have to bail on lunch?"

I laughed, relief still working its way through my veins, and nodded. "Yeah. It does. Let's go."

# CHAPTER ELEVEN

# BRENNAN

"Do I have to wear *all* of this?" Tariq scowled at all the pads I'd put on him. "I'm not a hockey goalie."

I laughed. "No, you're not, but yes, you do. And this too." I held up a helmet.

He huffed and rolled his eyes, but let me put on the helmet and adjust the strap. Some of the guys skated with the chin strap dangling to their knees, but Zafir would skin me alive if I let Tariq do that. Not that I would anyway—I'd seen one too many of those idiots regret it. And I'd had a nasty concussion myself even with a helmet.

So . . . Tariq was wearing a fitted helmet with a snug strap and about seven hundred pads on his various extremities. He'd thank me the first time he fell and didn't come up bleeding.

Once he had all his safety gear on, I grabbed my board and one for him, and we walked from the shop to the park. It was a fairly busy afternoon, with probably two dozen people skating, but they were on the more advanced end of the park. Tariq wouldn't be going near those ramps and half-pipes for a long time.

We found a section of flat pavement away from everybody else so I could run him through the basics. I would've preferred to do this in a parking lot somewhere, away from the distraction of other skaters—especially the ones showing off—and without the risk of someone clobbering him, but Bluewater Bay wasn't all that skateboard friendly.

*We let you have a park*, the attitude seemed to be. *No need for you to skate anywhere else.*

Whatever.

Tariq looked around at the other skaters, then shot me a glare. "How come they don't have to wear all this?"

"Because if they fall and break something, *your* dad won't kill *me*."

He groaned as only an exasperated kid could groan, but didn't argue.

"You ready to get started?" I asked.

He nodded.

"Okay, so it's going to be a little boring at first." I put my board down and rested my foot on it. "You're just learning how to balance and how to stop." I nodded toward the other guys. "That comes a bit later."

He frowned, probably disappointed he wouldn't be doing the really fun stuff right away, but he shrugged and put the board down at his feet. Mirroring me, he put a foot on it, and without a word, he looked up at me, the helmet shading his eyes as he waited for his first lesson.

The basics *were* pretty boring, but he hung on every word as I showed him how to balance and how to stop. Before long, he could start and stop without wobbling. He'd skate away from me, go about ten feet, then turn around and come back. Slow and easy.

Not far from us, a couple of intermediate skaters were doing ollies.

"Can I learn how to do that?" Tariq asked, watching the guys jump off the ground, boards and all.

I shook my head. "Not yet. Not till you're just a little more comfortable on the board." *And not until you've fallen a few times.* It was always better to learn to fall during the easy stuff. Bones didn't usually start breaking until the tricks with more speed and more air. An ollie was one of the most basic tricks, but this was his first time ever on a board, so he was a *little* too green for that.

He sighed. "Okay."

"We'll get to the fun stuff, don't worry. Once your balance is good and you're steadier, *then* we can start doing ollies." I gestured at the other skaters. "And once you get the hang of those, then you can start learning how to do things like kickflips."

"What's that?"

I stood on my board, tipped it up with one foot and, as I jumped up off it, spun it with the other so it flipped under me. I planted my feet on it in midair, and put it back down on the pavement, exactly where I'd started.

"Whoa!" He flashed a huge grin. "Is that hard?"

"It takes practice, but once you get the basics down, you'll get the hang of it."

His lips formed a silent O, and he looked at the board under his foot. I knew that look. Every skater I'd ever taught had had the same epiphany—and so had I—when they realized why they had to do all the stupid, boring basics. When they realized it opened the door to a bunch of cool tricks, suddenly it wasn't such a horrible thing to have to practice dumb things like starting and stopping. If he was anything like me, he was imagining himself jumping off railings and doing kickflips and all the crazy tricks my buddies were doing at the other end of the park.

As long as it kept him practicing the simple stuff . . . fine.

"All right." I nodded toward his board. "Let's have you go a little farther this time, and just a little bit faster."

He got on the board and pushed off. My heart skipped—*I said a* little *faster, Tariq!*

But if I called out to him, I might startle him and make him wipe out, so I just cringed and watched.

At the other end of the stretch of concrete, he stopped. It was a rough stop, but he stayed upright, so I kept my mouth shut. Then he turned around and started back to me. Again, he went faster than I wanted.

About halfway back, he wobbled a bit, the board fishtailing under him, recovered . . .

And toppled onto his hands and knees.

Panic shot through me even as the hard plastic smacked on concrete, reminding me that he was encased in the best armor a skater could buy.

I hurried to his side and crouched so I could touch his shoulder. "You okay?"

"Yeah." As he started to get up, I gently held his arm and helped him to his feet.

"And that," I said as I checked the pads to make sure they were still on straight, "is why you have to wear pads and they don't." I gestured at the other skaters.

"So when I get good like them, I don't have to wear these?"

"Uh . . ." I cleared my throat, making a mental note not to let him see me skating in shorts with no pads. "We'll take that up with your dad. How about that?"

"Okay."

We kept practicing, and after another hour or so, he wasn't tired and he wasn't bored. He was getting pretty good too—well-balanced, confident in his stops and starts, and taking some wide turns without much trouble. Even when the other skaters sometimes went barreling through—two of them narrowly missing him—he stayed steady on his feet. He started throwing wary glances toward the show-offs at the other end, but that was probably a good thing. Being aware of the other skaters was important.

After he'd made another trek around the flat area, I asked, "You want to try a really easy ramp?"

His eyes lit up. "Yeah!"

I led him to the gentlest ramp. It wasn't much—just a few degrees of incline on either side. Not enough to get him going too fast or out of control, but enough to teach him how to stay balanced when the ground wasn't perfectly flat.

"Okay, here's how you're gonna do it." I stood on my board on top of the ramp. "You just lean, and let your body weight move the board forward, and let gravity do the work." I demonstrated, going down the tiny slope and up the other side, then back to where he was standing. "You'll probably eat it a few times, but that's why you have pads on. Got it?"

He nodded. By now he'd fallen quite a few times, so he knew how to land, and he knew the pads would absorb most of the impact. He'd also smacked his butt on the pavement hard enough to know he wasn't invincible. He was developing just the right amount of caution for a beginning skater—he was protected from most scrapes and bruises enough to take some risks and try new things, but falling still wasn't fun and kept him from doing anything reckless or stupid.

At the lip of the ramp, he set himself up the way I had, though he had his arms out, and shifted his weight. The board didn't move for a second. Then it did, startling him, and he panicked, but I caught him as his board rolled lazily down the ramp.

"It's okay," I said. "We all do that a few times. You want to try again?"

He nodded and set up his board. The second time, he fell again, but the third time, he went down the ramp and up the other side without any trouble. He hadn't gained enough speed to come back up to where I was standing, but still, he'd done great.

"Awesome!" I grinned at him as he picked up his board. "You've got it."

"Can I do it again?"

"Of course. Do it as many times as you want."

He set himself up again. He stood for a moment, probably steadying himself, then started down the ramp.

Out of the corner of my eye, I saw the flash of a blue shirt and a red helmet. In my mind, I saw the collision before it happened.

And in a split second, it *did* happen.

Sven came barreling around a turn, going horizontally across the ramp Tariq was just about to climb. I didn't even have time to shout a warning before they collided. The sickening thud. The grunt of a boy hit way harder than he was expecting. The curse of a guy who knew he was going down.

They tumbled ass over teakettle. Boards went everywhere—I was pretty sure one tripped somebody else, but I was too focused on Tariq to even look.

And Sven landed right on top of Tariq, flattening him facedown on the pavement.

I was halfway to them before they'd fully landed.

"Shit!" Sven scrambled up onto his arms. "Oh shit. I didn't even see him!"

I ignored him. I could chew him out later but . . . Tariq.

The kid let out a sob. At least he was conscious—that was a plus.

"Hey. Hey." I put a hand on his back to keep him from coming up too fast. "I'm right here. Let's have you sit, okay?"

Arms shaking as he cried, he let Sven and me help him shift position. Tariq kept one arm close to his side and covered his nose with the other. I glanced at the spot where he'd landed, and the blood on the concrete made my stomach lurch.

Then he lowered his hand, and I realized the blood wasn't just coming from his nose.

And right there, front and center in the poor crying kid's mouth, was a gap where his front tooth used to be.

Oh shit.

"Tariq." I swallowed. "Hey, buddy. I want to make sure you're okay. Can you tell me where it hurts?"

He pointed at his face.

"Anywhere else?"

"My arm," he whimpered, sending a drop of blood and spit down his scraped chin.

"Oh! Here's the tooth!" Sven picked it up off the pavement and stood. "Let me go get some of that salt solution to soak it, and then you can take him to the ER and see if they can put it back in."

"Good idea." It was a blessing in disguise that we were so prepared for people to lose teeth. The shop kept some Hanks' Balanced Salt Solution on hand for exactly this kind of thing. If a tooth wasn't too badly damaged and we put it in the solution quickly, the dentist could usually put it back in the person's head.

Usually.

*Oh God.*

*Zafir is going to* kill *me.*

"I'm gonna take you to the doctor, okay?"

Tariq's eyes welled up all over again. "The doctor?"

"Sorry, kiddo." I touched his chin and turned him toward me. "I'll be right there with you, though. I promise."

"I want my dad!"

"I'm gonna call him. Okay? Sven's going to take care of your tooth, and we'll put some ice on you, but I'm calling him . . ." I took out my phone and held it up. "Right now. All right?"

He sniffed, pressing his swelling lips together, and nodded.

Even as I was pulling up Zafir in my phone, I turned to my friends. "Kim, go grab a couple of ice packs from the shop. Renee, can you get some damp shop rags?"

They took off running, and sent the call.

As the phone rang on the other end, I watched Sven carefully take off Tariq's helmet.

"Good thing you were wearing this, kid." Sven held up the helmet, revealing a nasty scrape across what would have been Tariq's forehead.

The kid's eyes got huge, and I swore I could feel the fresh panic rising in him.

"Tariq. Tariq, look at me." When he did, I softly said, "You're okay. We're gonna get you cleaned up and take care of your tooth." I squeezed his uninjured arm gently. "Just take a couple deep breaths, okay?"

He watched me, and slowly pulled in a breath.

On the phone, the call kicked over to voice mail.

"It's Zafir—you know the drill."

I took a deep breath. "Hey, Zafir," I said as calmly as I could. "Tariq had a little mishap at the skate park, so I'm taking him to the ER just to make sure he's okay. I mean, he's fine." *Sort of.* "But just to be safe. So, um, give me a call back."

After I hung up, I cringed. Great. That was exactly what he needed to hear when he checked his voice mail. Should I have told him about the tooth? No, that would've made him panic even more. Nothing said "your kid's okay" like ". . . except his front tooth." Might as well save that part until he made it to the ER. It wasn't like he could do anything about it either way.

"He didn't answer?" Tariq asked softly.

"He's probably driving," I said. "He's at work, remember?"

Tariq's shoulders sagged, and his chin quivered, but then he winced. He reached for it, but I gently stopped his wrist.

"Your chin's kinda scraped up," I said. "Probably better to keep your hand off it."

He nodded, and I realized he was still keeping one arm protectively against his side. Being very, very careful to speak calmly so he had no idea that my heart was beating *oh shit, oh shit, oh shit*, I said, "Does your arm hurt? Or your chest?"

"My arm." He pulled it in a little tighter, protecting it with his other hand. "It hurts."

Kim crouched beside us. "Arm? Can he move it?"

I put a hand on Tariq's to keep it still. "Let's just put some ice on it and let the docs see how well it moves. No point in jarring it any more than we have to."

Kim grunted. "Probably a good idea."

"We need to get him to the ER anyway. See if they can do anything about that tooth. Where's— Good, there he is."

Sven came back with a container of solution, presumably with Tariq's tooth in it, and some ice packs. "Take him over to the hospital in Port Angeles. They can fix it."

As I carefully helped Tariq to his feet, I asked, "They actually keep a dentist there?"

Sven laughed. "Yeah. Didn't used to, but I guess one of the *Wolf's Landing* stunt guys knocked a tooth out and had to wait forever, so they keep somebody around now."

"Must be a boring job," I muttered. But thank God they had somebody there.

"I think they keep the guy on call." Sven pulled out his phone. "I'll call the ER and let them know you're on your way so they can get him in."

"Good thinking." As it was, the hospital was thirty miles away—giving them a heads-up would hopefully keep Tariq from waiting much longer than he already had to.

"What about my dad?" Tariq asked.

I took out my phone. "I'll try him again right now. Let's go get in the car."

As we walked and I speed-dialed his dad, I kept my arm around him in case he got dizzy, but he seemed steady.

Zafir's phone went to voice mail again. Shit.

"I'll call his work when we get to the ER." I pocketed my phone. "I promise I'll keep trying."

Tariq just nodded, but didn't answer.

In Zafir's car, I strapped Tariq in and put some ice packs against his sore arm. Then I gave him one more and told him to keep it against his mouth.

Port Angeles wasn't *that* far away, but it felt like we had to drive all the way to Seattle. Every light was red, and though there weren't many cars out, the few that were had all decided to drive twenty below the speed limit.

I gripped the wheel and tried to stay calm. No point in scaring the kid any more than he already was.

I took a breath and forced a smile. "You were rocking your form, by the way." I glanced in the rearview. "A bit more practice, and you'll be on the bigger ramps with me before you know it."

"Really?" The ice pack muffled his voice.

"Yeah." I paused. "And I've fallen like that too. Everybody has."

"I didn't fall," he muttered. "That guy crashed into me."

"He did. You're right. And you were nailing that ramp before he did."

He mumbled something else that might've been "jerk."

Finally, we made it to the ER. I parked him in a chair by the fish tank, then went up to the triage desk.

"Can I help you, sir?" the nurse asked.

"Yeah, my friend's kid . . ." I nodded toward Tariq. "He took a spill on a skateboard. He's got a tooth out, and some cuts and scrapes." I glanced at him. He was still holding his left arm gingerly. "And he might've banged up his arm too."

"Oh, yes. Someone called ahead, so we've got the dental resident on her way in right now. She lives close by, so it shouldn't be more than five minutes. Do you have the tooth?"

I held up the container. "Yeah."

"Great. Thanks."

"Now, you said he's your friend's son?"

I nodded.

She pursed her lips. "We can't waste time getting that tooth back in, but before we x-ray him or anything, we're going to need consent from his parent."

"I'll keep trying to call his dad."

Her thin eyebrows rose. "Is he in the area?"

"He is, but he's at work. I've tried him a couple of times, but I'll keep at it."

I tried not to let Tariq see that I was starting to panic. I couldn't reach Zafir on his cell, and the girl who'd answered at the pizza place said he wasn't available.

*Come on, Zafir . . .*

While the nurse quickly took Tariq's vitals and ran him through some questions to assess if he'd conked his head, I left Zafir another message.

Right as I hung up, a woman strode into the ER. The triage nurse flagged her down.

"Dr. Pierce." She pointed at me. "This is the gentleman who brought in the boy with the lost tooth."

The woman extended her hand. "Hi, I'm Dr. Pierce."

"Brennan." I shook her hand and gestured at Tariq. "And that's Tariq."

"Do you have his tooth?"

"Yeah. We put it in some salt solution." I handed her the sealed cup. "That Hanks' Balanced stuff."

"Oh good." She took it from me. "How long has it been?"

"About"—I glanced at my phone—"half an hour. Maybe a little less."

"Perfect." She turned to Tariq and smiled at him. "Okay, sweetie. Let's have a look."

He opened his mouth, and it took everything I had to casually look away without letting him see that my stomach had tried to lurch into my throat. Hopefully he hadn't damaged his other teeth, but he'd definitely made hamburger out of his lip and gums. I suppressed a shudder.

Yep, Zafir was going to kill me. Tonight was my last night on earth. So screwed.

The dentist turned to the triage nurse. "Can you grab me a wheelchair, and we'll take him down to dental?"

The hairs on my neck stood up. "A wheelchair?"

"Hospital policy." She offered a reassuring smile. "Nothing to worry about."

*Says you.*

As she wheeled him down the hall, I stayed with him.

Tariq lowered the ice pack and looked at me. "Is my dad coming?"

"As soon as you get situated with the dentist, I'm going to call him again."

His eyes widened and started to well up again, but I squeezed his uninjured arm.

"It's okay, buddy. My signal's been iffy since we've been in here. But I'm sure he's on his way right now."

He watched me uncertainly, but then relaxed a bit. Okay, so it was a little white lie, but if it calmed him down, I'd tell him Santa Claus was in the next room.

*Which would be totally reassuring to a Muslim kid. Smooth thinking.*

In the dental department, he moved from the wheelchair to the dentist's chair.

I came down to his eye level. "Do you want me to stay in here with you while she works on your tooth?"

He glanced at my phone, then back up at me. "Yeah, but I want you to call my dad."

*Well, shit.*

Dr. Pierce turned to me. "It's going to take me just a minute to set up. If you want to step out and make the call, I'll probably be ready when you come back in."

"Perfect." I looked at Tariq again. "I'll be back in two minutes. All right?"

He nodded.

I patted his arm. "Back in a second."

Then I stepped out into the hall, and thank God, I had signal out here, so I called Old Country Pizza.

And waited.

# CHAPTER TWELVE

# ZAFIR

"He's *what*?"

"Did you get my message?" Brennan asked. "I—"

"No!" My heart was going crazy, my stomach sick with panic. "I couldn't answer my phone and— What's going on?"

"We're at the ER in Port Angeles," Brennan said quickly. "Tariq is fine. He really is. But—"

"What happened?" In a split second, my brain showed me every possible disaster that could have befallen my kid, and I was another split second away from vomiting unless Brennan started talking *fast.*

"I was showing him how to skate," Brennan said, "and one of the guys collided with him. God, Zafir, I am so sorry. I swear, I was watching him, and he was wearing a helmet, so—"

"How bad?" Visions of broken bones and gaping wounds flashed through my mind. "Is he okay? Is he bleeding?"

"He's walking and talking. Just shaken up a bit."

Well, that was something. But the ER? "Okay, but how *bad*?"

Brennan took a deep breath. "They want to do an X-ray of his arm, just to be sure. It's bruised, and he's got some road rash, but the doctor doesn't seem all that worried."

I swallowed. "Could you put him on the phone?"

"Uh, well . . ."

"Brennan . . ."

"Look, when they crashed, he got clocked pretty hard in the mouth. He's . . ." Brennan sighed, and quietly added, "He's got a cut lip, and, um, one of his front teeth . . ."

I winced. "Oh no."

"The emergency dentist is numbing him up right now to put the tooth back in. I'm . . . I'm not sure how well my signal will hold up, but I can try?"

"Okay. Okay. That's fine. Let me talk to him anyway."

"Hang on." Movement on the other end. Muffled voices. A female voice.

Then, "Dad?"

*Oh, thank you, Allah*. Eyes closed, I covered the phone so Tariq wouldn't hear my relieved sigh. Then I schooled my tone and managed, "Hey, kiddo. You doing okay?"

"It hurths."

I winced. "I'm on my way now. Can you hang in there for me?"

"Yeah." He didn't sound like he was freaking out. That was a plus.

"I'll be there as soon as I can. Can I talk to Brennan again?"

"'Kay."

There were muffled voices in the background again.

"Hey, Zafir?" Brennan said. "The nurses need to get your consent to do some X-rays and check him out. They're taking care of the tooth now, but they—"

"Yeah, yeah. Sure. Put them on."

The nurse quickly ran me through what needed to be done—putting his tooth back in and x-raying his arm—and asked if I consented. Then a second nurse came on and went through the same routine. Once they were satisfied they had my full consent to treat my son—yes, please!—they put Brennan back on the phone.

"The dentist is numbing him up right now," he said. "He's doing good. And I'll stay with him while they're working on the tooth."

I swallowed. "Okay. Great. Thanks. I'll be there as soon as I can. Just keep him calm if you can, all right?"

"Doing the best I can." With a hint of a smile in his voice, he added, "He's holding it together pretty good, though. Kid's a trooper."

We'd see about that. Tariq and doctors didn't mix very well, especially if there were blood or needles involved.

After we'd hung up, I shoved my phone in my pocket and hurried into the back office. "Hey, boss. I need to leave early. My kid's at the ER. I need to go get him."

"He okay?"

*Yeah, that's why he's at the ER. Really?*

"Took a spill and knocked out a tooth." I rocked from my heels to the balls of my feet. "They're still doing X-rays and stuff, but I need to get there."

Calmly, Pete craned his neck and looked out at the kitchen. "I'm short-staffed, but Mike's on his way—soon as he gets here, you can go."

I blinked. "But . . . my son's at the *ER*. In Port Angeles. I need to *go*."

"And he'll be here in fifteen minutes. Just hang tight."

*Hang tight?* Hang tight*? Are you* serious*?*

I knew better than to argue, though. It wasn't below Pete to find a reason to make someone stay when they needed to leave early. Laura had been stuck here a full hour last month when her boyfriend needed to be picked up after a car accident. Just because she'd lipped off at Pete when he hadn't let her go right away.

Teeth grinding, I left his office. It took all I had not to pace back and forth in the front of the restaurant as I watched the parking lot for Mike's battered old car.

*Come on, man. Don't be late tonight. Just this once, be on time.*

I'd never been crazy about Pete, but that resentment burned deeper with every minute he kept me here instead of letting me get to my kid. There was nothing I could do for Tariq, but I needed to be there with him. The longer it took for me to get there, the more he was going to panic. I still hadn't forgotten the time I'd needed to pick him up early from kindergarten because he was sick, and it had taken almost an hour because I'd been hung up at an appointment. To this day, I was haunted by the moment I'd walked into the nurse's office, and he'd burst into tears and sobbed, *"I thought you weren't coming!"*

Even now, as he was getting older and understood that delays and obstacles happen, his sense of abandonment was on a hair trigger. I was the only constant figure in his life, and any inkling he got that I was going the way of his mother or my ex-fiancée would send him into a panic.

I closed my eyes and took a deep breath. I'd talked to him. He knew I was on my way. He knew Port Angeles was a bit of a drive from Bluewater Bay. That had to mean something, right?

With each passing minute, it was tempting to just walk out of Old Country and never come back. My son needed me a lot more than I needed this abuse.

"Hey, Hamady," Pete barked. When I turned around, he pushed a loaded pizza bag across the counter. "I need you to take this one."

My lips parted. "But, I've—"

"You're not clocking out until Mike gets here, so you might as well earn your pay." He gestured at the pizza bags. "It's in the Sunnyside Condos. You can damn near walk. Won't take you long."

I was a heartbeat away from telling him where he could put the pizzas, the Sunnyside Condos, and the time clock, but I *needed* this paycheck.

So I gritted my teeth and took the bags.

All the way out to the truck, out of the parking lot, and down the road, I was beating myself up. This was my fault. Tariq wouldn't be in the ER, hurting and scared, if I hadn't stupidly left him with Brennan. I didn't like him skateboarding at all, and what had they been *doing* that put him in the path of another skater, and then in the hospital? How fast had he been going?

I ground my teeth until my jaw ached. I was an idiot. What was I thinking? Brennan and I barely knew each other.

Well, okay. We knew each other. We'd been making excuses to see each other every chance we had over the past few weeks, and I'd probably told him more about me than I'd told anyone in years.

But damn it, I trusted him with my kid for one afternoon, and now they were in the emergency room?

I thumped my hand on Brennan's steering wheel. What *was* I thinking?

Okay, so I was desperate. Kelly had left me in a bind, and Leyla's hands had been tied, and Brennan had offered a solution, and . . . and now my kid was at the hospital in another town. Probably wondering where I was. Probably freaking out, having visions of me just vanishing into the same thin air as his mom.

I whispered a prayer, asking Allah to keep Tariq calm, and parked the truck in front of the condos. After I'd double-checked the unit number, I collected the pizza bags and the bill and hurried to their door. It took all the restraint I had to not sprint up the stairs. With the way this day was going, I'd trip, drop the pizzas, and have to go back and get replacements, which would keep me away from the ER even longer because Pete would absolutely make me do the second run.

Or even better—I'd bust my ass, and wind up going to the ER as a patient.

So I took the stairs carefully, delivered the pizzas, and collected the money. On the way down, with no pizzas at risk, I ran. And I nearly did bust my ass on that bottom step, but I recovered, my ankle smarting just slightly. Not nearly enough to slow me down.

I drove like a bat out of hell back to Old Country, and as I pulled into the parking lot, I'd never been so happy to see Mike's blue Honda. For once in his life, he wasn't excessively late.

I ran into the store and dropped the pizza bags on the rack. Then I went to the cash register, where Isobel answered phones and took orders.

"Hey." I set my cash bag on the counter. "I need you to cash me out. Fast. Please. My kid's in the hospital and I—"

"I heard." Isobel glanced back, probably making sure Pete was out of earshot. To me, in a conspiratorial voice, she said, "Go. I'll tell Pete we settled up, and I'll give you your tips when you get here tomorrow."

"Are you sure?"

"I can drop them by your apartment later if—"

"It's fine. I trust you."

"Okay." She shooed me toward the door. "Go. Your baby needs you."

I didn't make her tell me twice. I darted into the back, clocked out, and left.

And as soon as I was in Brennan's truck, I put the pedal to the floor and drove over to Port Angeles. At that speed, it wouldn't take long to get there, but it felt like it took forever.

My throat was tight, my heart giving the engine's RPM a run for its money. All the way to the hospital, the terrified father and the admittedly-less-devout-than-I-should-have-been Muslim were at odds inside my brain, alternately praying for Tariq to be all right, and acknowledging that I understood Allah's will trumped mine.

*Please let him be all right. Inshallah.*

*Please don't hurt my son. Inshallah.*

*Inshallah. Inshallah. Inshallah.*

Finally, I made it to the hospital, and once I'd parked, I hurried inside. At the triage desk, I didn't even care that my voice was shaking and I sounded like I was on the brink of hysteria. "My son just came in. Tariq Hamady. T-A-"

"He's in room six." The nurse gestured for me to follow. "I'll take you back to him."

My body and brain didn't even know how to react to that. Relief that I'd see him in a minute? That he was in a room and not an operating room? Or a nauseating level of terror that may or may not have been rational because I had no idea how he was doing. How much had Brennan glossed over to keep me from panicking?

At room six, the nurse tapped twice on the door. Then she pushed it open. "Tariq, honey?" She gestured for me to go in ahead. "You have a visitor."

Before I'd stepped in, I heard him say, "Dad?"

His voice sent pure relief right through me, almost knocking my feet out from under me, but I stayed upright and went into the room. "Hey, kiddo."

He was reclining in the hospital bed, and sat up as he saw me. I hugged him gently, then stood and looked him over.

His face was a little bruised—it'd probably be more colorful in the morning—and there was some road rash on his chin and jaw. His arm was against his side, immobilized by a splint and several ice packs.

I swallowed. "How's your tooth?"

He flashed a smile. His gums were puffy and red, but every tooth was accounted for. That was a plus.

"They were able to put it back in," Brennan said. "The dentist will have a whole bunch of instructions for you for some follow-up stuff, but she seemed pretty confident that it went back in okay."

Nodding, I said, "Good. Good to hear. And the arm?"

"He just had X-rays taken," the nurse said. "He had a round earlier, but the doctor wanted a better look at his elbow."

Fresh anxiety shot through me. "What? Why?"

"She said she couldn't see one part of the joint well enough, and wanted to make sure there wasn't a chip or a fracture hiding in there."

"Oh." The panic slowly receded. "So . . . was there?"

"We should know shortly." The nurse put her hand on the door handle. "We'll keep you updated, but for now, he's fine to just rest and relax."

I nodded.

She left the room, and I turned back to my son. "How do you feel?"

He shrugged his uninjured shoulder. "Sore. Me and Brennan have just been playing a game."

I glanced at Brennan, and replayed what I'd seen when I walked into the room. I'd been so focused on giving Tariq a hug and making sure he was all right, it hadn't really registered, but now that I thought about it, I realized they'd been as relaxed as two people in a hospital room could be. Brennan had been holding his phone in front of Tariq, and I could see a paused game on the screen.

"Oh." I blinked a few times. "Well. Um. While we're waiting for the doctor, if you guys want to keep playing . . ."

They exchanged glances, and both looked at me.

"You sure?" Brennan asked.

"Yeah." I pulled up the empty chair. "Might as well pass the time, right?" And give Tariq something to focus on besides me being frazzled and shaky.

As Brennan started a new game, I kept my unsteady hands below the bed rail where neither of them could see. Not that they seemed to notice much, though. Once the game came to life, they were both focused, chasing little cartoon aliens around the screen and laughing hysterically whenever one exploded.

Watching them blew my mind. With all the visions I'd had of Tariq being in horrible pain and hysterics, this was what had waited for me—the two of them calmly playing on Brennan's phone. Sure, Tariq winced now and then, and every so often, they'd pause the game so we could adjust an ice pack for him, but he wasn't crying. He wasn't asking me over and over what had taken me so long.

He was just . . . chilling with Brennan and playing a video game.

I shifted my gaze toward Brennan. *How? How in the world did you do this?*

Well, whatever he'd done, it'd worked.

Tariq was going to be fine. He was calm. And I could breathe.

*Thank you, Allah, for watching over him.*

*And if he was going to get hurt today, thank you for putting Brennan at his side.*

# CHAPTER THIRTEEN

# BRENNAN

When all was said and done, the X-rays were clear. Tariq's arm wasn't fractured. He'd bruised it pretty good, and there was a little swelling in the soft tissue, but with some ice, rest, and ibuprofen he'd be fine.

The tooth was in place with a soft temporary splint, his gums stitched in a couple of places, and his mouth still numb. I didn't envy him when that Novocain eventually wore off.

Thank God Zafir was there—the instructions they gave him would've made my head spin. Antibiotics. Painkillers. Some sort of rinse he had to do a couple of times a day. Symptoms to watch for. Some complicated follow-ups with Tariq's dentist. I lost track of it, especially when someone mentioned that if he got an infection, he might need a root canal.

They handed Zafir a whole ream of instructions and information and insurance paperwork, and he just nodded, skimmed over them, asked questions, and played the role of the responsible adult that I sure as fuck wouldn't have known how to be.

And finally, after it felt like we'd been there for a week and a half, the ER released Tariq.

On the way out to the parking lot, Zafir and I switched our car keys back, but neither said anything. Tariq got into the backseat of his dad's car and buckled himself in.

Zafir closed the door and turned to me. My stomach was already a ball of lead, and facing him down now didn't help at all. With the doors shut, and as much privacy as a mostly deserted parking lot allowed us, I cringed inwardly. *Here it comes . . .*

He spun his key ring on his finger. "So, um. I should really get him home so he can get some sleep. Do you want to come back to my place for a while?"

I nearly jumped—that wasn't the question I'd anticipated. "Um . . ."

"I feel like I owe you," he said. "You took care of him for me."

*I'm also the reason we ended up here.*

I swallowed. Being around Tariq was fucking with my conscience, but I decided I would feel better if I knew he was home, in bed, and relaxed. "Sure. Yeah. I'll follow you, I guess. I'm parked . . ." I looked around. "Where is my truck?"

He pointed a couple of rows over. "Sorry. I just took the first spot I could find, so I—"

"Yeah, yeah. That's fine. I would've done the same." I shifted my weight and gestured toward my truck. "So, like I said. I'll follow you."

He got into his car and waited while I walked to mine. As he headed out of the lot, I followed, my heart thumping and my stomach twisting the entire time.

Now that the worst was over and Tariq was okay, I . . . wasn't. All the way back to Bluewater Bay and to Zafir's apartment, I kept replaying the crash over and over in my head, imagining every way it could have been worse. Sven was a featherweight compared to some of the other guys—what if one of the bigger skaters had crashed into Tariq? Or he'd hurt his neck? Or broken something?

Acid burned in my throat. Zafir had trusted me with his kid for half a goddamn day, and I'd handed him back bloody and dented. Why Zafir hadn't lit into me right there in the parking lot, I had no idea. Maybe he was just exhausted. Two jobs and an ER visit—that was a long day. Maybe he was saving it until we were behind closed doors and he could *really* read me the riot act.

My hands were sweaty as I steered into the apartment parking lot behind Zafir. I parked in a guest spot, and got out as Zafir was helping Tariq onto his feet.

None of us spoke on the way up the stairs. Tariq was a little sluggish now—they'd given him some painkillers, which must've really kicked in when he was in the car, and he was starting to get groggy. Hopefully they were helping with the pain too—poor kid.

Zafir keyed us into the apartment. As he shut the door behind us, he said, "I'm going to put him to bed. Shouldn't take long."

"Sure. Okay."

They headed down the hall. As they did, he kept a hand between Tariq's shoulders, probably steadying him as he shuffled along the carpet.

While Zafir put Tariq to bed, I stayed in the kitchen. I couldn't sit. Couldn't stay still. I leaned against one counter, then paced for a minute, then leaned against another one and drummed my fingers rapidly.

After what felt like half the night—but was probably more like five minutes—Zafir stepped into the kitchen.

I squirmed, my stomach twisting into even tighter knots. "How is he?"

Zafir shrugged. "He's all right. He'll probably be extra sore tomorrow, but he'll be fine."

I flinched. "Oh man. I'm glad he's okay, but . . . God. I am so sorry."

"Relax. He's fine."

"But he could've—"

"Brennan. Come here." He led me to the couch and sat, and patted the cushion beside him.

I wasn't so sure sitting would help with this restlessness, but I sat beside him and wrung my hands in my lap.

He touched my arm. "Listen to me. I know my kid. He's a wreck when there's blood, or if he has to go see a doctor."

I cringed. "I am so—"

"I'm not done," he said softly, and squeezed my arm. "When I got there tonight, he was completely calm and cool. I thought I was going to walk in and find him crying and freaking out because he was scared, and hurting, and wondering where I was. But he wasn't." Zafir smiled as he withdrew his hand. "I don't know what you did, but I can't even tell you how grateful I am for it."

"But the whole reason he was there was—"

"It was an accident. It happens."

"But I broke your kid!"

Zafir laughed. "And you've been skating long enough to know that kids bounce." He paused. "You want to know what he asked me while I was tucking him in?"

I nodded.

Zafir smiled. "He asked if this meant he couldn't skate anymore."

"And . . . does it?"

"My first instinct is to say he'll never set foot on a board again." Quirking his lips, he half shrugged. "But if he spent a few hours in the ER after having his tooth knocked out and his face scraped up, and he *still* wants to skate . . ."

I stared at him, not sure if I should laugh or what. Shifting uncomfortably, I lowered my gaze. "Well, he did seem to enjoy it."

"So I gathered."

Silence fell, and I wasn't sure what to do with it. Finally, I cleared my throat. "Listen, um. I know how emergency rooms can be, and dentists, so if you need any help, like with the bills, I—"

"No," he said sharply. "I've got insurance. Don't worry. We'll be fine."

"But if anything isn't covered." I met his gaze. "I'm happy to help. I feel *terrible*."

"You did help. More than you can probably imagine." He took my hand. "Thank you for keeping him calm while I was on my way. The emergency room could've been an even bigger disaster than him falling, especially when it took me forever to get there, but it wasn't. Because you were there."

"All I did . . ." I hesitated.

Zafir lifted his eyebrows.

I looked down at our joined hands, wondering why it wasn't weird that he was still holding on. "All I did was what I thought I'd want someone to do if I was a kid in the ER."

"Which is exactly what you should've done." He squeezed gently, then let go, and the cool spot where his hand had been—*that* was weird. Like it made more sense for him to put his hand back and leave it there.

But I couldn't bring myself to reach for him. "I guess . . . I guess I should get going. I know you need to get some sleep." I glanced in the direction of Tariq's bedroom. "I'm, um, glad he's okay."

Zafir smiled. “Me too. I’m glad he had you tonight.”

We locked eyes for a long moment. A long enough moment it should’ve been uncomfortable, but it wasn’t. Not really. Kind of awkward—like, what was I supposed to do now and why was my heart beating like this?—but not uncomfortable.

Then Zafir cleared his throat and dropped his gaze. “Anyway, thanks again. For taking care of him. It . . . it really means a lot.”

“Don’t mention it.”

# CHAPTER FOURTEEN

# ZAFIR

The next morning, I called in to work, then called the school and let them know Tariq would be out today. I'd made him an appointment at ten thirty so his dentist could check the tooth and the stitches, and we'd figure out the rest of the day from there. His attendance record was immaculate, and he was doing fine on his schoolwork—staying home to recover a little wouldn't hurt him.

As long as we didn't have to be anywhere for a while, I let him sleep in. Around eight, as I was drinking my first cup of coffee, I heard some movement at the end of the hall. I gave him another minute or so, then put some hot chocolate in the microwave for him.

Just as the microwave beeped, Tariq limped into the kitchen. I quickly schooled my expression so he didn't see the alarm that shot through me. The scrapes on his face had scabbed over, and his lips were puffy. He shuffled like he was sore from head to toe, which he probably was.

"Hey." I set the hot chocolate in front of his place at the table. "How you feeling?"

He winced as he sat down. "Hurts."

"What hurts?"

"Everywhere."

"Everywhere? Just bruised and sore? Or is it really bad?"

"Sore." The splint in his mouth gave him a subtle lisp, but it wasn't bad.

"Well, they sent some pain pills home with you. You need to eat something, though. Anything sound good?"

He scowled. "My mouth hurts."

"Oatmeal?"

He shook his head slowly.

That made sense. His gums and jaw were probably tender, and even chewing something that soft might hurt. But what else did I have in the house that he could eat? Despite having a father with no qualms about eating leftover cold pasta for breakfast, Tariq turned up his nose at eating anything before noon that wasn't a *breakfast* food.

*Almost* anything.

I grinned. "Hey, you remember all those times you wanted pudding for breakfast?"

His eyebrows rose.

"I think we can probably do that just this once."

Gingerly, he smiled, more on one side than the other. "Really?"

"You gotta eat something. But it's only while your mouth is healing. Okay?"

Tariq nodded. "Okay."

I took a few cups of chocolate pudding from the pantry, peeled off the lids, and put the cups on the table for him. Then I sat across from him with my coffee.

"So," I said. "I'm really, really sorry it took me so long to get there last night."

He shrugged and took a spoonful of pudding. "I was okay. Brennan showed me how to play that game on his phone."

"I saw that." I wrapped my hands around my coffee mug to keep from wringing them and letting him see how much of a wreck I was. "But I, um . . . I got stuck at work, or I'd have been there sooner."

"I know." He licked the spoon and put it back in the cup for some more. "Brennan told me."

"Did he?"

He nodded. "He said you couldn't talk while you were driving."

Oh. Well, I guess that did explain it. Neither of them could've known I'd been working in the kitchen the first few times Brennan called. That my phone had vibrated each time, but I hadn't dared so much as look at it while Pete was hovering over me and Isobel while we'd frantically remade a huge order that another driver had dropped. It was only after we'd finished it and sent it out the door that another coworker casually told me I had an urgent call waiting on hold.

*"Why didn't you tell me?"* I'd snapped as I'd hurried to the phone.

*"Because Pete was* right *there! I didn't want to get my ass chewed!"*

I'd muttered a few curses, taken the phone, and heard some words straight out of a nightmare: *"We're at the ER in Port Angeles. Tariq is fine. He really is. But—"*

At the breakfast table, I suppressed a shudder. Just as well Brennan and Tariq had assumed I couldn't answer because I'd been driving. My son didn't need to know that my boss and coworkers had no sense of urgency in situations like that.

I sipped my coffee. "Seemed like you were doing okay when I got there. I thought you'd be scared."

He smiled a little, though he winced. "I was. But Brennan said you were coming, and the stuff the dentist gave me made it stop hurting." He took another spoonful of pudding.

*I owe you big-time, Brennan.*

Once Tariq had eaten the first cup of pudding, I gave him a pain pill, which he washed down with his hot chocolate. He'd taken this particular prescription after he'd had his tonsils out, so at least I knew he didn't react badly to it. As long as he had something in his stomach, he wouldn't get sick. A little sleepy, maybe, but that was probably just as well—the more he rested today, the better he'd feel tomorrow.

As he started on his second pudding cup, I said, "So, it sounds like you were having fun before . . ." I hesitated. "Before you got hurt."

"Yeah." He grinned, showing the stitches and part of the splint in his mouth. "And Brennan's gonna show me how to do an ollie and—"

"An ollie?" I asked. "What's that?"

"It's where you jump off the ground with your board."

"I see." I took a sip of coffee. "And, uh, what exactly happened, anyway? When you fell?" Brennan had explained it, but I was curious how Tariq remembered it.

"He was showing me how to go up a ramp, and somebody crashed into me." Completely matter-of-fact. No sign that he was traumatized. As he scraped another spoonful of pudding from the bottom of the cup, he added, "The guy said he was sorry. And he found my tooth."

"Oh. Well that's . . . that's good."

"Yep. And Brennan said next time he'll teach me how to do an ollie, and once I learn to do that, I can learn to do a kickflip."

My stomach was still struggling with the idea of him being on a skateboard again at all. I wasn't sure I could handle finding out what a kickflip was, so I just smiled and nodded. "Sounds like fun."

His smile faded. "Can I really still skateboard? After yesterday?"

*No. I don't want you on any kind of wheels ever again unless you're encased in carbon fiber bubble wrap.*

I swallowed. "It's up to you. If you still want to, then when you're feeling up to it . . ."

"Can Brennan give me more lessons?"

"I don't see why not." I got up to refill my coffee. "Let's give you a chance to heal up first, but if you still want to, okay."

"Cool." He concentrated on his pudding for a moment. Then, as I was sitting down again, he asked, "Is Brennan your boyfriend?"

I dropped my very full coffee, but fortunately, it was only quarter of an inch above the table at that point. It landed right, if loudly, and splashed a couple of drops on my hand. "What?" I licked the coffee off my finger, thankful it hadn't been too hot. "My *boyfriend*?"

"Yeah." He held my gaze as I sat down. "You guys hang out a lot. Like you did with Chris. And Megan."

My heart flipped at the mention of my exes. "Well, yeah. We do."

He watched me, eyebrows up like he expected an explanation.

"We're friends." I laughed softly, wondering why it sounded—and felt—so fake. "We're not dating."

"Oh."

It was my turn to watch him. "Why? Do you . . . do you want us to be dating?"

"I don't know. I like him."

"Yeah, me too." I hesitated, then quickly added, "But just like a friend."

*Right?*

Tariq seemed to accept that. He didn't push the issue, and kept working his way through the last of the pudding in the cup.

I couldn't let the subject go, though. Tariq knew I hung out with both men and women, and he knew I dated both men and women.

He didn't automatically assume a close friend was more than that. But somehow, Brennan and I had made him wonder?

Was he seeing something I wasn't? Admittedly, I *was* getting pretty attached to Brennan. It had been a long time since I'd looked forward to someone's company like I did his.

But that didn't mean . . .

My stomach tightened as I wrapped my hands around my coffee cup. Even if I did have a connection with Brennan, there was one big problem: He'd met Tariq. And Tariq liked him. Which meant going out on that limb and dating was a huge gamble. What if things fell apart? What if Brennan spun the Wheel of Reasons People Don't Stay With Zafir, and I had to explain to Tariq why it was, yet again, just him and me?

Besides, there was no way Brennan was ready for anything more than friends. Up until recently, he'd been comfortable in his heterosexual skin. He was hanging around me because I understood the new skin he was in, and I didn't judge him, and I had answers if he had questions. We were becoming close friends. It didn't mean there was anything more going on.

I had to admit, though, that the bug Tariq had put in my ear was a persistent one. *Was* there something between Brennan and me? If there wasn't, could there be? And if there could, *should* there be?

*Easy, Zafir.*

I was an idiot for even thinking about it. Brennan had lived as a straight guy up until we met, and he was still dealing with a breakup. Just because we'd clicked and become fast friends didn't mean he was remotely interested in anything more.

Just because I couldn't stop thinking about him, and could trust him with my son, and couldn't wait to see him again . . .

That didn't mean *I* was remotely interested in anything more.

Right?

# CHAPTER FIFTEEN

# BRENNAN

I hadn't slept for shit. Over and over, I kept seeing Sven crashing into Tariq and flattening him on the ramp. When I was awake, I replayed what really happened—the crying kid sitting up with blood all over his face and his tooth missing. When I dreamed, it was worse. Broken bones. Realizing too late that I hadn't made him wear a helmet. Not being able to get him to the hospital while the clock ticked on that tooth.

By the time I dragged myself out of bed the next morning, I'd half convinced myself that those dreams were true and Tariq was way more fucked up than he really was.

As soon as I could see straight, I grabbed my phone and texted Zafir: *How is Tariq doing?*

Within a few minutes, he replied, *He got pudding for breakfast, so he's not complaining.*

I laughed. Pudding for breakfast? Damn, that actually sounded good. That kid had it made. Well, aside from the whole face-planting on the pavement thing, anyway.

*Glad he's doing better*, I wrote back.

*He is. He's looking forward to going to school. Thinks his friends will be impressed by war wounds.*

*LOL—welcome to having a skater in the house.*

*Great. Does that mean a cast will be a badge of honor?*

I grimaced. Probably best not to confirm that part to him quite yet.

I felt a lot better knowing Tariq was doing okay, though. I hoped like hell his tooth didn't give him any trouble—the last thing the poor kid needed was a root canal on top of everything else.

*Fingers crossed for him*, I wrote back.

Zafir didn't answer, so he was probably busy with Tariq.

And, anyway, I really needed to get off my ass and get ready for work.

Ten minutes before my shift started, I parked behind the store and headed inside. I hadn't even signed into the computer when my boss appeared.

"Hey, Bren." Colin's brow creased. "How's that kid? I heard you had to take him to the ER."

"He's good." I paused to clock into the system. "Tooth went back in, nothing's broken, and he's already itching to get back on a board."

Colin laughed. "Surprise, surprise."

"Yeah. I'm sure his dad is thrilled."

"You did reach him, right? I heard you were having trouble getting his dad on the horn."

"Yeah, yeah." I waved a hand. "He was driving or something when I called, but as soon as I got ahold of him, he came to the ER. Everything's good."

"Glad to hear it. You tell him if they need anything, let me know."

I nodded. "Will do."

From anyone else, I would've taken it as nervous damage control. Offering to help in any way so they could placate Zafir and keep him from suing. But I knew Colin better than that. He was one of those people who'd give the shirt off his back to help someone, and I had no doubt he genuinely felt terrible about Tariq getting hurt at his park.

Colin headed back out into the store, and I took care of a few inventory tasks for him before I also went out to the sales floor. Of course, by now everyone at the shop had heard what had happened, so they immediately started asking about Tariq. All through the first few hours of my shift, I was telling people that yes, the kid who fell yesterday was fine, and yes, we were able to reach his father.

Around one, Sven came in, and he didn't even clock in before he hurried up to me. "Hey, Bren. How's the kid?"

"He's okay." I patted the air. "They got the tooth back in, and now it's just a waiting game to see if it gets infected or anything."

"He didn't bust anything, though?"

I shook my head. "No. They x-rayed him twice to be sure, but he's good."

"Man, I still feel so bad." Sven grimaced. "I swear I thought for a sec the kid was dead."

I shuddered. "You're not that big."

"No, but neither is he. You're sure he's good?"

"He's fine. I talked to his dad this morning, and—"

The air pressure changed. We had all been conditioned to look when the door opened, since it could be a customer needing help, so we both turned.

And my heart stopped.

"Speak of the devil," Sven said.

"No kidding." I hurried across the store to Zafir and Tariq. "Hey, guys."

Zafir smiled. "Hey."

I looked at Tariq. "How you feeling, kid?"

He shrugged. "Eh."

Poor kid—the scrapes on his chin, nose, and jaw had all scabbed up and looked even worse than yesterday, and his lip was still puffy. There was even a faint bruise across his forehead, probably from his helmet hitting the pavement.

"So, um . . ." I cleared my throat. "This is . . . this is a surprise."

Zafir rested his hand on Tariq's shoulder. "We just came by to see how you were doing. After yesterday."

"Me? I'm fine. I'm not the one who . . . um . . ."

"Ate shit?" Tariq said.

"What?" Zafir's jaw dropped. "What did you say?"

Tariq looked up at him, eyes wide and innocent. "Ate shit. That's what they say when you fall."

Zafir shifted his gaze toward me and narrowed his eyes. "Really?"

"He didn't get it from me. I swear."

"Uh-huh." He eyed Tariq. "So where did you—"

"Hey, little dude!" Sven picked just that moment to join us. "How you feeling?"

Suddenly shy, Tariq shrugged, but didn't say anything.

"That was a gnarly spill," Sven said. "And you're already here? Back for more?" He put up his hand for a high five. "Tough kid!"

Tariq laughed and high-fived him.

Zafir winced. "Back for more," he said through his teeth. "Great."

I swallowed. "This . . . this kind of stuff doesn't *always* happen."

"That's promising, I guess."

Sven turned to Zafir. "Listen, um, I'm really sorry. I just looked away at the wrong time, and . . ." He gulped. "I'm sorry. If you need any help with the bills, or—"

"It's fine." Zafir smiled. "We're covered. But thank you. And don't worry about what happened." He nodded toward Tariq. "To tell you the truth, I think he's looking forward to showing off his battle scars at school."

Sven threw his head back and laughed. To me, he said, "You were right, dude. That kid is *born* to skate."

Zafir groaned. "Awesome. Well, maybe he could wear one of those next time?" He gestured at a rack of mouth guards.

"Yeah. I'll order one." I swallowed. "I, uh, didn't have any in his size, so . . ."

"It's okay." His expression softened. "Quit beating yourself up, Brennan. He's fine."

*But he could've been—*

"I know. I'm glad I didn't scare him away from skating though." I winked. "Sorry."

Zafir chuckled. "It was a valiant effort."

I was about to come back with something smart, but the door opened again. Instinctively, I turned, and looked past Zafir *right* when Aimee and Billy strolled in, hand in hand.

I bristled. We'd made up, but seeing her with him still rubbed me the wrong way.

Zafir glanced over his shoulder, then back at me. "Customer?"

"Ex-girlfriend."

He turned toward her again, and his lip twitched. Amusement? Annoyance? I had no idea. As he faced me, he said, "She comes by and visits you or something?"

"She's a skater," I muttered. "And we're the only shop in town."

He shifted his weight. "Should we, um, get going?"

"You don't have to."

"Actually—" He glanced at his phone. "I do need to take him home and give him another pain pill."

I winced. "I am so—"

"I'm serious," Zafir said. "It was an accident. And the way you handled it . . ." He smiled. "I can't really be mad about that, can I?"

"Well, no."

"It's all good. I promise." He turned to Tariq. "Come on. Let's go get you some more drugs."

"Okay."

To me, Zafir said, "What time are you off tonight?"

"Six." I paused. "Why don't I shoot you a text when I'm done? Maybe I could take you guys both out to eat."

"You really don't have to do that."

"I know. But it would make me feel a lot better about what happened."

Zafir held my gaze. Then a faint smile pulled up the corners of his mouth, and he nodded. "Sure. Okay. I'm not working tonight. But maybe we can just hang out?" He put his arm around Tariq. "We should probably give him a few days before we take him out to eat."

A weird mix of relief and excitement swelled in my stomach. "Okay. Perfect. I'll see you later?"

"Definitely."

They turned to go, and I exhaled. I did feel better after seeing Tariq up and around, and after Zafir's reassurance that he really truly wasn't angry. And now, all I had to do was deal with . . .

I cringed.

Aimee. And Billy.

And they were coming right this way.

He snaked an arm around her and shot me a grin. One of those grins where if I punched him in the mouth right then, there wasn't a jury in the land that would convict me of anything except not hitting him hard enough.

Billy started to speak, but Aimee beat him to it.

"*Billy.*" She shot him a look. "Don't."

The asshole huffed like a petulant kid, then walked away. Damn. They hadn't been together very long, and she could already order him around with a glare. Then again, maybe they'd been together longer than—

I shut that train of thought down before it could get very far. I was already annoyed that they were here. Didn't need to work myself up. Just having her here was enough.

"So." I cleared my throat. "What's up?"

"We need to talk about the apartment."

I slid my hands into my pockets. "Okay."

"Things fell through with my roommates. I'm still looking for a place, but—"

"Where are you staying right now?"

"Um." Her eyes flicked toward Billy, then to the floor, as if she hadn't meant to give herself away like that.

"Never mind," I muttered. "So, what about our place?"

She fidgeted. "I owe you for some of the bills, but . . . I kind of need first and last as a deposit for a new place."

"What do you want to do, then?"

She avoided my eyes, her lips twisting with obvious aggravation. "Can I wait to give you the money?"

"That's gonna leave me kind of short."

"I know. I'm sorry."

I wanted to tell her it was her problem, that this was her mess, but the truth was, I was on better financial ground than she was. I had a smallish savings, while she was struggling to stay afloat and put herself through school.

"Don't worry about it," I said quietly. "Just pay me when you can."

"Thanks. Also, I called the utility companies and had my name taken off the bills." She took a folded check out of her purse. "This should cover my part of those for the rest of that month."

"Thanks." I pocketed the check without looking at the amount. "The landlord gave me a new lease with just my name. So we're good there."

"Okay." She met my gaze, and my heart pounded. The weirdest part was this conversation was only slightly more awkward than the ones we'd had during the last few months of our relationship.

*We really were miserable, weren't we?*

"So. Um. Anything else?"

"No. I don't think so." She scanned the store, and when she'd apparently found Billy—he was chatting with Sven by the counter—she said, "I'm gonna go."

"Okay."

It didn't even feel weird to have her walk away without an obligatory peck on the cheek or the lips. All of that seemed like ancient history.

Good. That was how it needed to be. Time to move the fuck on.

I picked up a box of outdated magazines and started toward the back room to get rid of them. As I walked, I made the mistake of glancing at Aimee and Billy. He met my gaze, and smirked as he wrapped his arm around Aimee's shoulders.

*Smug bastard.*

It didn't hurt, though. It was what it was. Aimee had been my girlfriend, and now she wasn't. She'd cheated. She had him now. And I had—

My own thought startled me enough that I *almost* dropped the box.

She had Billy. I had . . . Zafir?

Shaking myself, I adjusted the box so I wouldn't drop it, and took it into the back room. After I'd set it on a table, I paused to get my brain together.

Zafir was filling that gap, wasn't he? He was the reason I'd barely spent any time thinking about Aimee, let alone pining for her or dealing with our breakup. Seeing her with Billy had only bothered me because the douche bag was obviously trying to rub it in my face. But the two of them being together didn't make me feel, well, anything. It was like the space she used to occupy in my brain had been filled with the excitement over seeing Zafir after I got off work.

Now that I put those pieces together, I couldn't help scratching my head and wondering how the fuck this had happened.

Not that it mattered. It had. I didn't have a clue what was going on with him, but I liked spending time with him. I liked his kid. I liked that he knew three girls in a row had dumped me for being sexually incompetent, and he didn't make me feel like there was something wrong with me. I liked that he still wanted to hang out even after things went south with Tariq yesterday.

I didn't know what the hell we were doing, but I did know one thing.

I liked it.

But . . . hello. Zafir was a dude. Asexual or not, I didn't date dudes.

Did I?

I couldn't imagine having sex with him. All I could imagine was being with him. As much as possible. Which, now that I thought about it, was how I'd felt about Aimee in the beginning. I never had that need to get into her pants. I'd just . . . wanted to be with her. When I wasn't with her, I couldn't stop thinking about her. When I was with her, I couldn't think at all.

Staring up at the ceiling, I gulped.

That was exactly what was happening with Zafir, wasn't it?

# CHAPTER SIXTEEN

# ZAFIR

Less than a week after his incident, Tariq was already itching to skate again. I held out until he had a clean bill of health from his dentist—no infections, no need for further work—and the splint had been removed, but about three weeks after he fell, I gave in.

This time, I came to the park with them, since I didn't have to be at Old Country for a few hours. While Brennan helped Tariq with his helmet and pads—and mouth guard, this time—I leaned against the railing and watched.

They were on a very small ramp at the end of the skate park where things didn't seem quite so extreme. Nothing too steep or high. The skate park equivalent of a shallow end, apparently.

Some of the other guys kept throwing glances toward Brennan and Tariq. At first, I was a little uneasy. Why were they so interested? But after a while, I realized they were just keeping an eye on traffic. They redirected other skaters so they'd stay on the far side of the park. If someone headed toward the tiny ramp where Tariq was skating, the guys would stop them and send them back the other direction.

They were doing the same with some other younger kids too. On a somewhat more advanced ramp than this one, two girls who were probably Tariq's age were skating under the watchful eye of one of Brennan's coworkers. No one went near them.

Slowly, I relaxed. Even if skating was inherently dangerous, it was comforting to know that people here took safety seriously, and that they were protective of the younger and less experienced kids. And Brennan had told me they'd all helped out when Tariq got hurt.

I released a breath and turned my attention back to Brennan and Tariq.

At the top of the ramp, Brennan balanced on his board, all four wheels in the air with only the end of the board making contact with the pavement. Then he shifted, and the wheels came down. He rode the board down the ramp, up the other side, and back to where Tariq was standing.

My heart was in my throat, but I forced my expression to stay neutral in case Tariq looked my way.

*Do I trust Brennan? He wouldn't actually make my kid do something dangerous, right?*

I turned toward the other guys. They were watching, but didn't seem alarmed. Then again, one of them had done a somersault in midair earlier, and another had wiped out before getting up and doing it again, so we might have had different definitions of "dude, that doesn't look safe."

I chewed my lip and watched my son again.

He stood on his board and started to shift the same way Brennan had, but he overcorrected. My heart lurched.

*No, no, no—*

The board buzzed down the ramp and up the other side, but Tariq was safely at the top, Brennan's arm around his waist as he got his feet back under him.

"You okay?" Brennan asked as he carefully let go.

"Yeah. Just screwed it up."

"It takes some practice. You'll get it. Don't worry."

Tariq nodded. He collected his board and tried again. This time, he didn't overcorrect, and I held my breath as he rode the board down the ramp. He made it partway up the other side, but then wobbled.

And fell.

I started toward him, but he casually got up, dusted off his knee and elbow pads, righted his board, and rejoined Brennan at the top of the short ramp. My heart was still racing, and he was already on the board, ready to try again.

Brennan patted his shoulder. "It's okay, dude. Falling is part of learning."

"I know." Tariq's brow furrowed. He tried the trick again, and this time, rolled down the ramp, up the other side, and back up to where

Brennan was waiting. His dismount wasn't perfect, but he didn't lose his balance and the board didn't get away from him.

"All right!" Brennan high-fived him. "Was it fun?"

"Yeah!" Tariq's grin made me laugh. Apparently he *had* found a new hobby. Right then, I was pretty sure I heard my bank account screaming for mercy. But hey, my kid was happy. I'd find a way to pay for the gear to keep him that way.

As they continued with their lesson, I sat back and watched. And I had to admit, I was watching Brennan almost as much as I was watching Tariq.

A weird prickly feeling climbed my spine. In the three weeks since Tariq's fall, I hadn't been able to shake the question he'd asked the next morning.

*"Is Brennan your boyfriend?"*

The more I thought about it, the more I was sure that, no, we weren't dating. But I kind of wanted us to be. And watching him with Tariq wasn't doing much to make that thought go away.

Everyone I'd dated had gotten along well enough with my son—I wouldn't have continued seeing someone if they didn't—but there was something different about the way Brennan and Tariq interacted.

Brennan had the kind of patience I rarely saw in someone who didn't have kids of his own. He walked Tariq through every step, and gently corrected him whenever he made a mistake. If Tariq fell—which he did several times—Brennan made sure he was okay, but didn't criticize him or tease him about it. When Tariq got it right, and he accomplished the trick he was trying to learn, Brennan high-fived him and cheered as if he was equally excited.

Brennan could do things with a skateboard that blew my mind. And yet, when my son managed to clumsily but successfully kick his board up into his hand while landing on his feet, Brennan congratulated him as if he'd just mastered one of the more complex tricks everyone else in the park was doing. But he also did it in such a way that it wasn't patronizing or condescending.

My mind wandered back to the night Brennan had called to tell me he and Tariq were at the ER. I'd had millions of horror movies rolling simultaneously inside my head—all kinds of visions of my son being hurt, scared, traumatized—and I'd walked in to find them relaxing over a video game. Yeah, he'd been hurt, and yeah, he'd been scared, but Brennan had him calm in spite of that day being the sum of Tariq's biggest fears. Without me, in a hospital, with blood everywhere . . . he was fine. Whether he was teaching him a trick or comforting him, Brennan had a calming effect on—

"Hey!" Brennan's sharp voice jerked me back into the present. My head snapped toward where he and Tariq were.

Tariq stood behind Brennan, cowering just slightly, and Brennan was right in another skater's face, stabbing a finger at him and snarling something I couldn't hear.

Heart pounding, I pushed myself off the rail and hurried closer.

"All right, all right." The other guy put up his hands and took a step back. "Take it easy, man."

Brennan shot him a murderous look, and the guy skated off in another direction.

"What's going on?" I asked.

Brennan shifted his attention to Tariq, squeezing his shoulder gently. "You okay?"

My son nodded.

My chest tightened. "Brennan? What's going on?"

He faced me. "Just some idiot who wasn't paying attention. He just got a little close. Clipped Tariq when he went by." He glared over his shoulder, but the other guy was staying well away. To me, he said, "That stuff *usually* doesn't happen here. Been a run of bad luck lately, but I'm going to talk to my boss about tightening the safety rules."

"Good idea." I looked down at Tariq. He had his board on the ground, and was testing it with one foot, arms out to the sides. Shrugging, I said, "Well, he doesn't seem to be any worse for the wear."

Brennan's eyebrows rose.

"Tariq," I said, "you want to keep skating, or are you done for the day?"

"I want to keep skating!" He gave us both puppy-dog eyes. "Please?"

I turned to Brennan and winked. "See? He's fine."

Brennan swallowed. Then he nodded. "Okay." To Tariq, he said, "You ready?"

My son nodded vigorously.

"Okay, you've got"—I checked the time on my phone—"twenty minutes, and then we have to go. All right?"

"'Kay, Dad."

I returned to my spot at the railing, and they continued skating. As Brennan guided Tariq through another skill, I kept replaying that weird exchange between him and the other guy. The skaters probably snarled at each other like that from time to time. A bunch of young guys on Red Bull and adrenaline? Yeah, that had to be par for the course. Someone got in Brennan's way while he was trying to give a lesson, and he put the guy in his place and sent him packing. He was annoyed. Territorial because someone had invaded his space.

It was *not* that grizzly bear protectiveness of a kid.

Was it?

After all, almost everyone here seemed to be vigilant about the kids. Some of the other guys even gave the idiot a dirty look as he returned to the more advanced side of the park.

I shook myself and watched Tariq's lesson. I was just reading too much into Brennan's reaction. Way too much.

*Wishful thinking, Zafir. Get over it.*

The next night, I was drumming my fingers on the counter at Red Hot. My shift would be over in twenty minutes, and I wasn't working at Old Country tonight. Since Brennan was also off, he was coming by to meet me. Then we'd pick up Tariq from the babysitter and go out to a movie.

In fact, Brennan was probably on his way right now.

My stomach fluttered. I kept glancing at the door, fidgeting as I alternated between watching for him and looking for something to do to pass the time.

Mostly, though, my mind kept gnawing on everything going on between me and Brennan. The more time we spent together, the harder it was to ignore that innocent question Tariq had posed over a pudding-cup breakfast.

*Was* Brennan my boyfriend?

And if he was . . .

My heart sank a little. Gnawing my lip, I played at the edge of the counter with my thumbnail.

Tariq loved Brennan. No two ways about it. Maybe it was just the novelty of having a semipro skater at his disposal to teach him tricks, but the two of them got along really well. All I had to do was mention Brennan's name, and my son's eyes lit up.

I was playing with fire. Tariq had been hurt too many times. I wanted to find someone and fall in love with them, but how many times could I let my son get *his* heart stomped on? How many times had I promised myself I wouldn't introduce a partner to Tariq until I was sure they'd stick around for a while?

But Brennan wasn't supposed to be a boyfriend. We were friends. And if I could get that through my head, I'd be a lot saner.

Funny—I knew before he did that he was asexual, and I'd still gone into this as if I were making friends with a straight guy. Someone who was completely off the table. I'd just assumed he was heteroromantic. However he identified, it had never once occurred to me in the beginning that we might connect like this. Otherwise, I never would have brought him anywhere near Tariq.

But I had, and now the cat was out of the bag. Tariq and Brennan hadn't just met, they'd bonded. Tariq obviously trusted him, or he would've been a hysterical wreck when I'd finally arrived at the ER that night.

Which left me two choices.

One, play it safe and stay friends with Brennan. Nothing more.

Two, let this thing happen the way it wanted to happen, and see if there really was something to the way my heart skipped whenever Brennan walked in the room.

This was one of those times I wanted to fall back on my faith—remembering that Allah had already decided how this would all play out. And if our relationship was even one He approved of, which would be a subject of hot debate if my father found out about this.

Same-sex relationship aside, from where I stood the future was a giant question mark, and what happened next hinged on what I did or didn't do. And I couldn't stomach the idea of just sitting back and letting things happen. Not when my kid was involved. Maybe that meant I sucked at being a Muslim, but I was determined to be a good father.

So was I being a better father if I distanced myself and Tariq from Brennan? Or if I let Brennan in?

The bell on the door jingled, and the hair on my neck stood up. We'd had a steady stream of customers all day long, but somehow I knew.

And when I turned, my heart skipped.

"Hey." Brennan smiled as he came up to the counter, skateboard under his arm as usual. "I'm a little early. I hope that's okay."

*I'm so glad you're here.*

"Yeah. Yeah." I cleared my throat. "Just, uh, have to wrap a few things, and then I'll be ready to roll."

"Sweet."

As she always did when Brennan came by, Violet practically shoved me out the door, and not five minutes after he'd shown up, we were heading to my car.

I glanced at the skateboard under his arm. "You really do take that everywhere, don't you?"

"Well, my grandma would shit herself if I brought it to church, but otherwise . . ."

We looked at each other and both laughed.

"You know, I could teach you too." He thumped the board with his knuckle. "If you wanted."

I eyed the board warily, then shook my head. "No, I think I'll pass. Tariq's tooth might not have deterred him, but I think it turned me off skating forever."

Brennan grimaced, his cheeks coloring. "How . . . how is that healing, anyway?"

"Oh, it's fine. I think it might've been a blessing in disguise, actually."

"What? How?"

"He had to go into the dentist for X-rays a few times to make sure it wasn't getting infected or anything." I shrugged. "After the second or third trip, he didn't bat an eye at going into the dentist's office."

"Well, I guess that's a plus. *I* still hate going to the dentist."

"Tell me about it." I shuddered. "So, I'll pass on skating, but Tariq obviously enjoys it." I paused. "Thanks for doing that for him, by the way. He's been having a ball."

Brennan smiled. "I'm happy to teach him. He's really got a knack for it."

"I don't know if that should worry me or not."

"Well." Brennan grinned sheepishly. "The very first time he skated, he got his tooth knocked out, and he still came back for more. So, uh, one of us created a monster. I'm not sure which."

"Great." I chuckled, then shrugged. "Hey, as long as he's happy and he's got someone to show him the ropes safely, I can't complain."

"I'll do the best I can."

"I guess this means I should start investing in some equipment for him, so you don't have to keep supplying him with loaners." I grimaced. "Maybe for his birthday. That gives me a few months to save up." *Which means I'll have enough for, like, one kneepad.*

Brennan rubbed the backs of his fingers along his jaw. "You know, I have an employee discount. I can hook him up with some starter gear, and then if he wants to get serious later . . ."

"I can't ask you to do that." I swallowed. "Even with your discount, I . . . probably can't swing it. Not for a while."

He shook his head. "It's no trouble. Whenever. Honestly, we can work something out, and my boss doesn't mind me letting you use the discount as long as we don't abuse it."

"Really?"

"Absolutely. I'd rather make sure Tariq's got the gear he needs."

"I . . . Thank you. It'll mean a lot to him." I paused. "And to me."

Brennan smiled. "Don't mention it."

We reached my car, and I drove us over to my apartment. As we stepped inside, I zeroed in on Tariq, who was playing a video game on the living room floor.

He paused the game and turned around. "Brennan!"

"Hey, kiddo!" Brennan's eyes lit up, and my stomach flipped.

*They really have bonded, haven't they?*

Tariq vaulted over the back of the couch.

"Hey!" I eyed him. "What have I told you?"

He stopped, lowering his gaze. "Go around the couch, not over it."

"Uh-huh." I gestured toward the living room.

With a slight pout—he knew better than to stomp or huff—he walked around to where he'd been playing, then came back to us.

"That's better." I smiled and ruffled his hair. "Grab your jacket. We have to go."

He disappeared down the hall.

Kelly chuckled as she gathered her coat and purse. "He's been pretty good about not jumping on the couch. But I'm not surprised today."

"Why's that?" I asked as I counted out her money.

"He's been crazy excited all afternoon about going out this evening."

Even as I chuckled, my stomach flipped again. "Has he?"

She nodded. "Hasn't stopped talking about it. Or, well . . ." She gestured toward his game. "Up until he started playing, I mean."

"Figures." I rolled my eyes. "The video game is like kid hypnosis."

"Doesn't just work on kids," Brennan muttered.

"You too?"

He nodded. "I sit down for ten minutes of *Call of Duty*, and the next thing I know, it's like next Thursday."

"So he's not going to grow out of it?"

Kelly laughed. "Sorry, Zafir. Little boys do not grow out of video games."

"Great . . ."

After Kelly left, Tariq came down the hall, pulling his jacket on as he did. "Are we going to eat before the movie? I'm hungry."

"Yes, we're going to eat before the movie." I looked at Brennan. "You in the mood for anything in particular?"

He shrugged. "I'm game for anything."

"Can we go to the Anchor?" Tariq asked.

"Oh, that place is awesome." Brennan shot me a puppy-dog look. "Can we? Please?"

I groaned. "Are you sure you don't want to go someplace with crayons?"

Tariq clicked his tongue. "The Anchor has crayons, Dad."

Brennan gestured at him and shrugged as if to say *See?*

Shaking my head, I gestured at the door. "All right, all right. Let's go."

We piled into my car, and I took us over to the Anchor. Tariq didn't give the kids' menu so much as a glance—he went straight to the regular menu and ordered the big fish and chips. I cringed, but it wasn't because I thought his eyes were bigger than his stomach. My sister had warned me about this phase—when a growing kid started eating everything in sight.

*"It's gonna get expensive,"* she'd told me a few months ago. *"Buckle up."*

*So it begins.*

"Have you ever seen a real cod, Tariq?" Brennan held up a piece of fish. "Because they're a lot prettier like this than when they're in the water."

"Really?" Tariq eyed him uncertainly, as if he wasn't sure if Brennan was yanking his chain. "Have you ever seen one in real life?"

Brennan nodded. "My brother caught one while we were out fishing. I'm surprised that thing didn't bite somebody. It was *nasty*."

Tariq blinked. Then he picked up a piece of cod and drowned it in tartar sauce. "They're ugly, but they taste good."

"Yes, they do." Brennan started to say something else, but Tariq suddenly pointed past him at the window.

"Look! That's Ari!"

Brennan twisted around, and I craned my neck. In front of the restaurant, a couple of guys walked past, oblivious to us.

"*Who* is that again?" Brennan asked.

"Ari Valentine," Tariq said. "He's on *Wolf's Landing*."

I arched an eyebrow. "How do you know who's who on *Wolf's Landing*?"

"Um . . ." His cheeks turned bright red.

I tried to scowl, but the sheepish look made me laugh. Rolling my eyes, I reached for my drink. "Okay, if you're going to watch it, maybe we should watch it together. So I at least know what's going on."

"But then we'll have to DVR like two seasons before you have time to watch it with me."

*Ouch . . .*

"You know . . ." Brennan cleared his throat. "Some of the techs and stunt guys from the show come to the skate shop. That's um . . ." Brennan gestured at Tariq. "That's why we had that stuff we put your tooth in. Most people have never heard of it, but the stunt guys swear by it."

"Well, I'm glad you had it," I said.

"Yeah," he said, a hint of shyness creeping into his voice, "me too."

And I was glad for the subject change, because Tariq seemed to forget about how little time I'd have to watch *Wolf's Landing* with him.

"Have you met them?" he asked Brennan. "The stunt guys?"

Brennan nodded. "Some of them."

"Do the actors skate?"

"Not many of them. I think the people running the show would get mad if one of them lost a tooth or something."

Tariq laughed. "They're wimps."

"Right?" Brennan sighed dramatically. "It's a tooth. I know a kid who had a tooth busted out, and was ready to skate the next day."

Tariq grinned.

I just chuckled and shook my head.

After dinner, we made our way to the movie theater.

In the auditorium, Tariq sat between us with a bucket of popcorn that was almost as big as he was. I didn't bother reminding him he'd just eaten.

*Guess I should start putting money away to feed him when he's a teenager.*

A few minutes after we'd sat down, the previews started, and it quickly became obvious that Brennan and Tariq had adorably similar taste in movies. The minute the screen lit up with explosions and slow-motion car chases, they were both on the edge of their seats, wide-eyed and slack-jawed. Then the next preview came along, trying to psych us up for a moody historical movie about . . . hell, I didn't know. I wasn't paying any more attention than they were because *boring*.

"Yawn," Brennan grumbled just loud enough for us to hear. "Aliens in the next five seconds, or I'm not going."

Tariq snorted. "If aliens landed there, they'd die of boredom."

Brennan and I both smothered laughs.

The painfully uninteresting preview finally ended, and the screen was once again alive with explosions and action sequences.

"I am so there," Brennan said to Tariq.

"Me too." Tariq looked at me, eyebrows up as if to ask, *Right?*

"Obviously," I said. "Though Brennan and I might have to go see it first. Make sure it's—"

"Dad." He rolled his eyes and sighed dramatically.

Brennan and I exchanged glances, and both chuckled.

The previews continued, and after about nine hundred of them, the movie started. Tariq was engrossed. So was Brennan.

Me? I had three or four brain cells following the movie, but the rest were focused on the two people beside me.

This was unnervingly familiar. Megan and I had taken Tariq out like this a number of times when we both had a night off. We'd all enjoyed it. I'd assumed things would stay that way, but they hadn't. Megan had left. Tariq had gotten hurt. So had I, but it was my choice to get involved with her. Tariq had been along for the ride whether he liked it or not, and when it was over . . .

I cringed, trying like hell to focus on the movie but failing miserably.

When I was alone, analyzing all of this from a distance, it was easy to say Brennan and I should be friends, and that I could keep us that way. It would be simpler, and less risky, and less stressful for my kid if things didn't work out.

But when we were in the same room, when I was constantly aware of his presence—even in my peripheral vision in the darkness of a movie theater—it wasn't so easy. I had no idea what we were doing. All I knew was that I liked it. If I was honest with myself, the only thing I would've changed was introducing him to Tariq so soon. If I'd thought this might turn into something more than friendship, I'd have kept them apart until I figured out what that something was. And if it had any staying power.

Because I was lying if I said I didn't want it to have staying power.

I glanced at Brennan, and swallowed. The truth was, wishful thinking or not, no one had given me butterflies like this since my ex-fiancée. I couldn't have *not* fallen in love with her if I'd tried.

So what made me think I could avoid it with Brennan?

# CHAPTER SEVENTEEN

# BRENNAN

That Sunday, Zafir and I headed to Seattle to try that asexual group again. We decided to take the Kingston Ferry, and thanks to Murphy's Law, we got there just in time to watch the boat pull away. The next one didn't leave for almost an hour.

Zafir parked in line and shut off the car. "We've got some time to kill. You want to go down to the beach or something?"

I shrugged. "Sure."

A path led from the ferry holding area down the seawall and to the beach, which was about thirty feet below the lot. We followed it down and walked in silence for a little while. The beach was deserted except for us. We wandered along the tide line, sand-covered rocks crunching beneath our shoes.

I kept an eye on the water. When the ferry came into view we'd have to head back up, but for now all I could see were some seagulls, a few small boats, and a black-topped red freighter in the distance. So we had time.

We had time, and we were on a damn beach, and I was with Zafir . . . and I couldn't relax. From the minute he'd picked me up this morning, I'd been a nervous wreck. All I could think about was everything that had kept me up the other night. What *was* this? What *were* we doing?

"You've been kind of quiet today." His voice startled me.

I stared at the rocks beneath our feet. "Sorry."

"It's okay. I just . . . Are *you* okay?"

*I don't know. I have no idea what's going on. Or why everything feels different when we're together.*

I stopped. So did he.

For a long moment, I stared out at the water, not sure if I was hoping to see the ferry, or if I wanted it to wait a few more minutes.

"Brennan?" he quietly prodded.

I took a deep breath. "I guess . . ." My stomach twisted itself into somersaulting knots. I had no idea how to say this. What I even wanted to say.

Zafir's hand moved, and I turned as he tucked a few strands of black hair behind his ear. He was still watching me, squinting a little against the salty wind, his expression offering absolutely nothing.

And before I could stop myself, I blurted out, "Why does it feel like we're dating?"

Zafir didn't even flinch. "Maybe we are."

My breath caught. "What?"

"Maybe we are." He shrugged. "I've kind of been wondering the same thing, to be honest."

Blood pounded in my ears. "So . . . what do we do?"

"Do we have to do anything?" That gentle smile nearly turned me inside out. "Do you want to change anything we've been doing?"

"No." The answer was effortless. No hesitation whatsoever. But it also spawned a million new questions that were suddenly banging around inside my skull. "I guess I'm just confused. I mean . . ." I swallowed hard. Somehow, I managed to look him in the eye as I whispered, "Where does it stop being friendship and become a relationship?"

"Wherever we decide it does. I mean, remember what we talked about—sex isn't the only thing that defines a relationship, right?"

"Okay. True. But I guess I'm confused about what *does* define one."

"Well . . ." Zafir stepped closer, right into my comfort zone, but I didn't back away, not even when his eyes flicked toward my lips, then back up to meet mine. "The only people whose opinions matter are yours and mine. So, it's however we want to define it."

"Kind of . . ." *Slow down, heart. Seriously.* "Kind of wondering how much control we have over it."

Zafir smiled. No—he grinned. "Some things do happen on their own. But we can control if we step on the gas or the brakes."

*Why do I feel like I'm stomping on both right now?*

He broke eye contact, and though he didn't step back, his cheeks darkened. Laughing softly, he looked out at the water.

"What?" I asked.

"I, um . . ." His Adam's apple jumped. Then he met my gaze again. "I'm trying like hell to reassure you that we can call the shots here, but the only thing I can think of is—" He hesitated. So soft I could barely hear him, he said, "Is how much I really want to kiss you right now."

Goose bumps shot up all over my skin. "Really?"

Nodding, he dropped his gaze again.

"That isn't weird? For . . . uh . . ."

"For asexuals to kiss?"

"Yeah."

He looked at me again and smiled. "Does it matter?" Arching an eyebrow, he added, "Especially since you're apparently more worried about whether asexuals should kiss than whether we should?"

"What? No, I'm—" *Curious. The word you're looking for is* curious. "I guess . . . no. I guess it doesn't matter."

"And who says it's sexual? It's just affection." He ran his hand up my forearm. "People can touch without it having anything to do with sex."

*But why does it feel so different when you touch me versus when other people do?*

I had no idea what to say. Or how to speak, really. Standing this close to him, knowing what was on the table, with curiosity inching past nervousness—I was lucky I could breathe.

Zafir's weight shifted, and rocks and sand crunched as he stepped a little closer. His shirt was a light breeze away from touching mine. He lifted his hand off my forearm, and I held my breath. Even before his fingers moved into my peripheral vision, I knew what was coming.

Eyes locked on mine, he touched my face. My heart was going impossibly fast now. I was vaguely aware that we were out in public, and someone might lean over the guardrail above and see us, but I didn't care.

His hand slid around to the back of my neck, and with the faintest pressure from his fingertips, he drew me toward him.

Our lips met.

And everything . . . faded.

The ocean was suddenly a million miles away. The seagulls were distant background noise. There were people and cars, but my senses were too busy exploring the softness of his lips. His stubbled chin hissed across mine, driving home that I was kissing a man for the first time in my life. That I was kissing Zafir. And I liked it.

Slowly, I wrapped my arms around him. Nothing about this felt as weird as I thought it should. It was . . . God, it was perfect.

He broke the kiss and our eyes met.

"Wow," I breathed.

"Yeah. Wow." He searched my eyes. "Does that turn you on?"

I swept my tongue across my lips. "It, um . . . not really, no."

Zafir's brow knitted, and he sounded more nervous than I'd ever heard him when he whispered, "But did you like it?"

"I—" My heart thumped against my ribs, and I caught myself missing the softness of his lips against mine. This didn't make any sense, but . . . "Yeah. I did like it."

So I pulled him back to me and kissed him again.

# CHAPTER EIGHTEEN

# ZAFIR

It was Brennan who broke away this time, and I shivered as we pulled apart. I'd been wanting to kiss him for a while now, and he hadn't disappointed.

His eyes flicked toward the water. "Damn." He scowled. "Here comes the boat."

*No!*

I turned, and sure enough, the green-and-white vessel was on its way toward the dock. We still had a little time, but not much.

Looking up at him again, I said, "I guess we should go back to the car."

Brennan nodded.

Damn it. The moment had barely started, and now it was over. Way too soon. But maybe he needed that. Maybe we both did. Test the water, then back off and decide if it was okay.

He cleared his throat. "We still have a minute or so, right?"

"Yeah." I glanced at the boat. "They still have to unload, and—"

He cupped my face and kissed me. When he broke away this time, he grinned. "That's all the extra time I needed."

I swallowed. "Oh. Okay."

His grin fell, and his forehead creased. "You don't mind . . . um . . ."

"Of course not." I laughed to make my lungs work again. "I started it, right?"

"Well, true. But . . ." He chewed his lip, staring at the rocks beneath our feet.

"Relax." I touched his arm. "We probably should get back to the car, though."

Brennan nodded. In silence, we hurried up the path and across the parking lot. The ferry was just pulling into the slip as we got in my car. Now I kind of regretted coming back so quickly—we could've stolen at least two or three more minutes—but it was better like this. No point in having to scramble to the car while the people behind us gave us dirty looks.

After the ferry had docked and unloaded, a worker in an orange vest directed us to start loading. We were one of the first to load, fortunately, so we didn't have to wait long.

On the boat, I pulled up behind the car in front of me, parked, and killed the engine. "So, do you want to stay here or go up on deck?"

Brennan looked right at me and slid his hand over the top of mine on the console. "I think I'd rather stay here."

My heart sped up. "Yeah. Yeah, we can . . . we can do that."

He smiled, but broke eye contact. With his hand over mine, we both stared out the windshield for the longest time. Even as the ferry pushed off and the usual recorded safety message played on the loudspeaker, we didn't talk. We didn't look at each other.

The silence was going to drive me crazy, though, so I finally cleared my throat. "That's . . . What happened on the beach—it's not going to make things weird, is it?"

Brennan laughed softly. Almost shyly. "This has been weird from day one, but . . ." He met my gaze, and yes, there was definitely some shyness in his eyes. "Weird isn't necessarily bad, is it?"

I shook my head. "Of course not. But it's not . . . like, awkward?"

"No." He paused. "Right?"

"It's not awkward for me."

"Good." He exhaled. "I guess it's just new." With a hint of a smirk, he added, "Is it weird for me to have my first kiss with a guy on my way to an asexual group?"

I laughed. "Seems kind of poetic in a way."

"Yeah, I guess it does." He chuckled as he slipped his fingers between mine. "And this doesn't mean we'll get our asexual cards revoked?"

"Just don't tell anyone," I said in a stage whisper. "Can't be too careful."

Our eyes met, and we both burst out laughing.

"To be serious, no." I brought his hand up and kissed the backs of his fingers. "There's nothing in the rule book that says physical affection is off the table."

"Wait, so there's a rule book? Do I get one of those tonight?"

"Nope." I lowered our hands to the console. "You have to recruit three more people."

"Oh. Well shit."

"It's not as hard as it sounds. You're actually my twelfth recruit."

"Really?" He furrowed his brow. "So, do you get, like, a toaster or something?"

I snorted. "Please. The toaster is your seventh recruit. After twelve, I'm getting a mystery box."

"A mystery box? That could be bad."

"Nah." I waved a hand. "Friend of mine got it last year and said it's just a couple of movie tickets and a free tub of popcorn."

"You'd think they'd make it a gag gift or something. You know, like a box of condoms and a stack of porn."

I snickered. "I wouldn't put that past these guys."

"Sounds like my kind of crowd."

"Uh-huh. Thought so."

The city of Edmonds was coming into view, so people were slowly returning to their cars. It would still be a few minutes before we docked, though, so I didn't start the engine yet.

Brennan ran his thumb alongside my hand. "So what about Tariq?"

I stiffened. "What about him?"

"I mean, do we tell him? That we're . . . uh . . ."

"He already knows, actually."

Brennan's eyebrows quirked. "Come again?"

"He's . . ." I laughed, looking out at the water. "He's kind of the reason I've been thinking about this a lot. He asked me a while back if you were my boyfriend." I hesitated, then turned to him again. "And I didn't quite know how to answer him."

"So it doesn't bother him?"

"Which part? Me having a boyfriend, or you being that boyfriend?"

Brennan half shrugged. "Either or."

"He knows I date both men and women, and he likes you."

"Oh. That's . . . that's good. That he's okay with us. And two guys in general."

I watched my fingers tracing his hand in the darkness. "He didn't even realize people thought same-sex couples were weird until someone at our mosque made a snide comment about it. He still scratches his head if someone acts like gay people are strange."

"Now that's some good parenting right there."

"Maybe a bit self-serving, in this case."

"Still."

Our eyes met again, and we exchanged subtle smiles.

And I wondered how I'd ever not seen that this would happen. That he'd ever been a stranger, or some guy I sort of knew, or just a friend.

It was like he'd always been *Brennan*. And we'd always been like this.

It just made sense.

The asexual group had a standing reservation at a hipster coffee shop in Seattle's University District, and when we showed up, a dozen people were already there.

"Zafir!" Alicia squealed as we joined them. She jumped up and threw her arms around me. "I haven't seen you in forever!"

"I know. I'm sorry." I hugged her back. "I've been working too much."

Clicking her tongue, she released me and gave a disapproving glare. "What have I told you?"

"Yeah, yeah, yeah." I rolled my eyes. "All work and no play makes Zafir miss out on spending time with Alicia."

"Exactly." She turned to Brennan. "I don't think we've met."

"This is my first time." He extended his hand. "Brennan Cross."

"Nice to meet you."

After they'd shaken hands, I introduced Brennan around to the rest of the group.

"So you live over on the Peninsula?" Sam asked.

Brennan nodded. "Yeah. Bluewater Bay. Like him."

"What do you do?" Jayson asked.

"I work in a skateboard shop."

Three of the others—Robyn and two guys I hadn't met before—perked up.

"You do?" Robyn asked.

"Yeah." Brennan smiled in his adorably shy way. "Mostly for the discount. I'm a semipro skater."

I thought the three of them were going to fall out of their chairs.

"Really?" one of the guys asked. "Oh, I have to hear about this."

Brennan looked at me, eyebrows up.

I touched his arm. "Why don't you grab a chair, and I'll go get us some coffee?"

"Sounds good."

I went up to the counter to get us each a cup of coffee. By the time I came back—well, no shock. Brennan already had half the group hanging on his every word.

I took the empty seat beside him and set our coffees in front of us.

He paused and turned to me. "Thanks. What do I owe you?"

"You can get the next one."

"That works." Then he turned to the others again, and as he picked up his story, he absently rested his hand on my knee.

"So," Jayson said. "You're one of those skaters we see on TV? Doing all the flips and tricks and shit?"

Brennan nodded. "Haven't quite gotten into the X Games, but I'll get there."

"How do you do that stuff, anyway?" Alicia asked. "I've seen skaters do all kinds of crazy things, and I can't even stand on a skateboard."

Brennan chuckled. "Lots and lots and lots of practice."

"He's teaching my son." I put my hand on top of his. "I'm with you guys—it looks terrifying and fucking complicated."

"Seriously." Robyn laughed. "Props to you, though. Being able to do it well enough to compete—that's impressive."

"Thanks," Brennan said. "What do you guys do?"

"I work in IT," Alicia said.

"Retail," Robyn said.

"You too?" Brennan asked. "That's how I pay my bills. What do you sell?"

"Car stereos, mostly." She wrinkled her nose. "Not as fun as it sounds."

"She's not kidding," Alicia said. "Tell him about that guy with the Maserati."

Robyn groaned, covering her face with her hands. "Oh God. That asshole."

Brennan laughed. "Well, now I'm curious."

"Jesus." She huffed. "So it started right before last Christmas . . ."

Before long, the conversation had devolved into everyone who'd ever worked in retail sharing their horror stories. Robyn had her Maserati-owning misogynist who thought she was trying to rip him off because she was jealous that he had money. Jayson had done his time in a camera shop in college, and had more than a few amateur photographers try to blame him—not their own lack of skills—for ruined wedding albums. Brennan told about how he still had to sell things to his ex-girlfriend and her new boyfriend. And of course I'd had my fair share of retail-is-hell experiences, so I told the story of the man who didn't understand why he most certainly could *not* return a Fleshlight that had quite obviously been used. Repeatedly.

"I think Zafir wins." Jayson laughed. "That's horrible."

"Just be glad you weren't there." I gestured toward the counter. "So, anyone up for a cream-filled pastry or—"

"Oh my God!" Alicia smacked my arm. "You're terrible!"

Brennan shook his head, snickering. "I see why you make the trip out here for this group, Zafir."

I just chuckled. Gathering my plate and empty cup, I said, "Seriously, though—anyone want anything?"

No one except for Brennan did, so I headed up to the counter to get myself some coffee and him a cappuccino.

While I waited in line, Alicia joined me.

"So," she said. "You and Brennan . . ." She raised her eyebrows.

My face burned, and the color probably gave me away. "Yeah."

"Cool." She smiled. "What a nice guy. And I didn't even realize you were seeing anyone."

*It's kind of a new development.*

"Eh, you know." I shrugged. "I haven't been here in a while, and I just met him recently."

*Really? Recently?* I looked past her and watched Brennan for a moment. *You haven't been here my whole life?*

"Do you think he'll come back?" she asked. "To the group?"

"He seems to be having a good time. So, maybe?"

"Cool. It'll be nice to see both of you again."

"Thanks. I really do miss coming out here. Just haven't had time."

"I know the feeling." She scowled. "I've only been to like the last two meet-ups. I missed three or four before that."

"Good to know I'm not the only one."

"Nope, and you have to come a million miles." She paused. "How's Tariq doing?"

"Good. Good." I gestured at Brennan. "Those two get along so well it's scary."

She sobered a little. "They've met already? I thought you hadn't been seeing him very long."

"Yeah. We were kind of hanging out as friends. I . . . To be honest, I didn't see us dating, so I didn't think anything of it. Brennan started giving him skateboarding lessons, and then we started being . . . not just friends."

"Oh. Well. That makes sense." She glanced at him, and shrugged. "I guess that must be tricky when you have a kid."

"It is. Believe me. It is."

She smiled again. "Well, I hope things keep going good. It's nice to see you with someone like him."

"Thanks." I shifted my gaze toward Brennan, and I swore my lips tingled from that last kiss on the beach.

Yeah, maybe I was taking a risk. But I liked what we were doing so far.

And I hoped, inshallah, that this kept right on going.

As we walked back to my car, I asked, "Did you have a good time?"

"I did." Brennan glanced at me. "You?"

"Yeah. I like this crowd. They're pretty chill."

He nodded. “I noticed that. They seem like good people.”

“The Facebook group has all the dates and times,” I said. “If you want to come back on a day when I can’t, I’m sure they’d love to have you.”

“We’ll see. I . . . kind of liked being there with you.”

My heart fluttered. “Likewise.” I stopped beside the car, absently turning my keys in my hand. “You know how my schedule gets, though. Don’t feel like you have to wait for me.”

“I know I don’t have to. But I think I want to.” He paused. “If the choice is between driving all the way out here to have coffee with them, and meeting up with you for an hour or so after you get off work . . .” He let his shy grin finish the thought.

I glanced around, and when I was sure we were alone—two guys couldn’t be too careful—I put my hands on his waist. He wrapped his arms around me and brushed his lips across mine.

“I’m not gonna lie.” He smoothed my hair. “I can honestly say I have no idea what we’re doing. I just know I don’t want to stop.”

“Neither do I.”

“Then I guess . . .” He took a deep breath, and a nervous smile curled the corners of his mouth. “I guess we don’t stop.”

I grinned. “I guess we don’t.”

# CHAPTER NINETEEN

# BRENNAN

So I was dating a man now. I had a boyfriend.

Whenever I stopped to think about it, the whole thing boggled my mind. I couldn't even take a minute to let it sink in that I was dating a single parent, or figure out how I felt about that part, because my mind kept going back to the fact that . . . I had a boyfriend. How the hell . . .?

But most of the time, I didn't try to pick it apart. I was usually too distracted by glancing at the clock and counting down the minutes until I saw him again. And when Zafir and I were actually together, I didn't question it. Dating him? Duh.

Things didn't even seem to change all that much. We still texted constantly. We still spent as much of our off-time together as we could. He still brought Tariq to the skate park, and I still gave the kid lessons.

I felt a little more conspicuous going over to Red Hot to meet him for lunch, or when he came into the skate shop, but only because we weren't pretending to be just friends anymore. No one else seemed to catch on. If they did, they didn't say anything.

It seemed like the only thing that had changed was that we weren't denying it anymore. We kissed when we were completely alone. Held hands in the car when it was just the two of us. Shared those little knowing glances sometimes, like we had some big secret that nobody else knew.

Yeah. I was dating a man. I was a dude's boyfriend.

And somehow, it made perfect sense.

Why didn't we start doing this sooner?

Well. Couldn't change the past, and we were doing this now, so I couldn't complain.

With both of our schedules being pretty crazy, we grabbed whatever time we could. Tonight—a Friday night—we'd met up after I'd closed my shop and he'd clocked out of his, and caught a late movie at the theater in town. I was starting to love movie dates again. This theater had armrests that lifted up, so Zafir would sidle up next to me and I'd wrap my arm around his shoulders. We'd spend the whole movie like that—no armrest biting into anyone's ribs, no one trying to get frisky in the dark. Fucking perfect.

Afterward, I drove back to his apartment to drop him off.

"Man, I can't believe they carded *both* of us," I said. "Do we really look that young?"

Zafir laughed. "I guess we do. But it's about damn time they carded you. I had to show my ID the last three times in a row."

"And when we went to that bar in Port Angeles."

He groaned dramatically. "That was messed up. I wasn't even drinking."

I snickered, and he elbowed me. I patted his arm. "Oh, come on. At least you've never had a cop ask to see your learner's permit."

"Well, no. Partly because I don't get pulled over."

"Hey. Hey. That's beside the point. Point is I was twenty-three and the guy thought I was out driving alone with just my permit."

Zafir snorted. "That's what you get for having a lead foot."

"Right. Like you're Mr. Follows-All-the-Traffic-Laws."

"Okay, fine. That's what you get for having a lead foot and getting caught."

"Jerk," I muttered. We glanced at each other over the console, and laughed.

I pulled into Zafir's parking lot, and stopped in front of the stairwell. As it always did, that little pang of disappointment worked its way into my chest.

"So, I guess I'll see you tomorrow?"

He smiled, but suddenly seemed a bit uncertain. "Yeah. I'm off at ten, so . . ."

"Great. I'll be there."

He nodded and reached for the door handle, but hesitated. He pulled his hand back.

"What's wrong?" I asked.

"Nothing." He met my gaze, and the smile was a little more genuine, but there was something there that hadn't been before. "I, um . . ."

I put my hand on his knee. "You okay?"

"Yeah. Yeah. But, um." He cleared his throat. "Listen, Tariq is at my sister's tonight." He swallowed, and gestured up at his apartment. "Which means we have the place to ourselves if we want it."

My pulse shot up, and he had to have felt my fingers twitch on his leg. Why did this feel like those times my ex-girlfriends and I had danced around the idea of having sex for the first time? Why was this happening with him? What the fuck?

"Um . . ."

He laughed softly, sliding his hand over mine. "I wasn't suggesting we sleep together, if that's what you're wondering."

"It was." I swallowed. "What . . . what are you suggesting?"

"I'm suggesting we *sleep* together." He squeezed my hand. "Like . . . sleep."

It took a second for that to fully register. "Oh."

"It's okay if you say no," he said. "I'm just—"

"Actually." I took a breath. "I kind of like the idea."

"Do you?"

I nodded. "I, uh . . . I guess I should park?"

He smiled. "Good idea."

I pulled into one of the visitor spots, and without a word, we got out and went up to his door. I'd been here enough times that just walking into his apartment didn't faze me one way or the other.

But my heart pounded on the way to Zafir's bedroom. Agreeing to this had made sense in the moment. Going through with it was somewhat more intimidating.

At the end of the hall, Zafir opened the door and gestured for me to go in ahead of him.

Okay, a lot more intimidating.

He flicked on the light, and I looked around. I hadn't expected him to have a gigantic California king or something, but the narrowness of the mattress made my spine prickle. We'd find out in a hurry if we were comfortable sharing a bed, that was for sure.

From behind, Zafir wrapped his arms around me and kissed my shoulder through my shirt. "You sure about this?"

"I'm . . ."

*No. No, I am not.* I put my hands over his. *What are we doing?*

"We really don't have to," he said. "It was just a thought. That's all."

"It's a good thought. I want to." I gently freed myself and turned around. "We're just sleeping, right?"

"Mm-hmm." He cupped my jaw and kissed me softly. "Physically, that's as far as I want to go. This isn't some ploy to trick you into doing more."

"No, I didn't think it was. I guess it's kind of a new thing."

"I get it. To be honest, I just . . ." He lowered his gaze, cheeks darkening in the dim light.

I tipped his chin up so we were looking at each other again. "What?"

Zafir swallowed. "I've been sleeping alone for a long time. And I guess . . ."

I pressed my lips to his. "I like the idea of not sleeping alone too."

He held eye contact for a moment, then smiled. "If you decide it's not comfortable, say so." With his chin, he gestured toward the door. "I've slept on that couch before, and I can do it again."

"I'm not going to kick you out of your own bed. If this doesn't work, I'll take the couch."

He pursed his lips, but after a moment, shrugged. "Let's see how it goes, and cross that bridge if we get there."

"Sounds good to me."

He kissed me once more, then let me go.

Sitting on the edge of his bed, I untied my shoes. As I took them off, I looked at him. His back was to me, and he was sliding the band out of his hair. It occurred to me right then that I'd never actually seen him with his hair down.

And then . . . it was. It hung a few inches below his broad shoulders, with a wave in the middle where the band had been holding it together. Immediately, I wanted to comb my fingers through it. Hair had never done much for me either way, but I wanted to touch his.

He turned around, and cocked his head. "What?"

*Was I staring? I was staring. Fuck. I* was *staring.*

"Um." I cleared my throat and broke eye contact so I could push my shoes aside. Then I stood. "Your hair is down."

"Yeah, I—" He gestured at it. "I don't sleep with it pulled back."

"But the rest of the time, you always tie it back." I couldn't resist, and tucked a few strands behind his ear. "It looks good when it's down."

He smiled, and actually blushed. "Thanks. It's just kind of a pain in the ass. Gets in my face all the time."

"Except when you sleep?"

"Yep." He smirked. "Now it's gonna be in *your* face."

We both laughed, and the tension in the room seemed to ramp up and dissipate at the same time. Like the joke had given us permission to breathe, but also made it real that we were going to be curled up in bed together. Which was good. And new. And crazy. And totally not something I'd ever pictured myself doing. And—

And I was supposed to *sleep* tonight?

*Here goes nothing.*

We stripped down to boxers and climbed into his bed.

Getting into bed with another man—especially when we were both half-naked—unnerved me, but the alternative was going back to my place and sleeping alone. The only thing I was absolutely sure of was that I wasn't ready to *not* be with Zafir tonight.

As we arranged the sheets and comforter, I cleared my throat. "So, do we just stay on opposite sides, or . . ."

"Are you comfortable being closer than that?"

Years of calling myself a straight man said that no I was absolutely *not* comfortable being closer than that.

But a few weeks of rethinking who I was—and spending as much time as possible with him—meant I was suddenly curious what it would be like.

I rolled onto my back and gestured for him to move closer. He killed the light, then slid toward me, and rested his head on my chest as I wrapped my arm around his shoulders. He slung his other arm over me, and I put my hand on his elbow, and we just seemed to fit together.

"This okay?" he asked.

"Yeah. It's nice. You?"

"Same."

Normally, I was scared out of my mind the first time I went to bed with someone. There was so much pressure. I had more performance anxiety in the bedroom than I did at a major competition. And the fact that we were down to our underwear didn't do much to back up his insistence that nothing was going to happen.

On the other hand, with two people in a smallish bed, it was going to get too hot if we wore more than this.

And usually by now, I was subtly bracing for the hand on my chest to start creeping downward. I could never relax until the other person was asleep. Except I knew that wasn't on Zafir's mind.

I wasn't nervous tonight. Now that we were settled in, this was . . . *easy*.

Surprisingly—and not surprisingly—this was nice. His skin was warm, his body heat comfortably mingling with mine. I caught myself listening to him breathe, my own breathing falling into sync with his.

The only thing that felt weird was the fact that it *didn't* feel weird to be lying in bed with him. And there was no mistaking I was with a man. Even with his long hair, which I couldn't stop running my fingers through, his shape was very male. A little smaller than me, just the right size to fit perfectly up against me with his head on my chest, but he was all planes and angles instead of soft curves like my ex-girlfriends. I was definitely in bed with a man.

When I tried to pick it apart and wonder if this was weird, or if it should have been, my brain kept going back to *It's Zafir—of course you're in bed with him*. Like the only thing weird about it was that this was the first time we'd done this. What the hell had we been waiting for?

The wait was over, though. Finally. Here we were. With no pressure to do anything except be here.

That was it. *That* was why I was so relaxed.

Whenever I'd gone to bed with one of my girlfriends, there'd been a strange feeling in my stomach. A mix of apathy and dread. And it wouldn't go away until she'd fallen asleep, and I knew I was off the hook for the night. Then I'd relax, close my eyes, and drift off.

God. How had I not realized what I was? What kind of idiot did it take to spend years stressing over sex, even dreading it sometimes, without realizing that, hey, maybe it wasn't something I wanted after all?

Except men wanted sex. All men wanted sex. The only variable was if they wanted sex with chicks, dudes, or both. Since I'd never thought twice about being attracted to another guy, obviously I was straight, and that was that.

Then along came this other option, and it made sense, and now I was in bed with a man and completely okay with it.

Which really *did* make sense. This was the part of every relationship I'd liked—the companionship. It made the sex worthwhile because afterward, we'd cuddle up and go to sleep together. My exes had all said they loved that I enjoyed cuddling. I'd just never been able to tell them—or myself, for that matter—that I would've been perfectly content to skip the sex and go right to this step. I'd never realized that was an option.

Turned out, it was. And now here I was. And here he was. And this was the best thing ever.

I put my arm over his. The other, I kept loosely around him as I stroked his hair with my fingertips.

He was already out cold. I didn't blame him. How he kept up with two jobs and Tariq—Christ, no wonder the guy was tired. And yet he somehow found time for me. A lot of time for me, now that I thought about it. Even when he was probably dead to the world.

And now I was next to him, slowly drifting off while he slept beside me, and I felt like the luckiest bastard on the planet.

# CHAPTER TWENTY

# ZAFIR

Between Tariq and Brennan, I would've killed for a few more hours in the day. Dividing my time between the two of them and my two jobs was . . . not easy.

Still, it was worth it. Brennan didn't seem to mind that we could go two or three days without seeing each other beyond our lunch breaks.

Brennan had filled in for Kelly again tonight, and to my surprise, when I came home, he'd cooked. Like . . . really cooked. Something that didn't come out of a box.

"What's all this?" I inhaled deeply. "It smells amazing."

"It's just some beef stroganoff my mom taught me to make." He paused, then quickly added, "And don't worry—I got the meat from that place down by the deli that has halal stuff."

I blinked. "You . . . Really?"

"Well yeah." He looked at me like I'd lost my mind. "You said you try to keep halal. I assumed that meant Tariq too. Right?"

"Yeah. Yeah. I just . . ."

"Tariq told me that's where you usually go. So we went down there earlier."

"Oh. Wow. Most people don't bother . . ." I shook my head. "Anyway. Thank you. Uh, what did Tariq think of it?"

Brennan laughed. "Let's just say you're lucky there's any left for you."

"Oh really?"

He nodded.

"You'll have to show me how to make it, then. He's finicky as hell, so if you've found something he likes . . ."

"Happy to share it. It's super easy."

"Well, you made it, so—"

"Hey. *Hey*. None of that." He paused. "You want a plate?"

"Yeah, definitely."

While I threw back a gallon or so of water like I always did after a shift at Old Country, Brennan spooned some of the stroganoff onto a plate. He made a smaller one for himself, probably since he'd already eaten.

"Where's Tariq?" I asked.

"Where do you think?"

"Reading?"

"Yep." He set the plates and a couple of forks on the table. "I loaned him some books, and haven't seen him since dinner."

I sat down as I opened my second bottle of water. "What kinds of books?"

"Just some sci-fi." He sat across from me. "Don't worry—I picked out the ones that are fairly tame."

"Eh." I took another swig of water. "He's been sneaking Stephen King since last year, so . . ."

Brennan laughed. "Yeah, well, I didn't feel quite right giving a kid a book that's wall-to-wall sex and violence."

"Much appreciated." I took a bite of the stroganoff. "Wow. This is *really* good."

"Don't sound so surprised."

I chuckled. "That wasn't what I meant."

"I should hope not."

We kept eating, and I made a mental note to make sure I learned how to make this. Finally—something besides the very, very small list of recipes I'd swiped from my sister.

Brennan pushed his empty plate away. "So, I was talking to my boss today. There's a big competition in Portland this summer." He held my gaze. "Maybe you and Tariq could come along."

I sat up. "Really?"

"Sure." He shrugged. "Tariq would get a kick out of the skating, and we could probably check out the town too. And it would be nice to have more than a few hours off at a time."

I blew out a breath. "A few days off sounds really nice. Could be pricey, though. Getting there, getting a hotel . . ."

"We could probably share a room. My sponsors pay for some of my expenses, so it wouldn't be that much."

It did sound tempting. And Tariq would be thrilled to have a vacation that involved leaving Bluewater Bay, watching people skateboard, and hanging out with Brennan.

"I'll have to see how things go," I said. "I have vacation time at Red Hot, but taking more than a few days off from Old Country is kind of a nightmare."

"They don't let you take off?"

"Well, it's more like what it does to my paycheck."

"Ugh. Yeah." Brennan grimaced. "I get that. Let me know—I'm going either way, but it would be great to have you guys along."

"I will."

After we'd eaten, I said, "Let me go check on Tariq and tuck him in. Then we could, I don't know, watch a movie?"

Brennan smiled. "Cool. He's already brushed his teeth and put on his pajamas, so he should be about ready for bed."

"Good. Thanks."

Sure enough, when I stepped into Tariq's room, he was in his pajamas, curled up on his beanbag chair with a ragged paperback in his hands. He was already a good third of the way through it too.

"Hey." I tilted my head, trying to read the cover of his book. "That one of the books Brennan loaned you?"

He nodded. "It's really good." He shot me the same puppy-dog look I was pretty sure I'd used to manipulate my parents at his age. "Do I have to go to bed?"

"Afraid so." I glanced at the pages he'd already turned. "If I let you stay up, we both know you're going to finish that tonight, and then you won't be able to function tomorrow."

Sighing, he slid a bookmark into the book and closed it. "Okay." He pushed himself up off the beanbag chair.

"So did you guys have a good time?" I asked.

He nodded. "Brennan's fun. He's a good cook."

"So I noticed. That stroganoff was really good."

"Yeah. Can you make it?"

"I can try." As he climbed into bed, I added, "We've got a few episodes of *Wolf's Landing* downloaded. Maybe we can watch them tomorrow night. Since I'm off."

He nodded, pulling up his covers. "Okay."

I still wasn't crazy about him watching that show, but obviously he was watching it with or without me. And over my dead body were we letting the whole season pile up before I made time to watch them with him.

After I'd tucked Tariq into bed, Brennan and I settled on the couch to watch a movie.

I yawned. "Fair warning—if I fall asleep on you, don't take it personally."

He laughed. "Eh, if you do, I probably will too."

"Then I won't feel so bad."

He kissed my temple. "So what're we watching?"

"Depends on what you're in the mood for." I turned on the TV and pulled up my small collection of movies. "I have a little of everything, and we can always download something."

"Let's see what you've got."

We scrolled through my list, and eventually, we settled on a dumb comedy. I turned it on, and he wrapped his arm around my shoulders.

"This is okay, right?" he asked. "If Tariq comes out?"

"It's fine." I rested my hand on his leg. "I'm pretty sure he wouldn't be surprised at all."

Brennan kissed the top of my head. "Smart kid."

I leaned my head against him again, and we didn't speak as the movie got started.

This was amazing. I was starting to get spoiled. It had been so damn long since someone had shared my bed, or since I'd been with someone who liked cuddling up in front of movies, and now I had him. Too bad we couldn't spend every night together, but I wasn't going to waste the nights we *did* have bitching about the rest.

As the credits rolled, I clicked off the TV.

I sat up and stretched. "So what did you think?"

"It . . ." He swallowed. "Wasn't bad."

I cocked my head. "You okay?"

"Yeah. Yeah." He shook himself. "Thinking, I guess."

"What about?"

As soon as he looked me in the eye, my spine prickled. Was this going to be one of those uncomfortable conversations? The let-me-down-gently or the put-on-the-brakes?

I put my hand over his. He didn't pull away, which was promising, but the way he absently rubbed his thumb alongside mine felt . . . halfhearted? Or was I just imagining things?

Finally, he met my eyes. "We've been doing this for a while." His eyes flicked down to our hands. "Is it normal to still be getting used to it?"

I moistened my lips. "Which part?"

"All of it, I guess. I've never dated a guy. I've never dated someone I'm not sleeping with." He paused. "I mean, sleeping with, like—"

"I know what you mean."

He inhaled slowly. "I like it. All of it. But sometimes I do have to kind of stop and think about it." He played with a loose strand of my hair. "Not like I want to bail. Just . . ."

"Trying to get your head around it?"

He nodded. "And I guess I've figured out the asexual part, but I'm still hung up on the other part."

"What other part?"

"Being, like . . . biromantic, or aromantic, or whatever." His Adam's apple jumped. "I'm still trying to work out—how do you fall in love with someone when you're asexual?"

*If you knew what I felt every time I look at you . . .*

I shrugged as casually as I could. "It's easy if you think about it. I have no desire whatsoever to have sex. I'm not repulsed by it, just not interested. But that doesn't mean I don't want a companion. And it doesn't mean I can't connect with someone. I don't have to be sexually interested in someone to feel like my world is better with them in it. It's a different kind of love than loving my sister or my son or my friends. It's like . . . this is a person who's come into my life and changed it, and I want them to stay."

Brennan held my gaze for a moment, as if searching for something in my eyes. "Have you ever felt that way about someone?"

I nodded, blood pounding in my ears. "Twice."

"Yeah?"

"The first time was Megan. And that . . . didn't turn out very well."

He kept his gaze fixed on mine. "What about the second time?"

My pulse went through the roof. Stomach all tied in knots and heart slamming into my ribs, I wasn't even sure my voice would function, but I tried anyway.

"I'm . . ." It took everything I had to keep looking him in the eye as I put a shaking hand over the top of his. "I'm not sure yet."

Brennan's eyes widened. He stared down at our hands, and I was sure he was about to pull his away and put some distance between us. Instead, he turned his over and clasped our fingers together. "You're serious?"

I nodded.

"Wow." His eyes lost focus. Though he didn't let go of my hand, I was still convinced he was about to sprint for the door. Me and my big mouth. Again.

I forced a quiet laugh to get my breath moving. "Is this another one of those times where I've thrown too much at you and—"

He kissed me softly. His hand warmed my cheek, and his gentle touch brought my pulse back down a little at a time.

He drew back and met my gaze. "No." He ran his thumb along my cheekbone. "It isn't too much."

"Are you sure?"

With a lopsided grin, he said, "I'm still here, aren't I?"

"True. You are." I ran my fingers through his hair. "I love you."

He brushed his lips across mine again. "I love you too."

My heart skipped. I wasn't sure if I was more relieved to hear him say it, or terrified of where things went from here. The words were out. No pretending we hadn't crossed this line. As if we hadn't already crossed a few dozen.

"I'd suggest having you stay again," I whispered. "But I'm not sure if Tariq's ready for that."

"Don't worry about it." He kissed me lightly. "We'll get there."

Oh yes. I had no doubt we would.

And I couldn't wait.

# CHAPTER TWENTY-ONE

# BRENNAN

After practicing a few jumps on the big half-pipe, I got out of the way for someone else to skate. My ankle was throbbing a bit anyway, and my back was starting to get annoyed, so it was as good a time as any for a drink.

A couple of my buddies had taken over one of the picnic tables, and I dropped onto the bench next to Kim. Sven was sitting on the table, nursing a can of Monster that was almost as big as his forearm, and Kim was icing his knee.

"How's that healing?" I gestured at his leg with my water bottle.

"Eh." He shrugged. "Doc says keep icing it, so . . . I'm icing it."

"Still hurt?" I asked.

Grunting, he nodded. "That's why I have to keep icing it."

"Smart-ass," I muttered into my drink.

He chuckled.

For a minute or so, we all watched the other skaters.

I tilted my water bottle toward the scrawny eleven-year-old who was currently practicing a complex trick on the edge of the smaller half-pipe. "Man, Sven. That kid you've been working with is *killing* it. He's going to be beating all of us before he's in sixth grade."

Sven laughed. "What do you care? You'll be retired by then."

"Fuck you."

"And hey, I gotta ask . . ." He turned to me. "Who's that dude you keep bringing around? He looks like the guy who works down at that porn shop."

I gulped. Was I ready to start throwing the word "boyfriend" around with my friends? "He's . . . a friend. I'm teaching his kid to skate."

"Uh-huh. But he's at the shop all the time, and his kid's not." Sven took a deep swig of Monster. "*Is* he the porno dude? 'Cause I know I've seen him before."

"Yeah, he works at Red Hot." I smirked. "How often do you go there if you know what the employees look like?"

"Whatever, dude." He rolled his eyes. "I went there with Jenn, and she thought he was that author kid. The one who hooked up with the guy who wrote the vampire series."

"Why?" I asked. "She think that guy is the only Middle Eastern dude in this town or something?"

He shook his head. "Who knows."

Kim laughed. "And why the fuck would he be working in a porn shop if he was with that dude? That guy's richer than God."

"She didn't think he worked there. She thought he was like a customer or something."

"Wouldn't surprise me if he goes there." Kim snickered. "You ever *read* those books?"

I turned toward him. "They're putting them on TV. They can't have that much sex in them."

"Naw, it's not much," Sven said. "But Jenn swears the lead dude wants to fuck the—"

"Hey, Cross!"

The voice made my teeth grind. "Oh for fuck's sake."

My friends both rolled their eyes.

As I turned around, Billy approached, smirking like the asshole he was.

So much for my chill mood. Gut clenched, I glared at him. "What do you want, Fallbrook?"

"Got something for you." He held up his phone. "Bet this is something you've never heard before." Before I could tell him I didn't give two shits, he tapped the screen, and immediately, my stomach lurched into my throat.

"What the fuck?" I snapped. "Who the hell records his girlfriend in *bed*?"

Laughing like the jackass he was, he stopped the playback. "Just thought you might want to hear what she sounds like when she's getting off."

"Dude." Kim wrinkled his nose. "That's not cool, man."

Sven nodded, lips curled in disgust. "Seriously. Way to respect your girl."

"Whatever." Billy nodded toward me. "Just busting his balls."

"Yeah?" Kim growled. "Maybe do that without using Aimee like that? Man, get the fuck out of here."

Billy snorted, shaking his head, and grumbled something as he walked away.

"Man, what a dick," Sven muttered.

"Seriously," I said through my teeth. "Aimee deserves way better."

They both eyed me.

Sven pointed at Billy's back. "You do know she was fucking him, right?"

Jaw clenched, I nodded. "Yeah. I know. She cheated on me. But now she's stuck with that asshole."

"Serves her right," Sven mumbled.

I didn't argue. I didn't have it in me. Those few recorded seconds of my ex-girlfriend in mid-orgasm had disgusted me. I couldn't imagine what made a guy think that was something he should record and then play back for other people. But it had also hit a nerve. Probably not the one Billy had been aiming for, but still . . . a nerve.

What *did* Billy do for her that I hadn't? I'd gotten her off plenty of times. Enough that I'd immediately recognized what I was listening to.

I searched the crowd for Aimee, and found her at the big half-pipe. She was focused on skating, and probably had no idea what her douche bag boyfriend was doing with a recording of her like that. At the moment, she was way too focused on her jumps, and on that double flip she'd been trying to master since long before we'd split up. She was getting there, too—the first flip was almost effortless now, and she was landing the second one, but kept losing her balance once she was back on the board. Flips like that were disorienting. She'd keep at it, though, and next year, she'd be unstoppable.

As I slowly released my breath, a knot grew behind my ribs. This was so weird. It hadn't been all that long since Aimee and I had been Aimee-and-Brennan. Holding hands. Living together. Mail addressed to both of us. Squabbling occasionally over taking out the trash or leaving dishes in the sink. Having sex like it was what we both wanted. Talking about things we might do in six months, a year, five years, as if it was just accepted that Aimee-and-Brennan didn't have such a short shelf life.

Now it seemed strange to imagine any of that had ever happened. It almost felt like those were someone else's memories installed in my brain, and the woman practicing double flips on the half-pipe was a stranger.

I took a deep swallow of water and got up to go back to skating. My ankle still hurt, but I felt like focusing on balance and wheels right now instead of—

*Balance and wheels.*

*Just balance and wheels.*

I was behind the register at the shop a couple of hours later, bored off my ass and playing on my phone, when the front door opened.

My heart dropped.

Aimee.

She strode right up to me, looking me in the eye. "Hey. Can we talk for a minute?"

"Uh . . ." I glanced around the store. Naturally, it was a slow day, and there were two of us on. And Sven was fucking off on his phone in full view of us, so I couldn't play the "we're super busy" card. Asshole.

Facing her again, I took a breath. "Yeah. Sure. What's up?"

She swallowed, her cheeks darkening a little, and she eyed Sven. Then she gestured for me to come with her.

Great. It was going to be one of those conversations.

I came out from behind the counter and followed her to the other side of the shop, between the racks of wheels and a display of helmets. "What's up?" I asked again.

Pushing her shoulders back, she met my gaze. "Listen, I heard what Billy did at the park. And I just wanted to apologize. I had no idea he was going to play that at you."

I lifted my eyebrows. "Did you know he was recording it?"

She scowled. "No."

"Then he's the one who should be apologizing. To you, not me."

"That's between him and—"

"Aimee, you deserve better than him."

Her features tightened, and her eyes narrowed. I knew that look, and bit my tongue—it was that defensive, venomous glare she'd always given me when she knew she was wrong and wanted to shut down the conversation before she had to admit it. When we'd argued in the past, I'd pushed her until she'd given in, but this time, I didn't. I didn't have a dog in this fight.

"I appreciate the concern," she said, her voice taut but calm. "Except I don't think my social life is really your business anymore."

I exhaled, then nodded. "All right. Fair. I was just concerned."

"I know." She cleared her throat, avoiding my eyes for a second. "And, um, listen . . . I'm sorry again for what happened. Between us." She paused before sheepishly adding. "What I did."

"It's okay."

"No, it's not. We had problems, but . . ."

"But it's given me time to do some thinking too."

"Really?" She cocked her head. "About what?"

"Well . . ." Was I ready to tell someone? Was I ready to tell her? The truth was, I'd always been able to talk to her about everything, and I had to admit, I missed that. And even though we were facing each other as tense-but-civil exes now, I still felt like I could talk to her. Hell. Why not? Then maybe I could quit keeping this to myself.

I wrung my hands, staring at them because I couldn't make myself look at her. "About who I am, mostly."

"About— What?"

Stomach twisting with nerves, I lifted my gaze. "Maybe you were right about me not being able to, you know, be what you needed."

She winced. "Bren. No. I was . . . I was trying to blame you because you caught me and—"

"Maybe, but it got me thinking. And I think you might've been unsatisfied because I'm just not into sex."

"Not into it? What do you mean?"

"I mean . . ." I swallowed, bracing myself to show a card I wouldn't be able to put back up my sleeve. "I'm asexual."

She blinked, eyebrows twisting in that *what the fuck are you talking about?* way. "Huh?"

"I'm . . . I'm asexual."

"Asexual? What does that even mean?"

"It means I'm not wired to want sex."

"What?" She laughed humorlessly. "Bren, that doesn't make sense. I've *seen* you get into sex."

I broke eye contact again, a sick, humiliated feeling clawing its way up my throat. "I get into making you—making my partner happy. But if I had the choice . . ." I shook my head. "I couldn't care less about sex."

Aimee stared at me and fidgeted. "So, what? All those times we slept together, I was making you do something you didn't want to?"

"Not at all." I held her gaze, wondering for a second when she'd become a stranger. "You wanted it, and I wanted you to be happy." I shrugged. "I enjoyed it. It's just not something I want for myself."

It had all made sense when Zafir explained it. And it made sense in my head. Or when we were lying in bed together, touching but not pawing, and everything felt like it was exactly the way it needed to be. Like literally *sleeping* with someone was all I physically wanted or needed.

But looking into my ex-girlfriend's eyes, watching the way her brow contorted and her head tilted as if I'd just said the most insane thing she'd ever heard . . . *did* it make sense?

Eyes squeezed shut, Aimee put her fingers to her temples and shook her head. "Bren. No. This . . . Do you hear yourself?" She dropped her hands and met my gaze. "I mean, I'm sorry I hurt you. I really am. And I know I hurt you bad. But that's no reason to swear off sex."

"I'm not swearing it off. I just . . . I just don't want it."

"Then how the hell are you supposed to be with a girl?"

"I—" *Am actually with a man, but something tells me you wouldn't react so well to that.* "I'll either find someone who's like me, or if she wants sex, then I'll keep her happy."

She narrowed her eyes. "A girl can tell when your heart's not in it."

*But she can't say something to me before jumping into bed with a guy whose heart* is *in it?*

"Bullshit," I said. "There was never a point when my heart wasn't in it. If we were having sex, I was into—"

"But you never wanted it. You never initiated it."

"Right. So why is it so hard to believe that I'm not wired to want it or initiate it?"

"I'm . . ." She chewed her lip. "It just sounds like you're jumping into something so you can write off what happened and not have to deal with it."

I swallowed. "What do you mean?"

"I mean . . ." She pulled in a breath and looked me right in the eye. "Listen, you know how they say you shouldn't make a huge decision for a year after someone dies? Like selling a house or something?"

I nodded.

"Maybe . . . maybe this is kind of like that. We didn't break up that long ago, and now you're completely changing your identity."

"I'm not changing my identity. This is me. It always has been."

Her brow creased. "Is it? Or is it just you trying to move on?"

"It's—" Well, it was a valid question. "The thing is, I was trying to figure out how to be a better guy for the next girl, and this is what I found instead. It made sense."

"Did it *really*?" She tilted her head a little. "Or did it just sound like an easier thing than—"

"Oh, it wasn't easy." I laughed dryly. "Trust me—it took some doing to get my head around it."

"So it was a nice distraction."

"It . . . No. No, it wasn't that. It . . ." *What was it, Brennan?*

She stepped closer and lowered her voice. "This sounds an awful lot like breaking up with someone and suddenly changing religions. Then you can tell yourself the breakup was a good thing because it led you to your new beliefs."

My blood turned cold.

"Just think about it, okay?" Aimee held my gaze. "Make sure you're not jumping into something to avoid something else."

Wordlessly, I nodded.

"I should go," she murmured. "Take care of yourself, Bren. I know I hurt you, and I can't change that. But I do want you to be happy."

*I am. Right?*

"I know," I said. "And I want the same for you."

We locked eyes. I didn't have to mention Billy's name again. I could see the irritation in the tightness of her lips and the slight narrowness of her eyes.

I cleared my throat and glanced toward the register. "I should, uh, get back to work."

"Okay. I'll see you around."

I just nodded.

She started to go, and panic shot through me. In my mind, I saw Billy waving his phone in my face with the audio of Aimee.

"Uh, Aimee?"

She turned around.

I hesitated. "This, um, stays between us, right?"

"Of course."

"Thanks."

A hint of a smile flickered across her face, and when she went to leave this time, she didn't stop.

After she'd gone, I released a long breath and returned to my seat behind the cash register.

And my brain went right back to the conversation we'd just had.

Was she onto something? Or was she dead wrong? The fact that I couldn't grab one option or the other and say "Yeah, this is the answer" made me uncomfortable.

Everything I'd learned from Zafir had made sense. And getting involved with him—that had made sense too. But I'd been at Red Hot Bluewater less than twenty-four hours after I'd caught Aimee cheating, and that night, before she'd even moved her stuff out of the apartment, I'd been googling all things asexual.

*"Yep, this is me,"* I'd decided within days—hours really—of "me" still being half of Aimee-and-Brennan. And every time I'd questioned it, one look at Zafir had put me back on the asexual rails. He was a nice guy. He was easy to talk to. He was relaxed, chill—everything I needed to regain my sanity after breaking up with Aimee.

But was that all? Did I just dive in way too far because, hey, if it felt good, why not take it all the way? "All the way" in asexual terms. Which didn't leave me feeling like anything was missing.

So did that mean there *wasn't* anything missing? Or was this like when I was back on my feet after fucking up my ankle? I hadn't dared skate right away. After being on crutches, though, and after being in that much pain, just being able to stand and walk had felt like heaven. Later, I'd gotten back on the board and started putting my joints at risk again, but at first, I'd sat out and let gravity fuck someone else up.

Was that what I'd done with Zafir? After three sexual relationships with women, one of which wasn't even cold in the grave, I had an asexual relationship with a man. No chance for sexual failure there. Asexuality meant I didn't have to feel like a loser who couldn't please a girl. An asexual boyfriend was the furthest thing I could get from a girlfriend without being alone.

My heart seemed to speed up and slow down at the same time. My stomach tried to turn itself inside out. Air moved through my throat, but it took work.

Oh God. Maybe Aimee was right.

Maybe I wasn't in love with Zafir . . . I was in love with breaking out of the cycle that kept hurting me.

And if that was true, then the longer this thing went on, the more it was going to hurt *both* of us when it was over.

# CHAPTER TWENTY-TWO

## ZAFIR

I couldn't wait to clock off from Red Hot tonight. I didn't have to work at Old Country, and though I felt a little guilty about spending the evening with Brennan instead of Tariq, I hoped he understood. And I *had* promised Tariq we'd spend my next day off together, just the two of us, and he'd seemed pretty excited about that. Plus he had another skating lesson tomorrow after school.

Tonight, though, it was me and Brennan, and by lunch, I was already counting down the minutes until my shift was over. And the end was getting close—fifteen minutes until quitting time.

By this point, I was itching to see him. My phone had been quiet for the last hour or so. The skate shop must've been busy again. Before that, we'd texted sporadically throughout the day. He also hadn't stopped by before going to work. Running late, apparently. I was a little disappointed, but such was life.

Five minutes before the end of my shift, the bell jingled, and my heart skipped. Sure enough, it was Brennan. Skateboard under his arm, chin a tiny bit scruffy, and . . .

Distant.

Our eyes met briefly, and he flashed a hint of a smile, but then he lowered his gaze and focused intently on a display of lingerie. Which, okay, that was a new product, and they were pretty weird looking to the untrained eye, but he seemed evasive. As if he weren't looking *at* the lingerie so much as looking *away* from me.

My spine prickled.

Long day. He might've had a long day. That would explain why he hadn't come by earlier and why his texts had been sparse. Right?

Now that Brennan was here, quietly hanging out near the door while I wrapped up a few things, time ground to a near halt. The last five minutes of my shift took longer than the previous eight-plus hours.

Finally—six o'clock.

I grabbed my phone and keys, clocked out, said good-bye to Violet, and stepped around the cash register.

"Hey," I said. "You ready?"

His head snapped up like he'd forgotten I was there, but he pasted on a smile—*you're not fooling anyone, Brennan*—and nodded. "Yeah. Let's roll."

We walked out through the front door. The bell seemed louder than usual. Almost like an obnoxious cricket filling in the background to let us know just how quiet we were being.

As the door banged shut behind us, we started up the sidewalk.

"So." I cleared my throat. "Where do you want to go?"

He looked around like the streets and buildings might offer an answer. When they apparently didn't, he shrugged. "I don't know. You?"

"Have you eaten?"

For some reason, it took him several long seconds before he quietly said, "Not since lunch."

We kept walking even though we didn't have a destination in mind. I tried to think of where to go and what to do, but all I could think of was him. His down-turned eyes and his tense posture made my blood run cold.

I halted. It took him two steps to realize it, but then he stopped abruptly and turned around, shaking himself as if he realized how oblivious he'd been.

I studied him. "What's wrong?"

"Hmm?"

"You're acting kind of weird." A queasy feeling started burning in my stomach. "Is everything okay?"

He met my eyes. Then stared at the pavement and sighed.

*No. No, everything is not okay.*

*Oh crap. I've seen that look on other people before.*

My heart sank lower and lower. Everything was definitely not okay.

"Brennan?" I prodded gently. "Talk to me."

He started to take a breath, and I had to literally bite my tongue to keep from saying, *No, no, never mind—don't say what you're going to say. Please.*

"Listen, um . . ." He gulped. "There isn't really an easy way to say this."

*No . . .*

"You're a great guy, but this . . ." He paused, looking anywhere but at me for a moment. Finally, he met my gaze. "This isn't who I am."

My throat tightened. "What do you mean?"

"Dating a man? Being asexual?" He raked a hand through his hair. "I'm . . . I'm *straight*. I always have been. I guess, I don't know, I needed to be someone else for a little while because Aimee fucked up my head so much. But I'm getting over her now. And I need . . . I need to get back to normal."

I couldn't even put my finger on the worst part of his statement. Every word was like its own poisonous little dagger.

"Normal?" I barely got enough breath behind the word to say it out loud. "I . . ." I didn't know what to say.

Brennan wouldn't look me in the eye. "I'm sorry. I think I tried to jump into this too quick. I mean, one day, I'm with Aimee. The next, she cheated on me. And then I'm asexual and dating a man and—" He exhaled hard. "I don't know. I don't know what to think. But I need some time to figure out what the hell I am."

"We can take things slower. We—"

"No." He shook his head, and though neither of us moved, the space between us seemed to be physically widening. "I need . . . I need to stop. I can't do this."

"Brennan . . ." Two syllables, and I ran out of air. What could I say? I knew all too well how hard it was to rethink your sexual identity. Who was I to tell him what he was or wasn't? Or insist that he'd obviously figured it out?

Sighing, he scratched the back of his neck and kept his gaze fixed on the pavement. "I'm really sorry. I guess I just got so into the idea of being asexual, I jumped in with both feet and never looked back."

"Until now."

"Until now." He nodded. "I mean, suddenly we were spending all our time together, and being with you was a lot more fun than pining over her."

*Gee, thanks.*

"So, it was just a way to distract yourself?" My voice sounded as hollow as I felt.

"Not . . ." He chewed his lip. "Not to distract me. But it was like, what we were doing, and calling myself asexual—it was so different from what I'd been doing with her. And what I did with her wound up hurting me, so I wanted something totally different and . . ." He waved a hand. "I needed to be asexual because that took all the pressure off me. It meant she was wrong about me being a dud at sex. And I think I got in over my head."

*Well that part makes two of us, doesn't it?*

"I'm sorry," he said. "I need to go back to the way I was before."

"Back to normal."

He winced, but only slightly. "Listen, you really are a great—"

"Don't." The word came out as more of a growl than I'd intended, but I didn't apologize for it. "If you want out, then go. You've said your piece. I'm not stopping you."

He looked in my eyes. "I didn't do this to hurt you."

"Then we'll chalk it up to unintended consequences, won't we?"

Brennan flinched, lowering his gaze.

I shifted my weight, thankful for this numb outer shell that was keeping all my emotions contained. They'd come barreling through eventually. With any luck, it wouldn't be right here in front of Brennan.

I cleared my throat. "So, I guess that's it?"

"Yeah." He looked at me through his lashes. "I guess, um, I should go."

*Please do.*

But I just nodded.

We locked eyes for a painfully long moment. Then he muttered something in the neighborhood of good-bye, and turned to go.

Not five steps away from me, he put the board on the ground, stepped on it, and pushed off.

My chest tightened. Rationally, I knew this was just his habit. The board was like an extension of his own feet, and whenever he wasn't walking with someone, he was skating.

But I couldn't help feeling like it was a means to put more distance between us. To get away from this conversation—from me—faster.

At the corner, he turned. He didn't look back.

And just like that, Brennan was gone.

# CHAPTER TWENTY-THREE

# BRENNAN

The worst part was over. I'd let him down as gently as I could, and gotten the hell out of there as fast as I could, and now . . .

Now I didn't know what to do. I hadn't thought that far ahead. The whole day had revolved around getting through my shift and working up the courage to break things off with Zafir.

Work? Check.

Breakup? Check.

So . . . what was I supposed to do now?

And, as I skated down the street, I couldn't help wondering when I was supposed to start feeling better.

*It's not going to happen overnight. And it's only been like two minutes.*

Yeah. Probably wasn't going to crash into someone to distract me from Zafir like I'd stumbled across him after Aimee. That lightning probably only struck once. And that was probably a good thing.

But what was I supposed to do now?

Skate. I needed to go skate. The guys and I were going up to Vancouver for a competition next month, and there would be potential sponsors there. This was a bring-your-A-game event.

To the park, then.

I cruised down the sidewalk, skating a lot faster than I usually did out here. Bluewater Bay's tolerance for skaters wasn't bad, but they didn't like us flying through town. Hopefully they'd cut me some slack this one time.

At the shop, I grabbed my helmet and pads. Then I headed over to the park and tried not to think about why Zafir and Tariq wouldn't be there tonight. And about this ache in my chest that hadn't gotten better since I'd skated away from Zafir.

It had to be done. It wasn't easy, but it was right. *Right? Right.*

*Right?*

*Fuck.*

I shook myself and focused. Pads on. Helmet on. A-game on.

The sound of wheels sliding across pavement, landing on pavement, skidding on pavement—that usually got my blood pumping.

Tonight it just made me . . . tired? That didn't seem right.

*Oh stop it. You're pathetic. Skate, motherfucker.*

So I skated.

As hard as I could. As fast as I could. Until I could barely put weight on my left ankle when I stopped. Until my knee was screaming.

I was about to drop my board and hit the half-pipe one last time, but Sven grabbed my shoulder.

"Whoa, dude," he said. "What the hell are you doing? You can barely walk."

"I'm good." Why was my throat this tight? "Just need to—"

"You need to take it easy." He didn't let me go. "You can't afford to fuck yourself up right now."

*Too late.*

*What is wrong with me?*

Sven squeezed my shoulder. "Why don't you take a break for a few?" He nudged me toward the picnic tables. "You look like you could stand to get off your feet."

I exhaled. Then nodded and stepped back from the edge of the pipe. "Okay."

At the picnic table, I leaned forward and covered my face with both hands. I was tired. That was all it was. I'd just skated really hard, and I was tired. My muscles were aching, some of them even quivering, so clearly this was all fatigue. Not because I'd just broken up with—

*Stop. Stop doing this to yourself.*

*Just stop.*

I squeezed my eyes shut and took a few long, deep breaths. All around me, there were people chatting, laughing, and shit-talking in between skateboards hitting pavement. I was used to that background noise here. I even recognized most of the voices.

And when a particular feminine voice cut through the noise, my stomach lurched.

Damn it. Aimee was here. And of course, where Aimee was, so was Billy. Just what I needed.

I wasn't sure why I tortured myself, but I lowered my hands and lifted my head, turning toward the ramp where the sound had come from.

There she was. There he was.

And they were fighting. Lovely.

The park was crowded tonight, and loud, so I couldn't hear what they were saying. Didn't really need to, though. Her arms were folded across her chest. She scowled at him, her lip curling whenever she lashed out at him.

And he really didn't seem to care. He wasn't taking her seriously, that was for sure. Whenever she'd snap, he'd laugh and make an exaggerated defensive gesture—putting his hands way up, taking a huge, theatrical step back.

My chest tightened. When Aimee and I had been together, I would never have let someone talk to her like that. Not that I'd have had to step in—she wouldn't have stood for it. But with Billy . . .

I shook my head and looked away. I didn't get what she saw in him. Where exactly didn't I measure up compared to him? Did it really go back to the sex? Because that was the only thing she'd ever offered as a reason to leave me for him, and it was the only thing I'd ever seen them doing besides fighting. Was he *that* good?

As I mulled it over, another thought crossed my mind: if she broke up with him right here, right now, would I take her back? Because if I thought about it, she and I had done a lot of sniping over the last year. It was better than the screaming matches I'd had with the girl before her, though, so maybe that was why it hadn't bothered me at the time.

The thought of going back to that exhausted me. I much preferred chilling with someone, shooting the breeze, laughing about stupid things.

*Like I did with Zafir.*

A lump rose in my throat, but I tamped it down.

That whole thing was too raw to think about. I needed some time to let it all settle in my head. Then I could be objective. Or something.

It hurt because it always hurt to end a relationship. That didn't mean it was a mistake. Sure, I'd enjoyed being with Zafir. I hadn't spent that time walking on eggshells, or trying to second-guess his mood and know what he wanted from me. It didn't really seem like he'd wanted much from me. It seemed like he was perfectly happy with my company.

*Just like I was perfectly happy with his.*

I shook myself and banished those thoughts. Scanning the park, I found Aimee again.

They'd stopped fighting, and were now standing side by side next to the small half-pipe, watching some younger skaters. When he put his arm around her, she didn't pull away. She didn't lean into him, so he wasn't completely out of the doghouse, but she let him slide his hand down over her butt.

*Way to be respectful, jackass.*

My heart stopped.

That was what I wanted? Which part of that was the "normal" I needed to get back to? Did I really take relationship advice from a woman who was still hanging on the arm of a man who laughed at her when she was mad? Someone who'd recorded her during sex and thought it was funny to play it back for other people?

Granted, she'd been right about people making impulsive, drastic changes during breakups or when they were grieving. They needed time to regroup and think and sort through things. Jumping into something else was a good distraction, but didn't do much for that whole regrouping and thinking thing.

But *was* that what I had done? Did it count as impulsive if it was making a change for the better? If she dumped Billy's dumb ass tonight, and tomorrow she made a decision not to date men who recorded her having sex, did that count?

And if I was the kind of person who had no desire for sex, and wanted to be with someone who didn't push me for sex, then was it really that impulsive for me to start calling myself asexual? Just because my relationship with her hadn't been cold in the grave, was it wrong to realize I was asexual and connect with a man? Did the timing automatically make it wrong?

Of *course* it had happened right after my split with Aimee. That was when I'd had a reason to go looking for answers about my shitty sex life, and that was when I'd stumbled across those answers.

And stumbled across Zafir.

Who had the answers.

Who had that snarky sense of humor.

Who had that smile.

And . . . Oh shit.

No, I wasn't impulsive when I'd started calling myself asexual or when I'd started dating Zafir. I was an impulsive idiot when I listened to my ex-girlfriend. When I took advice from the woman who thought Billy fucking Fallbrook was a decent enough human being to date, and having sex with him in our bed was any way to let me know we had problems.

When I somehow got it into my head that I should walk away from Zafir and go back to a normal that had never felt right in the first place.

*Oh God. Oh my God.*

In what *universe* did breaking up with Zafir make any sense?

Lately, the highlight of my day had always revolved around Zafir. Finding a reason to go into Red Hot just to see him. Ordering pizza for the guys just so he'd be the one to deliver it. Spending a day off with him and Tariq. Showing Tariq how to skateboard while his dad watched, trusting me despite the fact that I'd let the kid get hurt the first time.

All of that was gone. One conversation, and it was gone.

And sitting here now, watching Aimee with Billy, simultaneously replaying the last conversation I'd had with her and the last one with Zafir . . . I realized way, way too late how badly I'd fucked up and how much I'd lost.

She deserved much better than Billy, and I hoped she'd wise up to that soon. But since she hadn't wised up to it yet, and she'd admittedly fucked up by cheating on me . . . *why* was I taking any of her relationship advice to heart? She had about as much credibility in that department as I did.

Though I probably had less. A lot less.

Because for all her mistakes, she wasn't the idiot who'd cut Zafir loose.

I swore I could feel my heart shriveling up behind my rib cage. I'd had the sweetest, funniest, most amazing person right there at my fingertips, and what did I do? Left him with tears in his eyes and walked away as if that made any kind of goddamn sense.

*Oh God. What did I do?*

# CHAPTER TWENTY-FOUR

## ZAFIR

After Brennan left, I'd gone back to my car, but I didn't go home right away. I drove around for a while. Went down to the waterfront to stare blankly out at the ocean and Canada and the occasional seabird.

It wasn't helping. I wasn't sure what I'd expected to accomplish—maybe find some answers or feel better—but nothing was happening. Brennan had still dumped me. I still felt like shit. I even had half a mind to call in to Old Country and see if Pete needed another driver tonight. I was already miserable, so why not add to it and make some money while I was at it?

Eventually, I headed home, and I made it there on autopilot. As I pulled into the parking lot, I realized this was about the time I'd expected to be back anyway. Go figure. I probably should've just come home when I knew my evening was shot. At least then I wouldn't have had to pay Kelly for the two hours I spent burning gas I also couldn't afford. Staring at the ceiling, the wall, the TV—it would've been just as ineffective as the road or the water.

I parked. Went inside. Paid Kelly. Still on autopilot.

Then she left.

Standing there alone, I cringed. Now for the hard part.

Did he have to know now? Maybe it could wait until tomorrow. Let the poor kid sleep.

Except he was too perceptive. One look at me and he'd know something was wrong. Either I'd tell him now, or he'd spend the whole night wondering what I was keeping from him.

Outside his bedroom, I took a deep breath, then tapped my knuckle on the door. "Tariq? You ready for bed?"

"Yeah."

I pushed open the door. No surprise—he was sitting in bed in his pajamas with a book propped up on his knees. A novel, too. At this rate, he was going to be reading *War and Peace* or something by the time school was out.

"Time to go to sleep," I said.

He looked up at me with puppy-dog eyes. "Can I finish this chapter?"

I tried not to think about how he'd gotten those fading red scars on his chin and nose, and shifted my attention to his book. "How many pages are left?"

He thumbed through it. "Ten."

"How about finishing it tomorrow?"

"Okay." He sighed and slid his bookmark between the pages.

I took the book, put it on the nightstand, then sat on the edge of the bed. "You can stay up later and read this weekend. I'd let you tonight, but if I do, you won't be able to get up to go to school."

He frowned, but didn't argue.

Blood pounded in my ears. He was about to go to sleep. Was I really going to do this now?

Then I realized he was watching me. The frown had faded, and instead he was scrutinizing me. He also shrank back a little, pressing against his pillows and huddling in on himself like he sometimes did when he was nervous.

I took in another deep breath. "Listen, I wanted to talk to you about tomorrow. About skating after school."

He stayed focused on me with wide eyes, and I could already see the disappointment pulling the corners of his mouth downward.

I patted his arm. "I'll find someone else to give you lessons. Soon. I just . . ."

"What about Brennan?"

"Well, that's the thing. Brennan's probably . . ." Probably? Oh, there was no probably about it. "He's . . ."

"Did you guys break up?"

I winced before I could tell myself not to, and his eyes got even wider. "We . . ." Why was I beating around the bush? There was no point in trying to gloss over anything. My son wasn't stupid, and he was old enough that he understood these things more than I would've liked. Couldn't he have been naïve for a few more years?

"Yeah." I exhaled hard. "We broke up."

His sad face was more heartbreaking than getting kicked to the curb in the first place.

I squeezed his arm. "I'm sorry. I know you're disappointed."

He nodded. "Why?"

It took all the restraint I had not to visibly wince again. How was I supposed to explain to a nine-year-old that Brennan had left because being with me was *abnormal*? I'd very carefully raised him to see same-sex couples as being no big deal. How did I tell him that Brennan had decided our relationship was too weird to continue? That there was something wrong with us? That being with me was inherently less than whatever it was he'd had with the women who'd valued him too little to be faithful to him?

My heart sank. *I wish I knew.* "Sometimes these things just . . . don't work out."

"He broke up with you?"

Didn't quite stop myself from wincing that time. "He . . . wanted something different, I guess."

"Why wouldn't he think you're good enough?"

*Fuck. Tariq. You're killing me.*

Swallowing, I shook my head. "Like I said, he wanted something different. That's why people date instead of just getting married. So they can see if they really want to be together." I lifted my shoulder in the heaviest half shrug ever. "If it doesn't work, they move on until they find someone they do want to stay with."

"Oh."

This was one of those moments when my parents would've assured nine-year-old me that I'd understand when I was older. I didn't say that to him, though. Mostly because I didn't know how much older he'd have to be before he understood—obviously twenty-six wasn't quite there.

"We both need to get some sleep," I said quietly. "Maybe instead of going skating tomorrow, we can go out to Port Angeles. To that big bookstore."

That brought some life back into his eyes, and he grinned. "Can we?"

I couldn't help smiling. Patting his arm, I said, "Yeah. As soon as I get off work, I'll come home, and we can go."

The grin got even bigger. "Yeah!"

I laughed softly. My bank account wasn't really in "let's go to the bookstore" mode, but it gave him something to look forward to. I'd figure it out. "Will you be okay tonight? I know this is kind of . . ." *Something you've been through too many times already. I am so sorry, Tariq.*

He nodded. "I'll be okay."

"Do you want to talk about it any more?"

He shook his head.

"You sure?"

"Yeah."

"Okay." I leaned down and kissed his forehead. "Good night."

"Good night. Love you, Dad."

"Love you too."

I pulled the covers up for him, patted his arm once more, then stood and started to leave.

"Dad?"

One hand on the light switch, the other on the door, I twisted around. "Hmm?"

"We don't have to go back to the skate shop. If you don't want to."

I swallowed. "You want to keep skating, though."

"I know, but . . ." He lowered his gaze, picking at the hem of his comforter.

"It's okay," I said. "We'll find another one. I think there's one over in Port Angeles. Maybe . . . maybe we can go there after mosque this weekend."

He looked at me again and smiled in that way only kids could—as if my promise to find an alternate place to skate made everything okay. "Okay. Good night, Dad."

"Good night."

I turned off the light and stepped out into the hall. I left the door ajar, went across to my own bedroom, and left that door open a little bit too. He wasn't prone to nightmares anymore, but just in case he got sick or upset, I wanted to be able to hear him. Or see the glow of his flashlight if he tried to stay up reading again.

I chuckled softly as I toed off my shoes. I'd never imagined any child of mine would be the type who had to be told to stop reading and go to sleep. Then again, I'd never imagined he'd get hooked on skateboarding, either.

My laughter dried up. Tomorrow, I vowed, I'd start looking around for someone to pick up where Brennan had left off. If Tariq wanted to skate, I'd find someone to teach him. How I'd pay for it, or how I'd get him to and from a park . . . well, I'd figure that out too.

I peeled off my shirt and went into the bathroom to brush my teeth.

My own reflection made me pause. In the back of my mind, I could hear all the people who'd ever reminded me how much my appearance stood in my way.

*"They're not going to hire someone who looks like a terrorist."*

*"Girls don't want guys who are shorter than them."*

*"No offense, but I'm not into guys who look like you."*

Even my own father's voice was in there.

*"Long hair? No beard? It's like you don't want people to know you're a Muslim. Or a* man."

I closed my eyes and sighed. *Thanks, Dad.*

Was that why Brennan had hit the brakes? Because he couldn't see himself with me?

Well. Yes. But not because of how I looked. Right?

*"I need to go back to the way I was before."*

*"Back to normal."*

I pushed out a long breath. There was always something, wasn't there? Some reason why a person couldn't see themselves staying with me. Some sort of deal-breaker. If they got past my appearance and were okay with me being asexual, they balked at my lack of education and earning potential. If the Muslim part didn't scare them off, the single-parent part did.

Always. *Something.*

And yet, I hadn't seen this one coming. Brennan had struggled to make sense of his sexuality, but he more or less took it in stride now.

We'd clicked together. As friends. As more than friends. Admitting we loved each other.

And then . . .

Then it wasn't normal anymore.

The worst part, though, was realizing how normal we'd become to me. He'd become one of those people who seemed like he'd always been a part of my life. Waking up next to him, eating dinner across from him, shooting the breeze with him when he swung into Red Hot before he went to work, watching him interact with my kid—it had all become my new normal.

And it was gone.

Just like that, it was gone.

I swiped at my stinging eyes. Well, what had I expected? Resting my hands on the counter, I stared at myself in the mirror, silently demanding an explanation from my reflection. My tired, self-pitying reflection.

Wiping my eyes again, I sniffed sharply and lowered my gaze.

*Come on. This isn't going to help. Brennan's gone. He isn't the first and won't be the last.*

*This is all part of Allah's plan, remember? You'll find someone, inshallah. And if you don't . . . inshallah.*

Yeah, Allah had a plan, and I'd go with it, but that didn't mean this didn't hurt.

*Get a grip. Crying about it won't help anything.*

I didn't know why I tried to stop it. What was the point? It wasn't like it distracted me from feeling like crap—trying to hold back just made me feel *more* like crap. I'd kept myself stoic enough to face my son, and now it was just me, my reflection, and Allah.

All the frustration left over from my last few failed relationships bubbled to the surface, making the pain of losing Brennan burn even hotter. Going through those breakups, being dumped and deserted because I was never quite up to par, had been worth it when Brennan came along. When I'd realized they'd all been the wrong people for me because Brennan had been in my future the whole time, it had been like those painful splits had existed for no other reason than to make me cherish Brennan when we finally met.

And now . . .

I covered my eyes with one hand, gripped the edge of the sink with the other, and released my breath. A couple of hot tears slipped free, and before I could choke it back, so did a quiet sob. Somewhere in the back of my mind, I tried to tell myself this meant there was someone even better than Brennan coming along, someone I'd appreciate and cherish even more after all of this, but even my faith couldn't erase the bleakness I felt right then. It didn't matter who was coming along. The only thing that mattered was how hard it was to let go of the first person who'd—

"Dad?"

I spun around, realizing a split second too late that I hadn't done a damn thing to compose myself before facing Tariq.

Staring up at me in his Minion pajamas, eyes wide, he looked even younger now. Like when he was five or six and he'd come into my room after a bad dream.

"Hey." I wiped my eyes, though that probably didn't do a bit of good. "You're . . . You should be . . ." I cleared my throat. "You should be sleeping."

He didn't move. "Are you sad because of Brennan?"

Just hearing my son say my ex-boyfriend's name was like a punch to the gut. Why did I let them meet? Why did I let Tariq get attached to him?

Exhaling hard, I nodded, and when I spoke, I hoped he didn't notice how much my voice shook. "Yeah. I'm sorry. I didn't want . . ."

*I didn't want you to see me break.*

I crouched in front of him, so he was slightly above my eye level. Smoothing his ruffled hair, I said, "I'll be okay. It just hurts right now."

He held my gaze, and I wasn't sure if he was about to start crying too, or what was going through his mind.

What I didn't expect was for him to hug me.

"I'm sorry, Dad. It'll be okay."

I just hugged him tight, closing my eyes and whispering a thanks to Allah that despite everything I'd ever screwed up in my life, I'd been blessed with an understanding son who was wise beyond both our years.

I let him go, but kept a hand on his shoulder as I looked right in his eyes. "I'll be okay. We both will. And tomorrow, I'll start checking around for a new place for you to skateboard. Okay?"

My son nodded. "Okay."

"I'm sorry," I whispered. "I know it's rough on you. When I date people and it"—*blows up in my face*—"doesn't work out."

He stared at me with wide eyes that seemed like they were *just* about to start welling up. "What about you?"

"Well . . ." I thought quickly. "I won't lie. It hurts. But remember how we were both sad after Megan and I broke up?"

His lips tightened as he nodded again.

I squeezed his shoulder. "But then it got better? And we weren't sad anymore?"

Another nod.

"We'll get there this time too." *Right? Can someone please tell* me *we'll get there?* "It hurts right now, and that's okay. It's okay to be sad."

His chin quivered, and I wrapped my arms around him again.

"I'm so sorry," I whispered. "I wish there was a way to make this easier."

*There is, idiot. Don't introduce your kid to your partners.*

I flinched and held him tighter.

*Or don't fall for your friends.*

"We'll be okay," I said.

"I know." He sniffed and pulled back, wiping his eyes before he looked up at me. "Brennan wasn't mean to you, was he?"

My chest felt like it was going to collapse in on itself. I knew what he meant. Had Brennan been nasty and cruel? Had we fought? Screamed at each other? Had he said anything that couldn't be taken back?

I shook my head. "No. He was . . ." I swallowed as my brain replayed our conversation. "He wasn't mean about it. He just needed to move on." *To something more normal. Something better than me. Just like Megan. And Chris before her.*

"That's good. Right? That he wasn't mean about it?"

*Sure. Why not?* I nodded, concentrating on *not* gritting my teeth. "Yeah. It's always good when you can end on good terms."

Tariq gave a sharp nod and wiped his eyes again. No more tears followed. Maybe that was all he needed, at least for tonight, and I envied him for that.

"Can I go back to bed?" he asked.

"Yeah. Of course."

He started to turn, but paused and looked at me again. "We don't have to go to the bookstore tomorrow." His eyebrows pulled together. "If you don't want to."

I ruffled his hair, then gathered him into another hug. "We'll go. I promise."

"Okay."

I stood, dabbing at my eyes as subtly as I could. "Go get some sleep. Otherwise we'll be dragging tomorrow." *One of us might as well be functional.*

He nodded. "Good night, Dad."

"Good night."

He left the bathroom, and I listened until his door hinges creaked softly. Then I faced the mirror again, resting my hands on the sink.

I'd done a lot of things wrong in my life, and apparently I wasn't getting any better when it came to choosing people to date.

But I could live with that because, somehow, I hadn't screwed up my son.

At least I'd done something right.

# CHAPTER TWENTY-FIVE

# BRENNAN

It was almost eleven when I finally left the skate park, but I didn't pull into my apartment's parking lot. I circled the block a few times, my gut tightening every time I went past the driveway without turning.

Was I really going to go home, go to bed, and go on like nothing had happened? This wasn't something I could sleep off. I wouldn't wake up tomorrow and find that everything had returned to normal. If it was going to change, I had to be the one to change it, and why the hell was I spinning my tires instead of doing something?

Fuck it. I wasn't sleeping until I fixed this.

I turned around and drove toward Zafir's apartment. I blasted the radio and sang along, concentrating on lyrics and the road so I wouldn't think. Thinking would make me realize how badly this was going to blow up in my face, and then I'd turn around. No. I *had* to do this.

His building came into view. Heart thumping, I pulled into the parking lot. Immediately, I homed in on his car in its usual spot, and my stomach lurched. At least he was here.

I parked in a guest spot as if I had every right to be here, and got out.

Staring up at his apartment, I tried to imagine how this would go, but all that did was make me want to turn tail and run before he figured out I was here. I'd come this far. I was going through with this.

The lights were all off. Of course they were. Tariq had school tomorrow. They both had to be up early. Zafir didn't have the luxury of dropping everything and driving to someone else's apartment to wake them up and spill his guts. He did, however, have the brains to not torpedo something amazing so he'd *have* to drive over and spill his guts.

I could text him. Call him. See if he was awake, or wake him up.

No. I didn't want him to think—know—I was a fucking coward.

So, despite my throbbing ankle and my lack of a backbone, I walked up the stairs. More like limped. Were there always this many steps? It was only two flights, but it felt like fifty. Whatever. Not turning back.

At his door, I stopped.

*Okay. I can do this. Just knock, apologize, say your piece, and . . . and hope for the best.*

Holding my breath, I raised my hand to knock.

But then I hesitated.

Tariq. Was he here?

I couldn't remember if he was staying at his babysitter's tonight, or if he was home. If he was home, then he had to know by now. It had been painfully obvious how much I'd hurt Zafir, and unless he was an Oscar-worthy actor, there was no way he could keep that hidden from Tariq.

My chest ached. What had Zafir told him? Did they both hate me now? If they didn't, they should. God knew I did.

My shoulders sagged, and a lump rose in my throat. I wanted to fix this, but I couldn't take the chance of Tariq being home. The apartment was too small for us to be absolutely sure he wouldn't overhear us. If he knew we'd split up, then me walking through the door would be enough to upset him. If by some chance he didn't know, he'd figure out something was wrong as soon as Zafir and I started talking.

Blood pounded in my ears. There was no way in hell I was sleeping tonight unless I fixed things with Zafir, but that was my fault. Not Tariq's.

Sighing, I turned around and started back down the steps.

# CHAPTER TWENTY-SIX

# ZAFIR

This was one feeling I could've done without experiencing again for the rest of my life. All morning long, I'd felt . . . drained. Not like I had when I'd been up most nights with a newborn. That kind of bone-deep exhaustion wasn't fun, but this was like all the life had been sucked out of me, and someone had beaten the crap out of me for good measure.

I'd felt it when Megan left. I'd felt it when Tariq's mom left.

But whether I felt like crap or not, I had to get my son to the bus and get myself to work. So I made myself stumble out of bed. Take a shower. Shave. Make coffee. Drink coffee. Make more coffee. Drink more coffee.

Some mornings, I had to drag Tariq out of bed and nag him every step of the way until he finally dressed, ate some breakfast, and ran for the bus.

Today, as I was eyeing the clock and forcing some coffee into my queasy stomach, he came into the kitchen . . . fully dressed, hair combed, with his shoes on.

I blinked. "Morning."

"Morning." He sat down at the table and poured himself some cereal.

I sipped my coffee as I watched him. "Are you, um, doing okay? After . . ."

"'Cause of Brennan?"

Somehow, I kept myself from wincing. "Yeah."

He shrugged and took another bite of cereal.

"You . . . want to talk about it?" I asked.

He shook his head. I didn't push. I didn't really want to talk about it either, though I would've if he'd needed to. When he was ready, he'd tell me. He always did.

After breakfast, while I cleaned up the dishes, he disappeared into his bedroom. When he came back out, he had his backpack on his shoulders and a small armload of books.

"These are Brennan's." He held them up. "I need to give them back to him."

I forced myself not to flinch. He'd just gotten these, and even though he was a speed reader, he couldn't have finished more than one of them. Letting them go now was just one more way for this whole thing to sting him.

"I'll take them back." I gestured at the table. "Put them by my keys, and I'll take them by the skate shop."

Without a word, he put them next to my wallet and keys.

"You should get to the bus," I said. "It'll be here in a few minutes."

He nodded. Then he looked me right in the eye and said, "We'll be okay, Dad."

I forced a smile. "I know. Have a good day."

He smiled back, hugged me, and took off to catch the bus. As soon as he was gone, I dropped into a chair at the table, rested my face in my hands, and sighed. He could test my patience at times, but it was like he knew when I desperately needed him to have it together because I didn't. Sometimes I wondered who the adult was in this house. There were certainly days when he was stronger than me, and today was one of them.

Guilt gnawed at me—he was too young to pull this much weight. I would *definitely* find him a new place to skateboard soon. No way was he missing out on something he enjoyed because my love life was crap. I owed him that much.

And I owed him a stable income and health insurance, which meant I needed to snap out of this and go to work. I hadn't had to pull him together this morning, so I didn't have any excuse not to pull myself together.

Though it took a stupid amount of effort, I got up from the table and shuffled back to my bedroom. I brushed my teeth, pulled my hair back into a ponytail, and put on my shoes. Wallet, keys, phone—ready to go. The books for Brennan went too, but I wasn't sure I'd make it to the skate shop to return them today.

I actually felt somewhat accomplished as I got in the car. When the alarm had gone off, I'd been tempted to pull the covers over my head and be a lazy, self-pitying slug all day.

But I'd made it this far. That meant I could get myself from home to Red Hot. Which meant I could clock in and do my job. That would get me to lunch and then . . . well, I'd see what I had left.

Fifteen minutes later, I parked in the alley behind Red Hot and let myself in through the back door.

I groaned. I was too fucking tired, but . . . time to adult. Time to work. I had to. Getting dumped by a guy I'd let myself get attached to was no excuse to be stupid with my family's financial security.

Violet didn't ask. The minute I walked into the shop, she took one look at me and said, "Honey, I need you to audit the back stock inventory. Why don't you take care of that, and I'll stay on the sales floor?"

*Yes, please.* "You sure?"

She gave me a knowing look, as if she saw right through to everything that had happened with Brennan. "I'll be fine up here." She nodded toward the back. "Go."

"Yes, ma'am." I had no idea what I'd do without a boss like her.

In the stockroom, I found the clipboard of inventory sheets and got to work. I didn't have the brain cells to count above about ten today, but I was still grateful Violet had put me on inventory duty. Better to have me in here, counting dildos and condom cartons instead of handling cash or dealing with customers.

So, I sat cross-legged on a table, piles of boxes on either side of me and a clipboard balanced on my knee. I perused the inventory sheets. She'd made notes on a number of items whose inventories didn't match what was in the computer. My job was to count the physical stock to double-check that we had accurate numbers for those, then go through sales records and shipments to see where the discrepancy came from.

An hour or two into my shift, I was in the middle of narrowing down where a case of vibrators had gone—turned out one of us had forgotten to take them out of the inventory after shipping them to another store—when Violet poked her head through the doorway.

"Zafir?" she said. "Brennan's asking for you."

I bristled, momentarily tempted to toss her the biggest dick-shaped object within reach and suggest she tell him to go fuck himself with it. But I didn't. Sighing, I put the clipboard aside and stepped down off the table.

She held out the shop's portable phone.

Oh. Well. At least he wasn't here.

As I took the phone, I asked, "You mind if I take a few minutes? I'll shorten my lunch break to make up for it."

Violet glanced toward the sales floor, and I could almost hear the pieces coming together in her brain. As she met my gaze, she said, "You do whatever you need to do, and we'll settle up later."

"Thank you," I whispered. She left, and I put the phone to my ear. "Hello?"

"Hey, it's me." He cleared his throat. "Can we talk for a minute?"

*I'd rather not.*

"All right. Talk."

He pulled in a deep breath. "I wanted to say I'm sorry."

*For which part?* I bit it back, though.

When I didn't say anything, he continued, "I think I made a mistake."

"Oh really?" It came out more sarcastically than I'd intended it to. I didn't apologize.

"I just . . ." He paused for a few long seconds. "I kind of freaked out. But it was a mistake. I—"

"Don't," I snapped. "It's done. It's over."

"Zafir, can we—"

"I'd really rather not." I closed my eyes and gritted my teeth. Maybe he had a valid case, and he really had just fucked up, but I didn't want to hear it. I was too fucking raw to hear it, because I could still hear everything he'd said yesterday. "I'm not a yo-yo," I said. "You can't just tell me I'm—"

"I know," he breathed. "Believe me, I know. Like I said, I freaked out. But I was wrong."

"Yeah." I shrugged. "You also left."

"Can you just listen to me?" he pleaded.

"No." I tightened my jaw, hoping that kept the tremor out of my voice. My eyes didn't sting yet, but I had a feeling that wouldn't last long. "I can live with you hurting me. I can even forgive and give second chances. But not when you hurt my kid."

"Zafir, I swear I never meant to hurt you or Tariq. I swear."

"It doesn't matter if you meant to or not," I snapped. "I can be reckless with myself and I have nobody else to blame if I get hurt. But him? No. There's no second chances there." And there was that sting in my eyes. I swallowed hard, hoping my voice stayed even. "I've already had to explain to him that his mother is gone, and that the woman who promised him she'd be his stepmother is gone, and I still don't know how to tell him *why*."

I clenched my teeth even tighter to keep my voice from shaking, but it didn't help much. "He's nine years old, Brennan. That is way too young to have to understand why there's a revolving door on his life. And if you think I'm going to give you the opportunity to—"

"Zafir, I didn't do this to hurt either of you. I know you're trying to protect him."

"But you want me to make an exception for you?"

"No! I . . ." He blew out a breath. "I know I screwed up. I—"

"No. We're done."

"Zafir—"

"No. There's nothing left to talk about. And I need to get back to work."

With that, I hung up the phone, set it down, and went back to the inventory sheets that were suddenly blurry and didn't make sense and—

"Zafir?" Violet's voice this time.

I exhaled. I wiped my eyes and swallowed, and my boss gave me a moment to collect myself before she spoke again.

"Things didn't work out with him?" she asked softly.

"You could say that."

She put an arm around my shoulders. "You okay, sweetheart?"

*I have to be. My son is depending on me.*

"Yeah." I scrubbed a hand over my face. "I'll . . ."

"There's still plenty of inventory left," she said. "Why don't you stay on that for a while?"

I released a long breath. This woman was a saint. After she'd gone back to the sales floor, I shut the back room door and leaned against it. Eyes closed, I let my head fall back, and just stood there for a while. A million emotions vied to take over. I wanted to break down crying again. I wanted to throw something. I wanted to apologize for turning him away. I wanted to call him back just so I could tear into him again.

But I didn't.

Because everything went back to Tariq.

I wouldn't waste any more time on Brennan now because I couldn't risk my job.

I wouldn't take him back because I couldn't risk him hurting Tariq again.

Rolling my shoulders, I pushed out a breath. Nothing about this was easy, but it was the right thing. For myself and for my kid. Someday, I'd understand why we'd had to go through this. What was up ahead in the future that Allah had decided we couldn't get to without getting past this obstacle first.

For today, all I could do was start putting it behind me.

I hoisted myself up onto the table again.

Balanced the clipboard on my knee.

And kept counting.

# CHAPTER TWENTY-SEVEN

# BRENNAN

In the driver seat of my parked truck, I stared at the phone. I probably shouldn't have been surprised. Maybe I wasn't. Maybe it was the fact that even if you knew it was coming, a kick in the balls still hurt.

Sighing, I shoved my phone in my pocket and got out of the truck so I could get to work. Maybe it was too soon. I'd dumped him, then tried to come at him again before he'd had a chance to dust himself off. What if I gave him a day or two to cool down, then tried again? What if I emailed him instead?

All I knew was that this couldn't be how it ended.

*Oh yes, it can. If I fucked up that badly, this could definitely be how it ends.*

I wasn't ready to give up, though. I gave him a few days before I tried to reconnect, but didn't get anywhere. He ignored my calls. A couple of texts went unanswered. It was tempting to call him at one of his two jobs, but I'd already done that once. No, I was pretty sure the only way I was going to talk to him was face-to-face, but where was the line between one last shot and being a stalker?

"Hey. Cross." Fingers snapped in my face, startling the crap out of me.

I shook myself, and my surroundings came back into focus. How long had I been standing next to the half-pipe, staring off into space?

Colin cocked his head. "You skating today or what?"

I looked down at my board, which was resting against my leg. At the half-pipe, which suddenly made me feel even more tired than before. Then I turned to him and sighed. "I don't think so."

He furrowed his brow. "What's going on? You've been a space cadet all morning."

"I'm . . ." My shoulders slumped. I couldn't think of a lie, and I sure as hell wasn't telling him the truth. Not that it mattered. Whatever the reason, there was no way in hell I was skating today, because my head wasn't in the game. "I'm sorry, I've—"

"You've got Vancouver coming up soon." He put a heavy hand on my shoulder. "This isn't a good time to be fucking off."

"I know. I know. And I'm . . ." I swallowed, avoiding his eyes as I tried to keep my voice from showing how close I was to breaking. "I just have some personal shit going on."

He exhaled, nostrils flaring slightly like they did when he was annoyed. "You gonna have it squared away before we go to Vancouver?"

I nodded. "I'll be good by then."

"You'd better be."

"For now, do you mind if I clock in early?" I gestured in the direction of Skate of Juan de Fuca. "Since I'm not doing shit here?"

He scowled, then rolled his eyes. "Whatever. At least you'll be useful there."

*Thanks, boss.*

Though he was right. If I wasn't going to practice for the event he was sponsoring me for, I might as well go make him some money at his shop.

Without saying good-bye to anyone, I skated over to the shop and clocked in.

"You're early," Sven said as I came out of the back. "Thought you were skating today."

"Yeah, I was. But I can't focus, so I figured I'd just get to work."

"Can't focus? What's up? You and your dude break up or something?"

My knees almost dropped out from under me. "Huh?"

"What?" He blinked.

"You . . . My dude?"

"Yeah." He shrugged. "Your boyfriend. That guy with the ponytail and the kid."

My jaw dropped.

Sven laughed and clapped my arm. "Oh come on. We all knew."

I stared at him. "Really?"

"Yeah. Why? We weren't supposed to know?"

"Uh . . ."

"Dude, we don't care if you're gay. Long as you pull your weight at the shop and you skate like you do . . ." He shrugged. "Nobody cares who you're doing, man."

I was too stunned to try to explain that I wasn't gay and I wasn't—hadn't been—doing anyone. "Oh. I guess I didn't realize anyone had figured it out."

"We're not as dumb as we look, man."

"Guess not." I forced a laugh. And now I felt even lower than before. I'd been so focused on going back to "normal," and everyone around me had already accepted what I was. After I'd carefully introduced Zafir as a friend, and made sure we never did any PDAs where someone might see it, they'd figured it out anyway.

Were we that obvious?

God, of course we were. How could we not be?

Well, for starters, I could stupidly break up with him and kill the whole thing.

My throat tightened, and my eyes suddenly stung. What the fuck was I doing here? Sitting behind the cash register at the skate shop with my thumb up my ass wasn't going to bring Zafir back. Going to Red Hot and talking to him probably wouldn't either, but at least that stood a chance.

"You know what?" I turned to Sven. "Can you hold down the fort for a few? I need to go take care of something."

"Sure." He shrugged. "It's pretty dead right now anyway."

"Cool. Thanks. I'll, um, be back as soon as I can."

Without another word, I hurried out the front door. Then I got on my board, pushed off, and skated like hell down the sidewalk.

"Hey!" someone shouted as I blew past a row of shops. "Slow down, idiot!"

"Sorry," I called over my shoulder, but didn't slow down. After today, I'd be back to a sane, law-abiding skater. But I had to get to Red Hot Bluewater *right now*.

A block later, I was there, and I skidded to a stop in front of the sex shop. My heart sped up.

*I can do this. I have to do this.*

I took a deep breath, then stepped in through that familiar black-papered door.

Violet looked up from behind the register, and her expression instantly hardened. "Can I help you?" The words were laced with *Get the fuck out of my shop.*

"I . . ." I gulped. "I need to talk to—"

"He's not here today," she snapped.

*What? I could've sworn he was scheduled all week.*

*Maybe he called in. Was he that upset? Was Tariq sick?*

"Anything else?" she asked tersely.

I chewed my lip. "Could you, um, let him know I—"

"I'll pass it along."

"Okay." I took a step toward the door. "Thanks. I'll—"

"Violet, I can handle this." Zafir's voice sent a chill right through me. A second later, he stepped around the end of an aisle and into view. Our eyes met. "What do you want?" His tone wasn't nearly as hostile as his boss's. Tired, if nothing else, which matched the dark circles beneath his eyes.

"I just want to talk. For a minute."

He turned to Violet. Neither of them said a word. She scowled, then shrugged and shifted her attention back to something on the counter.

Facing me again, Zafir said, "Let's go in the back."

He didn't wait for me to respond, but turned on his heel and started toward the back room. With my heart in my throat, I followed.

Violet shot me a glare as I walked past. How much he'd told her, I had no idea, but obviously enough to give her one hell of an opinion of me. A well-deserved one, too.

In the back room, Zafir closed the door between us and the sales floor. Then he folded his arms across his chest. "All right. Talk."

"I wanted to apologize."

"Again?" His tone was quiet, but carried plenty of venom.

"Maybe do it right this time," I said.

His eyebrows flicked up a little. That was the only response he gave.

I cleared my throat. "I freaked out. It wasn't your fault. I . . . I let some shit get under my skin and make me question things, and that was a *huge* mistake."

No response.

"I am so sorry," I went on. "I was so scared of not being normal. That there was something wrong with me, and that this was something I'd gone into impulsively as a way to get over Aimee."

"Impulsively?" he snapped. "We were friends for *ages* before we called it anything more than that. You had plenty of time to get your head around whether or not you were ace. So was that the part you jumped into? Or this part?" He gestured at himself, then me.

"The whole thing. All of it." I moistened my lips and tried like hell to keep my voice even. "The thing is, I don't care about being normal. I care about you. How I feel when I'm with you. And I am so, so sorry I hurt you. And I'm . . . I mean, I'm still not totally sure what my sexuality is. I just know that I love you. I've never felt anything close to this with anyone but you." I gulped, struggling not to lose my nerve. "I wanted to be normal until I realized normal meant living without the only person I've ever loved like this."

His Adam's apple jumped.

"I'm sorry, Zafir."

He shook his head. "I've been with enough people who were embarrassed of me for one reason or another. My ex-fiancée didn't like people knowing she was with an uneducated guy who'd be stuck in retail for the rest of his life. One of my exes hated telling people I had a kid. And believe me, you aren't the first guy who didn't want people to know he was dating a guy. Or who introduced me as a 'friend' because deep down, that's all I was."

I flinched like he'd smacked me. "I'm not embarrassed of you. I mean, hell—my coworkers knew we were dating, and I never said a word. I don't care if they know." I paused, trying to collect my thoughts enough to actually make sense. "This was about *me*. I started second-guessing myself, and thinking I'd jumped into being asexual because it was easier than dealing with my breakup."

"Didn't seem like it was easy for you to accept that's what you were."

"It wasn't. But it was a distraction." I shook my head. "Except it wasn't just a distraction. This is who I am. And I love you."

He straightened a little, setting his jaw. "But how do I know, especially after this shit, with you freaking out over what's 'normal,' if this really *is* what you want? What if it *is* some impulsive rebound thing?"

I studied him. "So now you don't think I'm asexual?"

"I didn't say that. But you're asking me to give you a second chance. How . . ." He avoided my eyes for a second. "I guess what I'm asking is how long do you think I want to be introduced as your friend before I start wondering if that's all I really am to you?"

I gnawed my lip for a moment. "Here's the thing. Ever since I started dating, I've been looking for the right person, and I thought that meant a woman. Someone who I wanted in bed, and then fell in love with and wanted to have a family with. I had this person in my head who'd be perfect. She was a woman, and we were amazing at sex, and . . ."

I shook my head, and when I went on, I was talking fast. Almost too fast. "I had it all wrong, Zafir. The whole time, the right person for me was nothing like I pictured and wasn't in any of the places I was looking. It was just . . . you. And if I introduce you as my friend, it's because that's what you've been from the start. I haven't even known you that long, and you're my best friend. You get me. That's *why* I fell in love with you."

His breath hitched just slightly. Mine was gone. For the longest time, we stood in silence, and I didn't know if I should keep talking or wait for him to respond. And if I was supposed to keep talking, what was I supposed to say? It was all out there now. All laid out on the table.

*Give me something, Zafir. This is all I have.*

The silence kept going. He looked away. Then I did.

Finally, I found one last reserve, and quietly said, "I also realized that when I'm with you, it really doesn't matter what's weird or normal. You accept me. You have from day one. I was stupid to take that for granted or walk away from that. I thought I was terrible at being in bed with my exes, but I ended up being terrible at being in love with you. I just . . . Can you give me another shot?"

He lowered his gaze. "It's not that easy."

"What do you mean?"

He swallowed, then met my eyes. "It's not just me, Brennan. Tariq's part of the deal too. And when he realized you were gone . . ."

My heart dropped. "I'm sorry. I want to make this up to both of you."

Once again, Zafir went quiet. He tightened his arms across his chest, and looked anywhere but right at me. Even from a few feet away, I was pretty sure I could physically feel his walls going up.

"There's one more thing," I whispered.

He exhaled sharply, but didn't say anything.

I gulped, wondering how much longer this thin ice would hold. "The day I broke up with you, I almost came by your place to talk to you. That night, I mean. I wanted to fix things."

His eyebrows rose.

I went on: "I knew there was no way I was going to be able to sleep until I did, and I wanted to do it in person. So I went over, and I made it to your door, but I couldn't make myself knock. I . . ." I was talking fast now, not even sure if the words were coming out in the right order. "I got all the way to the door, but then I left. I couldn't do it."

He held my gaze, but didn't speak.

I inhaled slowly. "And I left because . . . because I didn't want to upset Tariq."

Zafir blinked.

I stared at the floor between us. "I was all ready to knock, and I knew what I wanted to say, but then I realized that he'd hear us. And I . . . couldn't do that to him."

He was quiet for a moment, and when he spoke, his voice was gentler. "Really?"

"Yeah." I moved a little closer, and braced myself as I met his gaze. Something—I couldn't say exactly what—had softened in his expression, but I didn't dare let it get my hopes up.

Still, I'd already gone out on a limb, so what was going out a little farther?

With an unsteady hand, I reached for his face. He didn't pull away. When my fingertips brushed his skin, we both jumped, but otherwise, he stayed still. Cautiously, I let my palm rest against his cheek.

Zafir closed his eyes.

"I'm sorry," I whispered. "There's really nothing else I can say except that you're everything I didn't know I wanted. And I found you even though I was looking in all the wrong places. You don't owe me a thing, and I know you have to protect your son, but is a second chance too much to ask?"

Zafir swallowed.

"We don't even have to tell Tariq right away," I went on. "If you want us to just be friends when we're around him, I'm okay with that. Whatever you think is best."

I cringed. Whatever he thought was best probably came down to me fucking off and him moving on with his life. But it was out there. Nothing to do but wait for him to make a move.

Finally, he released a long breath and met my gaze. "You're serious, aren't you?"

"Of course I am."

Two, three, four quiet seconds went by, and then he wrapped his arms around me.

"To answer your question," he whispered, holding me tight. "No, a second chance isn't too much to ask."

Squeezing my eyes shut, I held him close and buried my face against his neck. "I love you, Zafir."

"I love you too." His words were as shaky as I felt. He nudged me to lift my head, and when I did, he kissed me gently. "I missed you."

"So did I." I smoothed his hair. "Like crazy."

He smiled, but it faltered, and then a worried look creased his forehead and tightened his lips. "I have no idea what to tell Tariq. If we start again, and it doesn't work out, then . . ."

I took his hand in both of mine. "I'm serious—maybe we shouldn't tell him right away. Or, you know, tell him we're friends again. Because even if this doesn't work out, I *would* like us to be friends again. And stay that way."

Zafir smiled, cupping my face. "Me too." He kissed me again, then glanced toward the door. "I, um, should probably get back to work, though."

"Yeah. Same here." I chuckled sheepishly. "I . . . kind of ditched my coworker to come here."

"Really?"

I nodded. "It was bugging me too much. The way I'd left things with us." I stroked his cheek with the backs of my fingers. "I had to come see you and fix this."

Zafir closed his hand over mine. "I'm glad you did."

"Me too."

"I'd suggest getting together after work tonight, but . . ." He took a breath. "I need to sit down with Tariq and tell him we're friends again. He needs to know."

I winced. "This is really bothering him, isn't it?"

Grimacing, Zafir nodded.

"I'm sorry."

"I know." He kissed me lightly. "But he'll be okay. And so will we."

*Thank God.*

"So, text me when you've got some time?" I smiled cautiously. "Maybe we'll grab lunch tomorrow?"

"Lunch sounds good. I'll definitely text you." He paused. "And I'll let you know how things go with Tariq."

"Thank you."

"For the moment, though . . ." He nodded toward the door. "Get back to work."

I saluted with two fingers. "Going back to work. And you too, slacker."

Zafir laughed. "I'll see you tomorrow?"

"I'm looking forward to it."

# EPILOGUE

# ZAFIR

*A Year Later*

I was just wrapping up at Red Hot when my phone buzzed with a text from Brennan.

*Can you swing by before you go to work? Tariq's order came in.*

I didn't have to be at Old Country for another hour.

Grinning, I texted back, *Be there around four thirty.*

I was almost as excited as Tariq would be when he found out about this. He had no idea Brennan and I had ordered him his own custom skateboard. Or that we'd also gotten him a new set of elbow pads to replace the one he'd cracked earlier this year, and kneepads since his old ones were starting to get tight. Brennan had even ordered a smaller version of the jersey he wore when he competed, complete with sponsor names.

"Chatting with Brennan?" Violet asked.

"Yep. Tariq's birthday present came in."

"Why don't you go ahead and go, then?" She smiled. "You two haven't seen much of each other lately anyway."

That was true. Some of the other drivers at Old Country had gotten fed up with Pete and quit, so those of us who were left had to pick up extra hours. Great for the paycheck, but man, it was wearing me down.

"Okay," I said. "I'll see you tomorrow?"

"Yep. Go."

"Thanks, Violet!"

I left Red Hot and started walking up the sidewalk toward Skate of Juan de Fuca. Hard to believe we'd stood out here a year or so ago and broken up—that was all a distant memory now. We had ups and downs like any couple, but nothing like that massive hiccup we'd had last year. Brennan had introduced me to his friends and teammates, none of whom seemed to bat an eye at him dating a man. He didn't bother spelling out that he was asexual—the fact that they accepted our relationship was enough for him. They didn't need to know anything more.

Tariq hadn't been sure what to think when he'd realized Brennan and I were friends again. We spent a few months that way, letting him get used to things before we eased him into the idea that we were dating. For a couple of weeks after that, he was frosty toward Brennan, and he'd confided in me one night that he was scared Brennan was going to leave.

Eventually, though, he'd warmed back up to him. Brennan started occasionally staying over. When that went well, he stayed a few times a week. In fact, if he wasn't closing at the skate shop, he'd go to my place while I was at Old Country. Kelly wasn't thrilled about losing a few of her evenings, but it eased some of my financial strain.

And I had to admit, there was something exceptionally sweet about coming home and finding the two of them watching a movie together, or playing video games, or poring over Tariq's homework at the kitchen table. I couldn't even count the number of times I'd walked in to find them both lounging on the couch, noses buried in books. That had been happening a lot lately, especially since Brennan had started letting Tariq borrow some of his science fiction and fantasy novels.

*"Well, Mr. Hamady,"* Tariq's teacher had told me during a parent-teacher conference not long ago. *"Your son is definitely the first fourth grader I've had do a book report on Tolkien."*

The memory made me chuckle as I continued toward Skate of Juan de Fuca. Maybe if my parents had let *me* hang around the skaters when I was a kid, I'd have started reading a few grade levels ahead.

At the skate shop, I opened the door and stepped inside.

And the whole place went quiet.

I glanced around. The employees all quickly went back to whatever tasks they'd been working on, and their conversations started again, but . . . weird.

"Hey, Cross!" his boss called into the back. "Your dude just got here."

A second later, Brennan came limping out of the back room. He'd twisted his knee during a competition a couple of weeks ago, so he was still hobbling around in a brace. He was getting better, though. The doctor had told him to stay off his board for six weeks, but I had a feeling Brennan would be back to skating in the next few days.

*Idiot.* I chuckled to myself. Between him and Tariq, I figured I might as well buy stock in one of those companies that manufactured ice packs.

"So," I said. "It all came in?"

"Most of it." Brennan grinned. He leaned down behind the counter and picked up a stack of boxes, which he set beside the register. Then he came around to where I was standing, and dug a box cutter out of his pocket. "They back-ordered the pads, but the helmet and board came in."

"Awesome. Can I see the board?"

"Yeah, yeah." He started cutting open the box, and excitement swelled in my stomach. Though I had no real interest in skateboarding, we'd been plotting for weeks to get Tariq the custom board along with some other gear for his birthday. Now that the order was finally in, I couldn't wait to see it.

In a few months, this thing would be scraped and scratched all to hell, but today, it was brand-new. One of Brennan's buddies had sketched a knights and dragons design, since Tariq loved fantasy and science fiction, and the company had put that design on the board.

"That thing is wicked cool," Sven said, pausing as he went by us. "He's gonna love it."

"Yeah, he is," I said. "Can't wait to give it to him."

"Well." Brennan carefully put the board back in its box. "Hopefully everything else will be here by then. Assuming he hasn't outgrown them already."

"Right?" Tariq was going to bankrupt me when he really started in on the growth spurts. His school clothes were killing me already. And when it came to skating gear—well, good thing Brennan had an employee discount.

"So you really think he'll like it?" Brennan asked.

"I think he's gonna love it." I smiled. "Thank you. For getting all this."

He smiled back. "There is, um, one more thing." He pushed a small box toward me on the counter, and shyly added, "This one's for you, though."

"Me?" I eyed him as I took the box. "You guys aren't going to give up on getting me to skate, are you?"

"Are you surprised?"

"No." I lifted the flaps and reached inside. "Knowing the two of you, nothing surprises me any—" Cold metal met my fingertips. I looked into the box. "What the . . ."

"You didn't think I'd forgotten *your* birthday is two weeks before his, did you?"

"No, but . . ." I pulled out the simple silver ring. "Is . . ."

"Yes, it's that kind of ring." Brennan took my hand. "I'd, um, get down on one knee, but . . ." He gestured at the brace.

In disbelief, I stared at the ring. At him. I realized Brennan's coworkers had all gone quiet again, and they were watching us. No one made a sound.

"You . . ." I struggled to find my breath. "Are you serious?"

He gulped, then nodded slowly. "Completely." He paused, then sighed dramatically and gestured down again. "I mean it—it's aching like a motherfucker today, so I couldn't—"

I laughed. "That's not what I meant."

"I know. And yes, I'm serious. You're the most amazing person I've ever met." He brought my hand to his lips and kissed my fingers. "Will you marry me?"

"I . . ." I glanced at the ring, then at him. "You know this means being a stepparent too, right?"

"I do." He straightened a little, an odd grin curling his lips. "Hey, I kind of like the sound of that—I do."

"Me too," I whispered. "And yes, I will."

He released a breath, and as everyone around us started applauding, he gathered me in his arms. "I love you, Zafir. And I always thought there was no way in hell I'd be a stepparent, but that was before I met Tariq. I want us all to be a family. Especially 'cause it . . ." He swallowed. "It kind of feels like we already are."

A lump rose in my throat. "Holy shit."

"*Now* are you surprised?"

Laughing, I nodded. "Yes. I am." I cupped his face in both hands and kissed him. "You pretty much just blew my mind."

"Mission accomplished." He paused. "Oh, and there's a little bit more."

"*More*?"

"Yeah. Not the most romantic thing in the world, but I crunched the numbers, and if we pool our money, we can easily live close to Tariq's school. Plus it turns out my shop's insurance is cheaper than yours, even if all three of us are on it." He grinned. "And if we're living together, we'll be paying less rent. Bills will be combined. All of that." He squeezed my hand. "Which means you won't have to work two jobs anymore. Not unless you want to."

The numbers all flashed through my mind—how much I made, how much I threw at bills every month. If my rent were cut by a third . . . and my insurance was cheaper . . . and the bills were split . . .

He was right. Money would still be tight, but we'd both learned to be frugal.

"I could quit Old Country," I whispered.

"Definitely. Then you'd have more time to spend with Tariq."

My knees shook. I was already overwhelmed by his proposal. Now he was offering me even more. A ticket out of that awful, toxic, exhausting second job. Just thinking about quitting, I could already feel the knots in my shoulders relaxing. And I'd get to spend more time with Tariq. More time with Brennan. More *downtime*. Period.

"I don't even know what to say right now." I laughed softly. "Mind blown."

He smiled and kissed my forehead. "You said yes. That's all I was hoping for."

"I definitely said yes." I ran my fingers through his hair. "Guess we'll have to think of a good time to tell Tariq."

"Yeah," Brennan said with a grin. "I guess we will."

I kissed him again. "And, uh, when we get there, it's up to you what you want Tariq to call you. Megan tried to push him to call her Mom, but . . ." I shook my head. "He didn't like that."

"He's called me 'Brennan' all this time. I don't see why that needs to change."

"If you're both happy with it, then it doesn't." I cradled his face in both hands. "You are, without a doubt, the best thing that's ever happened to us."

"Likewise." He hugged me tight. As he let me go, he glanced up at the clock. "Damn. You probably need to get to work."

I looked up and groaned. "Damn it."

"You want me to come by after your shift is over?"

"Definitely."

"Text me when you're off?"

"Will do."

"Sweet." He gestured at the ring in my hand. "You want to wear that? Or wait?"

I glanced down at it. "Kind of think I should wait until you've got one too."

Brennan grinned. "I'm game."

"Cool. Okay. I should go, or I'm going to be late."

"What're they going to do?" He winked. "Fire you?"

"A dude can dream, right?" I pulled him to me again and kissed him lightly. "I'll see you later tonight. I love you."

"I love you too."

One more kiss, and I headed out of the shop. Usually, I was grumbling to myself and dreading the evening on the way to Old Country. Tonight would be miserable just like every night at that place, but that was okay. My days there were numbered.

Because, inshallah, I was marrying the most amazing man ever. Inshallah, my son was getting the best stepparent I could have possibly prayed for.

And my family's future looked amazing.

A BLUEWATER BAY STORY

## EXPLORE MORE OF BLUEWATER BAY

Starstruck
*L.A. Witt*

There's Something About Ari
*L.B. Gregg*

Hell on Wheels
*Z.A. Maxfield*

Lone Wolf
*Aleksandr Voinov and L.A. Witt*

The Burnt Toast B&B
*Heidi Belleau and Rachel Haimowitz*

Wedding Favors
*Anne Tenino*

The Deep of the Sound
*Amy Lane*

When to Hold Them
*G.B. Gordon*

Rain Shadow
*L.A. Witt*

Stuck Landing
*Lauren Gallagher*

Selfie
*Amy Lane*

How the Cookie Crumbles
*Jaime Samms*

Lights, Camera, Cupid!
*Valentine's Day collection, featuring: SE Jakes, Amy Lane, Z.A. Maxfield, Anne Tenino, and L.A. Witt*

For more, visit:
riptidepublishing.com/titles/universe/bluewater-bay

Dear Reader,

Thank you for reading Ann Gallagher's *All the Wrong Places*!

We know your time is precious and you have many, many entertainment options, so it means a lot that you've chosen to spend your time reading. We really hope you enjoyed it.

We'd be honored if you'd consider posting a review—good or bad—on sites like **Amazon, Barnes & Noble, Kobo, Goodreads, Twitter, Facebook, Tumblr,** and your blog or website. We'd also be honored if you told your friends and family about this book. Word of mouth is a book's lifeblood!

For more information on upcoming releases, author interviews, blog tours, contests, giveaways, and more, please sign up for our weekly, spam-free newsletter and visit us around the web:

**Newsletter**: tinyurl.com/RiptideSignup
**Twitter**: twitter.com/RiptideBooks
**Facebook**: facebook.com/RiptidePublishing
**Goodreads**: tinyurl.com/RiptideOnGoodreads
**Tumblr**: riptidepublishing.tumblr.com

Thank you so much for Reading the Rainbow!

RiptidePublishing.com

Thank you to Heather the Dentist for helping me put Tariq's tooth back in.

Lead Me Not

*Writing as L.A. Witt*
Rain Shadow (a *Bluewater Bay* story)
Starstruck (a *Bluewater Bay* story)
Noble Metals
Precious Metals
Falling Sky
Finding Master Right
The Left Hand of Calvus
Static
The Tucker Springs stories

*With Aleksandr Voinov*
Market Garden series
Unhinge the Universe
Hostile Ground
Lone Wolf (a *Bluewater Bay* story)

*Writing as Lori A. Witt*
The Tide of War

*Writing as Laurn Gallagher*
Stuck Landing (a *Bluewater Bay* story)
Razor Wire

See L.A. Witt's full booklist at: gallagherwitt.com

Ann Gallagher is the slightly more civilized alter ego of L.A. Witt, Lauren Gallagher, and Lori A. Witt. So she tells herself, anyway. When she isn't wreaking havoc on Spain with her husband and trusty two-headed Brahma bull, she writes romances just like her wilder counterparts, but without all the heat. She is also far too mature to get involved in the petty battle between L.A. and Lauren, but she's seriously going to get even with Lori for a certain incident that shall not be discussed publicly.

Website: gallagherwitt.com
Twitter: @GallagherWitt

CPSIA information can be obtained
at www.ICGtesting.com
Printed in the USA
LVOW12s2125040716
495097LV00004B/112/P